HURRICANE CREEK

BY
GARY BARGATZE

Warfield

Happy Hollow

Upcoming titles in the *Your Winding Daybreak Ways* series

Hollow Rock

McGill

Cabedelo

Thunderwood

Babylon, A Human Requiem

For more information about the series, visit the author's website: www.garybargatze.com

HURRICANE CREEK

GARY BARGATZE

Rigor Hill Press

Rigor Hill Press, LLC
www.garybargatze.com

ISBN-13: 978-0-9909499-6-1
LCCN: 2015911678

Editorial Credit: POP Editorial Services, LLC
Cover Design by Alan Pranke
Interior Design by Biz Cook

Printed in the United States of America

For Dylan and Sean, who rekindled the light

HURRICANE CREEK

1

WHEN MY UNCLE moved us back to Memphis, the children stopped coming by to play. I was going on seven, and it was the first time I ever felt loneliness. It wasn't the way it had been a year earlier, when Uncle Aaron tried explaining that Mama had died of the fever, Grandpa and Aunt Amanda had burned up in a fire, and I would be living with him, his new wife, and her three sons in Nashville until Grandpa's old house could be rebuilt. I was too young to grasp what Uncle Aaron was trying so hard to say. In my mind I expected Mama, Grandpa, and Aunt Amanda to be at the door welcoming us back to Memphis. And even after that didn't happen, I held out hope they would all return home by Christmas.

So innocence trumped the truth until I realized the present would no longer mirror the past. I suspect if I had been older or if I had been brave enough to ask Uncle Aaron, we would have innocently concluded that church members dislike their children consorting with sinners forsaking the Sabbath. Blame my innocence on youth; blame Uncle Aaron's on his justifiable ignorance of local affairs. After all, he hadn't lived in Memphis since leaving for the university in '73. Neither of us sensed the world shifting beneath our feet, and even if we had, I doubt we would have realized these seismic changes had nothing to do with religion and everything to do with money, politics, and race.

But it was my new Aunt Jane who first experienced the shift from Reconstruction back to what the good old boys called "Redemption," or returning the social order to the way it was before the war. It was not until much later I understood the meaning of a dinner conversation between Uncle Aaron and Aunt Jane only days after returning to Memphis.

"As usual, the supper's delicious, dear," Uncle Aaron said.

Aunt Jane looked up from her plate, smiled half-heartedly, and replied, "We make do with what we can get our hands on. Fresh meats and vegetables are hard to come by in South Memphis."

"South Memphis? The shops on the old Fort Pickering site? Why are you going there? My family never went to South Memphis. We always walked the few blocks up to the markets around Court Square. Those folk had everything in season. Only time they closed or had shortages was during the quarantines for the yellow jack. . . . You go uptown from now on. Once you see the shops up there, you won't be going back to South Memphis anymore."

"Things are different here than in Nashville, Aaron," Aunt Jane replied.

"Different? How so?"

"I was treated with respect back home."

"As indeed the widow of a United States Senator should be treated. And one of only a handful of freedman senators in the whole country, I might add! But, Jane, what's different about Memphis? Someone show you disrespect? You know

I'll straighten that out right away."

"It's not something you can fix, Aaron. It's bigger than one person saying or doing something hurtful. It's a general feeling around here that things are upside down and we Negroes should get back in our place on the plantation."

"My God, what got you to thinking like that?"

"The very markets you were talking about, the ones up on Court Square."

"The markets? I don't understand."

"After enrolling Marcus, Daniel, and Lil' Jim in the Kortrecht Grammar School this morning, Lil' John and I went uptown to those markets. First stopped at Mr. Bentley's—"

"No wonder why," Uncle Aaron interjected. "He always had nice displays on either side of the door."

"Well, we went in to look around. Number of white folk chatting. They took one look at us and turned away. Got awfully quiet. Didn't say a word."

"What'd you buy?"

"Nothing."

"Nothing? That's the best market in that part of town."

"We just turned around and left. I could tell we weren't wanted there. We were out of place."

"You saying because of your color, Jane? I've known Mr. Bentley a long time and probably everyone else who was in the shop. I really don't think it's color. He's always been good to me." Uncle Aaron heaped another serving of potatoes on his plate before continuing the conversation. "So after you left Mr. Bentley's, where'd you go?"

"Stopped at a second market on the other side of Court

Square. Little old lady with a stooped back was out front sweeping the walk."

"Had to be old Miss Hardy," Uncle Aaron suggested, taking a big bite of food. "She's the nicest lady. Gave me a piece of hard candy every time I went in there with the Taylors. She must've treated you well."

"No, not so well, Aaron. The old woman followed me into the store. There were several ladies in there looking around. As I walked back toward the meats she had hanging above the counter, your kind old Miss Hardy approached me, smiled nervously, and whispered in the sweetest voice, 'Child, not to offend, but you folks are now shopping in South Memphis near where the old fort stood. You have just as much down there as we have here. You might want to give it a try.'" Aunt Jane arched an eyebrow and looked pointedly at Uncle Aaron.

"I can't believe it! Mr. Bentley? Miss Hardy?"

"You've got to believe it, Aaron," Aunt Jane insisted. "It happened. It's true."

"I don't understand, Jane. You're implying it's all about color. It can't be. I stopped in day before yesterday to say hello. I went to their shops, among others. I spoke with Mr. Bentley and Miss Hardy directly. They were as nice as they'd ever been. Talked about the good ol' days before I left for the university."

"It has everything to do with color!" Aunt Jane exclaimed. "Don't you see, Aaron? It's different for you. They've known you a long time. You're mulatto, fairly light-skinned, and to top it off, your adoptive parents were white. You told me the church had accepted you and your sister into the fold. Now why was that? I'll tell you! The Taylors were members; the minister chose them to be your parents after finding you and your sister wandering about in the Hollow; and most importantly, they were white. You see. Your blackness was forgiven, allowing you to move freely among the elites."

Realizing his skepticism was only making matters worse, Uncle Aaron tried steering the conversation away from the shopkeepers' motives and back to the facts. "So what did you do next?"

"Since we weren't making any progress with your friends in Court Square, Lil' John and I did what the old woman suggested we do—we went to South Memphis." Aunt Jane then leaned in toward her husband and asked, "Have you ever had the occasion to visit there?"

"Maybe once or twice a long time ago."

"Well, it's a shantytown, if you ask me. We walked up and down Shelby, South, and Main looking for the markets Miss Hardy was talking about. Markets? Shops? Not on your life. Mostly taverns and bars. Filth in the streets. No sewers. The stench of the municipal dump. Lots of temporary huts and hovels just thrown together to get people out of the cold and rain. Probably hold at most two people if you're lucky. And permanent houses? Yes, saw some. But the largest was no more than twenty feet by forty—two stories, four or five rooms—but not for just one family. More like three or four. The streets were swarming with Negro veterans out of work. Nothing to do, just drinking and insulting any of us women who dared walk through the district alone. I'm sure if you saw it, you wouldn't have me going there anymore. Finally found a small market—meats, fruits, vegetables—everything on the cusp of going bad. Asked the proprietor if he had anything better than this in stock. He smiled, lifted a curtain, and said, 'Absolutely—for a price.' The food was nothing special, Aaron; but I paid what he was asking. So I've got to tell you, in Memphis we make do with what we can get our hands on."

Uncle Aaron looked down, placed his fork alongside his second helping of potatoes, and after a long silence, apologized. "I'm sorry, Jane. We'll find a way to make this right. I'll go with you to South Memphis, or I'll go to Court Square myself, or we'll find a friend on the commission to lend us a hand."

"A white friend, Aaron?"

Wishing to preserve harmony without fully conceding the point, Uncle Aaron relented, "Yes. If need be, a white friend."

After staring into their respective plates for the longest time, Aunt Jane slid her hand over on top of her husband's. She truly loved Uncle Aaron; and besides, she had also learned a great deal from her late husband about political savvy and conciliation. She squeezed Uncle Aaron's hand and assured him, "We'll find a way. We always do."

After a pause she said, "But, hey, it wasn't all bad news in South Memphis today. Remember I said I enrolled the boys in the Kortrecht Grammar School before going up to Court Square? It will get them some schooling before the spring semester ends and help them adjust more quickly this coming fall. The new school building's impressive—two stories, all brick, lot of windows letting the light in. Spent some time with the principal and the boys' teachers, and I have really good feelings about them. They're all our people, Aaron. You can tell they want what's best for the children. They're well educated, enthusiastic, and dedicated. Principal Sampson sets the tone for the classrooms. He's a visionary. He said his objectives are building the students' 'mental stamina' and cultivating their 'brain force.'"

"Laudable goals, Jane, but how does he propose to achieve them?"

"Mr. Sampson said success is tied to so much more than memorization and book smarts. So the teachers have begun instructing the children in what he called 'life skills'—how to think and study, instilling perseverance and self-application. They've begun requiring the students to prepare their studies at home. He said the native powers of Negro children are of the highest order; but unlike the white students, the Negroes lack the ability to envision a bright future. They don't see the counting rooms, the business houses, and the mercantile exchanges spurring them on to success. Mr. Sampson believes we must teach our children to aspire and brace their minds for hard study and mental labor. Teach them the value of reading and discipline, how to avoid the sirens' songs of the ballroom and the festival."

"But when you met with the boys' teachers, did you get the sense the principal's vision was really being transferred to the classroom? You know how it is—the idea's easy; the application's hard."

"I was thrilled, Aaron. It was inspiring. All three teachers—a Mr. Lott, a Miss Dickinson, and a Mrs. Wilson—all echoed Mr. Sampson's goals and aspirations. You could tell they really cared about the students."

Uncle Aaron smiled, patted his wife's hand, and said lightheartedly, "Well, when you stop to think about it, today wasn't a complete disaster after all, was it, dear? The school sure helped put everything else in a little better light."

Aunt Jane wasn't smiling and responded firmly, "Aaron, don't make light of what I was saying about the meat and vegetables. It's not easy making do with what we can get in South Memphis."

"I'm not making light. I gave you my word, and I'll keep it. We'll find a way to make it right. All I'm saying is it's better to have a problem with the shops than with the teachers. So while our children are learning to dream, you and I will tackle the South Memphis markets."

And then it was Uncle Aaron's turn to sense the shift from Reconstruction back toward Redemption and the ways of doing business before the war. I don't know how he did it, but he managed to keep the news from Aunt Jane for some time. It was one of his strongest traits; he never liked divulging bad news without having a positive plan in place to address the problem.

I clearly remember the evening he gave Aunt Jane the news. It was during that first summer we were back in Memphis. We had finished dinner. Uncle Aaron told us he wanted to speak with Aunt Jane about "grown-up matters" and sent all of us children back outside to play. One thing I learned early on from my cousin Marcus was how important it was to listen in when the parents were discussing "grown-up matters." So the four of us boys quickly exited and hunched up outside the dining-room door to learn the grown-up secrets.

"I've had some bad news, Jane. The governor called me in early last week for what he called 'a chat.' He asked me to take a seat and first thanked me for my 'outstanding' liaison work between his office and the commission government here in Memphis. He said he was so happy his son had recommended me for a position in his administration. I don't know if you remember my telling you, but his son and I attended the university together over in Sewanee. My sister, Amanda, had introduced us our sophomore year. She was studying at Mary Sharp College in Winchester just down the road from Sewanee."

"I remember," Aunt Jane said and urged Uncle Aaron to continue.

"Well, before getting to the nub of the matter, the governor first reminisced about all the times I'd stayed with the family at his Winchester estate, how much they enjoyed my company. Said he and his wife thought of me as a 'third son,' and it was that feeling of family that demanded he speak with me urgently and confidentially.

"He said the question of handling the state debt had now hopelessly fractured the Democrats. While one faction wanted to maintain the state's credit at any cost, the other was in favor of repudiating the debt and saying to hell with the creditors. He said he'd tried working a compromise but had failed to bridge the differences. He then explained what he planned to do. First, he was going to reject both positions and then he was going to include a pledge in the party platform for the upcoming Democratic State Convention."

"A pledge to do what?" Aunt Jane asked.

"To follow the people's will as determined by the November elections."

"So he was going to campaign for reelection promising to follow the voters' wishes?"

"Not quite. That's where the bad news comes in. He then exploded the bomb. He's gonna tell the convention delegates he'll not accept their nomination to stand for reelection."

"My God! Not accept the nomination? Not stand for reelection? Why on earth . . . ?"

"He said the Democratic Party is deeply divided; the Republicans are on the rise; and the newspapers are portraying him as a failure, since he hasn't solved the debt issue during his term. He said he feels very comfortable with his decision to retire and plans on returning to his Winchester estate and resuming his law practice."

"To be honest, Aaron, I think the late Senator Rodgers"—which is how Aunt Jane referred to her first husband when making political points—"I think he would have followed the same path up to the point of rejecting the nomination. Despite the division in the party and the newspaper editorials, I think the senator would have become the party's standard-bearer and run a strong race promising to do the people's will. He always said you have to give the edge to the incumbent; people vote for the devil they know rather than the one they don't. On the other hand, I know politics is a blood sport. It can wear you down. Maybe it was more personal than anything else."

"I think you've hit on it; he's just tired out. You could

see it in his eyes. He kept comparing his term to his service during the war. A lot of references to the battles, especially Murfreesboro where he lost a leg."

"The news is startling, Aaron, but what's so bad in it for us?"

"The governor called me in to fire me, Jane. He didn't exactly say it that way—said something much more diplomatic, something about 'relieving me of my duties for my own good.'"

"Firing you for your own good! That doesn't make any sense at all. Even if the governor thinks the Democrats will lose the election, he must know a new state Republican administration would be much more in your corner, much more pro-Negro. . . . The governor knows you're mulatto, Aaron; it would be so easy for him to recommend you to the incoming administration."

"That's what I thought; but the governor pointed out the problem's at the local level rather than the state."

"How so? Despite your mixed heritage, you've never mentioned having had any problems with the local Democrats here."

"That's exactly how I responded, emphasizing no one either elected or appointed has ever treated me poorly while doing my job here in Memphis. The governor smiled, nodded, and then explained his thinking. 'I know, I know. I wouldn't expect otherwise,' he said. 'Remember before the war, I was a Unionist and strongly against succession. But once the vote was taken to secede, I remained loyal to Tennessee and its rights. Yes, I joined the Confederates and fought hard to defeat Lincoln's men. And as I hope you've learned about me over the years, my decision to fight and even sacrifice a limb for the rebel cause had nothing to do with the Negro. For me it was all about the central government telling us in the states what we could and couldn't do.' Then he added, 'Having read the Constitution while studying the law, I knew our founders intended we have a federalist system. The Constitution describes what Washington can do; and everything else falls under the states' control. I resented those boys in Congress running roughshod over us.'

"The governor was fired up then. He went on, saying, 'After the war, I went back to practicing the law, while others fought hard politically against the Reconstruction. These southern elites resented the laws Johnson and then Grant and the Republicans forced on them—Negro suffrage and the like. The white folk saw their voting majority disappearing before their eyes. So if no majority, then no Redemption and no return to the old ways of the antebellum South.' Then he looked at me and said, 'I'm sure you know what they did to regain control. They did everything they could to suppress the Negro vote—the Klan, biased editorials to stir rebellion, intimidation, assault, destruction of property, and even murder. I'm not saying the politicians were involved directly; they plied their trade in the legislature passing bills permitting segregation on the trains, in the hotels, and any place of entertainment. And you and I know there are more bills coming. They're talking now about literacy tests and laws requiring examination and registration of voters twenty days or more before elections.'

"When he finished, I politely challenged the governor's premise. I suggested the Memphis commission members and their staff had never bothered me personally or tried interfering in my liaison work, that they'd always treated me with respect.

"The governor leaned forward to firmly rebut my personal experiences with the politicians. 'They haven't bothered you or interfered with your work *yet.* Just wait. If the Republicans gain control of the governor's office and the state legislature, which I believe they will, then I'd bet things will quickly begin to change. Don't you see?' he said. 'The Memphis locals are Democrats. I'm a Democrat and leader of their party. They're all politicians. They play along to get along. But what'll happen when a Republican governor is sworn in? They'll become insurgents pushing back subtly behind the scenes. They'll undercut you any way they can. And before you know it, they'll openly be calling for your head. The charge will be incompetence; there won't be a word about race.'

"The governor stood up, signaling our meeting was ending. As we walked over to the door, he put his arm around my shoulder and said, 'You know, Aaron, we've spoken before about how much we have in common. We both lost our fathers early and have worked really hard to get where we've gotten today. I admire you for that, and I want to see you succeed. I believe you should find something you'd love doing for a lifetime. But something outside this political war zone—outside the line of fire.' He extended his hand, wished me luck, and said I'd always be welcome in his home."

After a brief pause to turn the page, Aunt Jane opened the next chapter: "We can always live off Senator Rodgers's inheritance until you find suitable work."

"I appreciate the offer, Jane, but you know how I'd feel about that."

"Okay, Aaron, you've got something up your sleeve. I know how this is going to work. You've presented the problem as the bad news and now you'll offer a credible solution as the good. So what's the good news, Aaron? What are you going to do?"

Employing his usual modus operandi, Uncle Aaron responded enigmatically: "What I've dreamed of doing ever since I was a boy and what I studied at the university."

"You know very well that's not telling me much. I believe you said you majored in English. You could do any number of things. Stop teasing and tell me!"

The sphinx continued, "I believe I told you about making acquaintances with Ed Shaw while doing my commission work."

"Ed Shaw? The Kentucky freeman who operates the saloon?"

"Oh, he's done a lot more than that, Jane. Studied the law; won election to the city council; became wharfmaster; and during Reconstruction, he pushed the politicians to hire Negro teachers and pass stronger civil rights laws."

Growing exasperated with Aaron's response, Aunt Jane exclaimed, "You've told me everything I would ever want to know about this Mr. Shaw without even beginning to answer my question! What are you going to do, Aaron?"

"Well, after getting the word from the governor last week, I went to speak with this bartender, lawyer, politician, and activist. Mr. Shaw's so dynamic; so full of ideas. Without spilling the beans about the governor's intentions or fully revealing my reasons for leaving my position, I asked him for some fatherly advice. 'I attended the University of the South and majored in English, Mr. Shaw. Ever since I was a child I wanted to either write or get into journalism. But the closer I got to graduation, the more it looked as though I was destined to teach. Weren't many opportunities for young writers or newspapermen. The obvious fallback position was teaching. My adoptive father, whom you may have known, Preston Taylor, was headmaster and cofounder of the Westminster Academy near Court Square.'

"'Yes, I knew him; he was a good man,' Mr. Shaw said. 'We first met at the Howard Association during the '73 fever epidemic. It's just awful what happened to him and the rest of your family. That damned fire. You begin to believe the adage that no good deed goes unpunished. And everyone I know, white and Negro alike, respects what he did for you and your sister. As usual, though, we fail praising good deeds until the saints have left us. . . . I'm sorry, please go on.'

"I started again. 'So I thought I was destined to teach until I inadvertently landed the liaison position with the current administration. But I believe it's time to move on now. The political wheels have begun spinning too fast. You've worked in and outside the government. You've worked for others and started your own businesses. Honestly, I'm seeking your best advice.'

"Mr. Shaw smiled broadly and began the cross-examination. 'I believe you said you'd always wanted to be a writer or a journalist, correct?'

"'Yes.'

"'I believe you said you majored in English with this dream in mind, correct?'

"'Yes.'

"'I believe if there were an opening in one of the city's leading activist journals, you'd seriously consider applying for the position, correct?'

"'Yes. . . .'

"'And if the owner-editor actually offered you the job along with a stake in the business, you'd accept right away, correct?'

"'Absolutely! It would be the opportunity of a lifetime.'

"Mr. Shaw extended his hand and exclaimed, 'Welcome aboard, Mr. Editor!'

"'Editor?'

"'Editor of my *Memphis Weekly Planet*.'

"'I don't believe this is happening,' I said.

"'Believe it, Aaron. With everything I've got going on right now, with all the political intrigue engineering an unholy alliance with the Democrats, I don't have time to write, edit, and run the shop. It's yours now. So do us both proud.'"

Everything became awfully quiet in the dining room. I was nearest the door. I poked my head around the corner to sneak a peek. Aunt Jane was now sitting on Uncle Aaron's lap. She was hugging and kissing him over and over again. His hopeful message had clearly overwhelmed her annoyance with his tortuous journey home.

2

UNCLE AARON BURST into the dining room carrying an armload of newspapers. He walked directly up to the head of the table and placed the towering stack next to his plate. "Sorry I'm late again, Jane. I wanted to make sure this edition of the *Planet* got out the door on time. The *Almanac*'s calling for a lot of rain, so I wanted the readers to have it in their hands for the weekend. . . . I'm really hungry. I haven't had anything to eat all day but an apple. Is supper about ready?"

"I just have to get things on the table," Aunt Jane replied and then, quickly turning to me, said, "Lil' Jim, run upstairs and fetch Marcus and Daniel for supper." She turned back to Uncle Aaron and said, "You'll be happy to know the boys are religiously following their teachers' orders and getting their homework done. But I can't believe how much they're giving the children every night. Mr. Sampson really meant it when he said he wanted to brace their minds for hard study and mental labor."

"What about Lil' Jim here? No homework?"

"He's younger. Doesn't get as much as the older boys. But just as soon as he gets home, he gets right at it. He's already finished his assignments for tonight."

I puffed out my chest and smiled proudly as Uncle Aaron

tussled my hair.

"Just curious, Aaron; why'd you bring home so many copies of the paper?" Aunt Jane asked.

"It's a surprise for you and the boys after dinner."

Aunt Jane looked over at me again and said impatiently, "Lil' Jim, do as I told you! Fetch the boys before everything gets cold!"

Knowing better than to cross my aunt, I ran out of the kitchen in an instant.

Not long after devouring second helpings of beans, cornbread, and banana pudding, Uncle Aaron picked up the top copy from his stack of papers, held it up high, and announced, "I want all of you children to know I wrote a long article in this week's paper. I wrote it for y'all. It's about our history. And, Marcus, I expect you'll value much of what I'm gonna say. For the rest of you boys, I suspect you'll understand little of this now, but I believe one day you'll pick up one of these copies and remember you were here in this room as I described what I'd written for y'all and all the Negro children throughout the South."

"May we have a paper now, Father?" Daniel asked.

Uncle Aaron shook his head and responded, "Not yet, son. I'm putting this stack high on the shelves in the parlor. When you boys get a bit older, I'll give you your own copies."

"So what's it about, dear?" Aunt Jane asked eagerly.

"Some of the ideas you and I have been batting around on weekends. The headline and subhead describe the gist: 'Casting Off the Yoke and Standing Firm: Our Past, Present and

Future in Memphis and the Post-War South.' I was thinking of Saint Paul's letter to the Galatians when I drafted the headline. He wrote, 'For freedom, Christ has set us free. Stand firm, therefore, and do not submit again to a yoke of slavery.'

"I spent a good three months researching and drafting the article and decided I'd open with a little-known incident in our history. It grabs the reader's attention and illustrates our unending quest for freedom. Here's how I began the piece:

"'Some 350 years ago the first of our people stepped onto America's shores in South Carolina. They didn't come of their own volition. Their Spanish masters had dragged them here in chains to help settle a colony, San Miguel de Gualdape. But after only several months of a bitter winter, the Spaniards began feuding among themselves. Our people seized the opportunity to rebel, cast off their yokes, and sought refuge among the natives. Within weeks of the revolt, an epidemic struck the colony, forcing the Spanish masters to sail for home and leave their slaves behind to breathe the fresh air of freedom.'"

"I like it, Aaron. You're right. I suspect few have heard of San . . . San . . ."

"San Miguel de Gualdape."

"Over three hundred and fifty years ago?"

"Yes, settled in 1526."

"Senator Rodgers shared a lot of his history books with me, but I've never heard of the Gual . . . Gualdape colony. You know you're right, we all want to learn. And when you read something unusual, it does grab your attention. Engages the mind. . . . Sorry for the interruption, Aaron. Please, tell us more about your article."

"Yes, right. Well, in the next paragraphs, I show how succeeding generations were not so lucky. How the agrarian economics of the South influenced politicians to act in favor of landowners, and gradually trapped our people in centuries of misery. I discuss John Casor's failed freedom suit, which perversely changed his status from human being to a freedman's property for life, and then I move beyond his individual case to the onerous slave codes broadly defining the status of slaves and the rights of masters. That's when I quote one of the many barbaric provisions from South Carolina's 1712 code, which became the model for many of the other colonies." He stopped, looked at the article, and read aloud:

> Any slave evading capture for twenty days or more will be publicly whipped for the first offense; branded with the letter R on the right cheek for the second offense; lose one ear if absent for thirty days for the third offense; and castrated for the fourth offense. If female, she will be whipped, branded on the left cheek with an R and lose her left ear.

"My God, Aaron! The children shouldn't be hearing this! Let's excuse them. Discuss it with them when they're older."

"No, Jane. I want them to hear, to remember today, even if they don't yet fully understand all we're saying. What did Mr. Sampson say? Ah, we must 'brace their minds.'"

"I don't know if there are other difficult passages; but for the children's sake, please try to be discreet. Remember, they'll read the article for themselves when they're older."

"Point taken, Jane. There may be several more rough spots, but I'll do my best to tone 'em down."

To be honest, we boys were anxious to hear the "rough spots," but we knew better than to let on. We sat quietly and continued listening as Uncle Aaron and Aunt Jane discussed his article in the *Planet.*

Aunt Jane said, "So after Casor's freedom suit and the slave codes, where'd you go next?"

"To the founding documents: The Declaration and the Constitution."

"That's curious. Why the Declaration?" Jane asked. "It didn't carry the weight of law."

"You're right, but it carried an implied promise for our people. 'We hold these truths to be self-evident, that all men are created equal, that they are endowed by their Creator with certain unalienable Rights, that among these are Life, Liberty and the pursuit of Happiness. . . .' Since the Declaration said everyone was created equally and endowed with certain unalienable rights including liberty, our forebears naïvely believed they would also be treated fairly under a new form of government. So thousands of our people joined the patriot cause to ensure freedom for everyone.

"But as I write in the article, 'The Declaration's implied promise wasn't kept, and our ancestors' dreams weren't realized. In the eyes of the framers, the Negro's sacrifice wasn't enough to merit freedom.'"

"There wasn't any progress at all? Even with the Constitution?" Aunt Jane asked.

"As I point out in the piece, there was progress only in the North. Indigo, rice, and tobacco were too important to the fledgling national economy. So during the Constitutional Convention, the South sought and received exemptions concerning slavery, and those provisions were clearly spelled out in the document. I discuss them in detail—I want everyone to realize how money corrupts politics and bends dreams back toward the earth."

"So you're saying the reward for our sacrifice was the status quo?" Aunt Jane asked.

"Exactly. But we now know the pendulum began swinging back our way for a brief period beginning when we were kids. You and I lived through a time our people dreamed of for centuries."

"So where'd you go after the Constitution? To the Proclamation?"

"Yes, and then the Thirteenth Amendment abolishing slavery, which the states ratified after the war in December '65. Early 1866 is the pivot point for the article."

"The pivot point?"

"Yes, when the pendulum hesitated for a brief moment and then began swinging back in the opposite direction, away from freedom and back again toward despair and de facto enslavement. It's really the main thrust of the piece."

"So you think the pendulum began swinging back in early 1866? I don't understand. That's at the very beginning of the Reconstruction Era, before the late Senator Rodgers was elected and more than a decade before you were appointed liaison to the Memphis commission. Besides, historians say the decade after the war was when we made a lot of progress . . . . So what happened in early '66?"

"A riot."

"Where?"

"Unbelievably, it happened here, in Memphis. And the riot played a big role in slowing the progress we'd begun making throughout the South."

"You know I didn't grow up here, so I've never heard of it. What happened?"

"Pure and simple, it was a race riot. Began on May 1, lasted through May 3, in of all places, South Memphis, near the old Fort Pickering site. Tensions boiled over between Negro veterans and the white police. Conservative newspapers like the *Avalanche* blamed the start of the violence on the 'unruly behavior of colored soldiers around white folk.' I think a more accurate explanation would be Memphis elites resented living under Union control from '62 until the end of the war. And what the citizens found most galling was living under martial law enforced by three regiments of Negro soldiers. The white folk believed the social order had been turned on its head. They felt they were being overrun and controlled by Negroes. You see, after the Proclamation, our folk had fled the plantations and flooded into Memphis seeking protection behind Union lines.

"And added to that long-standing resentment was the ongoing struggle for jobs between our people and the Irish laborers. I found a supporting quote from the superintendent of the Freedmen's Bureau who said there was a conflict of labor between the Irish hack drivers, dray drivers, porters, laborers, and so on, and our folk employed in the same occupations. The Irish felt a great deal of bitterness knowing that southern gentlemen actually preferred hiring Negroes over them."

"Sounds like human nature—people resisting a new order of things, tensions grew, tempers flared and finally boiled over into violence."

"Yes. But it was more than that. After those first skirmishes on May 1 between the Negro soldiers and the police, the conflict grew into an ethnic battle between Negroes and the Irish over jobs and then into a full-blown race riot pitting white against Negro. During the second and third days of the violence, white firemen, laborers, and small business owners joined the Irish and expanded their target from the Negro regiments to Negro civilians, institutions, and property in South Memphis."

"Anyone hurt? Was their much damage?"

"Yes, plenty of victims and a lot of destruction according to a congressional report. It said by the time military authorities had declared martial law and detached a large force of white troops to restore order, approximately fifty Negroes had been killed, seventy-five wounded, five women . . . ah . . . assaulted, and more than a hundred people robbed. And as far as the institutions and the property go, the report said the rioters burned four churches, twelve schools, twenty businesses, and nearly a hundred houses."

"My heavens, Aaron. That's awful." I could see anguish on Aunt Jane's face.

"I'm very clear in my article about the deaths also. Many of them were executions. The congressional report quoted witnesses seeing, for example, one of our folk standing outside his house watching the hubbub in the streets, minding his own business, when two white fellows walked up, hit him in the head with a stick, and then fired a glancing shot to his head. Seeing his injury was minor, they fired a second round into his belly and then asked the dying man if he had any firearms in his house. . . . Oh, there are a lot of stories like that: rioters bursting into Negro houses, asking the owners if they had served with the colored troops, and then regardless of the answer, shooting them through the temple at point-blank range."

"Aaron, please! The boys," Aunt Jane exclaimed.

"I'm sorry, I'll be more discreet. . . . Without going into detail, I'll just say the report includes testimony from two Negro women whose house was invaded by seven men. The white posse ordered the women to fix supper for them; and after having their fill of ham, eggs, and biscuits, they pulled out their pistols and ordered the women to . . . ah . . . submit to their will. If they refused, the men said they'd kill them and set fire to the house."

When I turned toward the all-knowing Marcus to decipher this grown-up talk, he just nodded and winked, signaling he would fill me in later.

Uncle Aaron continued his narrative. "As the posse was leaving later that evening, one of the invaders spotted a red, white, and blue quilt draped over a chair. He asked the owner if she had quilted it before or after the Yankees came to town. She answered honestly, saying she had sewn it after Grant took the city. The intruder said, 'You Negroes have a mighty liking for the damned Yankees; but we'll kill you and you'll have no liking for anyone anymore.' He cocked his gun and aimed it at the woman, but for some reason he showed pity. He lowered his Colt, laughed aloud, and exited into the street."

"All the cruelty? Why? How'd you explain it in your piece?"

"Memphis was sending a message to the Negro and the rest of the South."

"A message?"

"Yes, and I explain this in the article. It was all about setting new boundaries, establishing limits to what Negro folk could say and do in the future. Other southern cities understood the message well. The riot here precipitated similar violence all over the South. The white folk were telling us they'd define our emancipation to their liking and they were hell-bent on returning to the old order."

"But we showed our resilience, rebuilding the schools, churches, and businesses."

"Yes, Jane. But there were scars. I didn't realize it growing up. The Taylors had pretty much sheltered me. But our folk here had witnessed firsthand the elites' determination to reestablish our subordination. And following the riot, the conservative newspapers wasted no time openly pounding the point home. Here, listen to this quote I found in the *Avalanche* only two days after order was restored: 'The chief source of all our trouble being removed, we may confidently expect a restoration of the old order of things. The Negro population will now do their duty. . . . Negro men and women are suddenly looking for work on country farms. . . .Thank heaven, the white race are once more rulers in Memphis.' You see, Jane, they wanted all of us to act like Austin Cotton."

"Austin Cotton?"

"A freedman. Found his testimony in the congressional report. Believe me, I've included it in my piece. Even thought of using his statement as the title for the article."

"What'd he say?"

"The investigators asked him why he hadn't been harmed while others had been killed or wounded. He answered, 'No one abused me because I was humble as a slave almost. I have heard them say to me, "You are right, Uncle; you are humble, just like a slave."'"

"Sending us right back into slavery!" Aunt Jane exclaimed. And then remembering her experiences in South Memphis, she added, "And you, Aaron, acted like I was out of my mind when I said South Memphis had turned, but now you see I was right. I just didn't know it started so soon after the war .... Now tell me, after pointing out the pendulum had begun swinging back, where'd you go with your argument? Reconstruction?"

"To that time period, but not Reconstruction per se; more about what the southerners were doing to regain control. I speak briefly about the Klan starting as a social club, how the enfranchisement of Negro men in '67 radicalized the Klan, who saw the Negro vote as a threat to the old order, especially after our folk turned out and swept a number of Negroes into office, including your Senator Rodgers, which you know all about. I then talk about how the night riders stepped up the violence to intimidate us, to discourage us from voting in the future. And I emphasize it didn't take long for their plans to work: by 1870 white conservatives had regained control of the state legislature and begun reversing the liberal laws passed during the early years of Reconstruction."

"Forgive me, Aaron, but the way you put it, it all sounds so discouraging, bordering on hopelessness. Is this the message you want our children and others to take from your article?"

"Jane, you know me better than that—the 'eternal optimist,' as you say. Would I ever write a discouraging or hopeless piece? Do I see a challenging situation? Certainly. But do I think our position is impossible? Absolutely not."

"Where's the hope then? Tell me, because I just don't see it."

"Toward the end of the piece when I discuss the way forward."

"And what are you proposing?"

"First I explain that the way the elites have rigged the system, the answer doesn't lie in politics. Perhaps in the long run, but not for now."

"How can we get anything done without exerting political power? Having been a senator's wife, you know how I feel about politics. What else is there that can change things?"

"We've got to think in steps, Jane. Short-term objectives leading to long-term goals. We have to set the foundation. Since we don't have political clout, it'll take some time; but slow and steady wins the race. They've built a dam, and you know what water does; it always seeks a way around it."

"So how do we make it better for the boys here? I've seen what's going on in South Memphis and I don't like it."

"We have to keep doing what we're already doing and encouraging other Negro families to do the same. It really struck a chord with me, that conversation you had with Principal Sampson. I've borrowed some of his ideas and phrases for the article. I hope he won't mind having helped a fledging journalist with his first piece. It's all for a good cause."

"Having met the man, Aaron, I'm sure he'd be honored and understand your heart's in the right place."

"As I was saying, I believe Mr. Sampson has it right. For as long as I can remember, our public schools have been separated from the white schools. Even during Reconstruction the goal was separate but equal. And from what I could tell doing my liaison work, the state legislature and the Memphis commission met their commitment to Negro schools. The problem hasn't been with the money; it's been getting our folk to send their children to school and then keeping them there. Getting the parents and teachers working as teams to build—what'd Mr. Sampson say?"

"Building 'mental stamina' and 'brain force.'"

"Yes, teaching them life skills: how to think and study, how to persevere and work independently, getting them to study at home . . ."

"You've included all these ideas in your recommendations?"

"I have . . . and so much more. In fact, it was Mr. Sampson's comment about the lack of vision—"

"Envisioning a bright future?"

"Yes."

"I know. That struck me too. And he wasn't just talking about the children lacking vision. He was including the parents as well."

"Yes. And if he has that right, how could we ever have successful parent-teacher teams? How can the schools succeed, if the parents can't envision their children becoming professionals, starting their own businesses, or working in the counting rooms and mercantile exchanges? You see, what's missing here is the parents' grasp of the connection between their children's education and financial success."

"Many will say you're dreaming, Aaron; trying to erase the effects of more than two hundred years of servitude. They'll ask, 'How could there be any initiative, any aspirations left in these people?'"

"I'm not buying their pessimism, Jane. You and I know Mr. Sampson's assertion is credible—his belief that the native powers of Negro children are of the highest order. But before including the claim in the article, I had to find evidence to support it. You know how much research I've been doing. Well, I finally found it: an 1865 census of southern occupations. There were twenty thousand skilled white craftsmen and tradesmen at the end of the war. And how many Negro craftsmen?"

"I don't know. I'm sure it's less."

"And just as I thought as well. But I'm glad you're sitting down. The census said there were *a hundred thousand* Negro tradesmen, and most of them were former slaves. That's a five-to-one ratio, Negro to white. There were turpentine farmers, carpenters, carters, coopers, bricklayers, blacksmiths and the like. . . . Puts that gloomy notion to rest. Our people have the initiative and the skills to succeed.

"And can you imagine what a formal education could

mean? Many of our children becoming professionals, entrepreneurs, business owners. You see, that's been much of the problem. Most of our folk have been channeling their skills and money into the white man's wallet. Our children must learn to see themselves owning the businesses rather than working for them."

"But, Aaron, there's a barrier I can speak to personally. I hope you've addressed it. Remember, the late Senator Rodgers owned his own business prior to getting into politics; had ten employees doing the cooking and catering. I clearly recall the sleepless nights at the beginning, wondering whether he'd get the money to meet the payroll and expand the business. Being charitable to the white folk at the bank, they felt Mr. Rodgers was too big a risk; but being realistic, odds are they'd already heard from the white caterers that it wouldn't be in the bank's interest to float our loans, that is, if they wanted to continue receiving the other caterers' deposits."

"That's exactly where I went with the piece. I write, 'Besides political repression and white terrorism, there's also the potent issue of economic oppression to address.' I explain how the white-run banks have continually limited our access to capital."

"Well, how do you suggest increasing our access to capital?" Aunt Jane interjected.

"Negro banks. Owned and operated by our people for our people." Uncle Aaron smiled at his own cleverness.

Aunt Jane wasn't giving in. "All right. So we will create Negro banks. Any other ideas to increase capital?"

"You're on the right track, Jane. In so many words I suggest the elite's resistance to the Negro banks will be quick and strong. So I've proposed a backup plan: Create financial cooperatives to fund Negro startups in manufacturing, real estate, and insurance. Build a consortium of Negro businessmen to invest in enterprises, which will provide employment for our people. It'll be hard for white folk to stop us on all fronts having diversified into manufacturing, banking, insurance, and real estate, and that's not to even mention all the craftsmen, tradesmen, and professionals who will now have access to loans to start their own small businesses."

It had been a long time since I saw Uncle Aaron so fired up. Aunt Jane's face also lit up to hear him speak so passionately.

"Now let me tell you about the summary, where I paint the overall vision," Uncle Aaron continued. He looked at his paper and read: "'Effectively educate our children; persuade many of them to become entrepreneurs; and after they've accumulated wealth, encourage them to leverage it politically to the benefit of all our people. Teach them to remember our past, to face the present, and foresee a brighter future. Our challenge as parents is to ensure our children know the legal, economic, and political strictures we've faced for centuries. And with that knowledge they can develop their own strategies to resist and ultimately prevail. As the psalmist wrote, "I will utter dark sayings of old, which we have heard and known, and our fathers have told us. . . . We will not hide them from our children, so that the generations to come might know them too."'"

Tears welled up in Aunt Jane's eyes. She leaned over, wrapped her arms about Uncle Aaron's neck, and whispered, "Amen, Aaron. Amen. I'm so proud of you."

3

AS THE BIRTHDAYS passed, I became more isolated. I became a stranger in a familiar land. I increasingly realized I could go where my family couldn't. I could walk uptown to the markets without causing a stir. The white folk were none too friendly, but that was because I was young and nameless. It had nothing to do with my appearance. You see, unlike the rest of my family, my physical features and skin color resembled a white person's in every way.

But unfortunately, my looks cut two ways. I no longer felt comfortable at school, at home, or in South Memphis. It wasn't so much a reaction to hostility. It was more a feeling of neglect and always being the odd man out. The South Street shopkeepers stared coolly. The Negro teachers rarely included me in classroom exercises. The students reluctantly added me to their playground teams. Aunt Jane and Uncle Aaron addressed most of their dinner questions to their children. And my cousins rarely invited me into their rooms to talk or play. I remember overhearing my Aunt Jane's sister describing my situation: "You know, Jane, there's just too much cream in that java to my liking."

So I didn't live from day to day but from year to year. From one oasis to the next, each surrounded by a vast sea of loneliness. My refuge? The idyllic week Thomas spent here each summer around my birthday. As far back as I could remember, he was like an older brother or the father I never knew. He had once lived here in my grandfather's house until the fire killed Grandpa and drove Thomas away. Grandpa had hired Thomas to teach English at Grandpa's school, but after the first wave of yellow fever hit Memphis in '73, Thomas resigned his post to study medicine. Thomas and Mama later worked together as a team treating scourge victims during the siege of '78.

When Thomas left Memphis after the fire, he promised me he'd come back every year to visit; and he kept his promise. The first couple of summers he returned, Thomas stayed with Doc Landrum, who'd been a partner in their medical practice. When he began staying here at the house, Uncle Aaron and I had Thomas all to ourselves. For reasons I never understood, Aunt Jane always seemed to plan her visits back home with her boys for the week Thomas was coming to town.

During those first couple of years when Thomas just dropped by for visits, there always seemed to be some tension in the air. Aunt Jane was courteous enough with Thomas, but she didn't project the warmth she usually shared with everyone else, even with strangers. I never really understood her detachment. Was she feeling put upon having to entertain a guest who dropped in for hours and stayed for supper every day he was in Memphis? Did she resent Thomas spending more of his time reminiscing with Uncle Aaron and me than conversing with her and her boys? Or was it because of

Thomas's whiteness, a troubling whiteness like mine?

While Uncle Aaron was at the office working on the *Planet*, Thomas and I would find something stimulating to do. As the years passed, the excursions became increasingly more remarkable—like steaming up the Mississippi to Fort Pillow; attending an outdoor lecture at Rhodes College; and rowing over to President's Island to explore the old freedman's camp. But there were three very special places we shared every year that evoked discussions and memories of my mother.

The first was the old Court Square between Main and Second Streets near my grandfather's private academy. Thomas said it was Grandpa's favorite spot; he called it the soul of Memphis. When I got a little older, I could see why. As you enter the refuge, time slows and the din of commerce disappears. Mature cypress and cedar trees arc the yew-lined paths. The August air is moist and laden with a thick scent of magnolia and rose.

Thomas and I always left home early to secure prime seats at the noontime concerts, especially when the cornetist Joe Dobbins was playing and leading his Young Men's Brass Band. No matter which of the many paths by which we chose to enter Court Square, we always positioned ourselves at the base of a large cast-iron fountain topped by the standing nude of Hebe, the Greek goddess of youth. And there were several other advantages to sitting along the edge of that granite foundation: feeling the cool mist cascading from basins at Hebe's feet; feeding the voracious catfish prowling the depths below; and knowing I was seated where Mama had sat weaving dreams for an unborn son.

The second site we visited every year was Central Park, where we would catch a home game between the Memphis Reds and either Birmingham or Macon. Going to a Reds game every year was special for both of us, but I believe it was for different reasons. While I had really fallen in love with baseball and enjoyed getting autographs after the games, I think it gave Thomas a chance to reminisce about a rare, carefree summer day he'd once enjoyed watching baseball with my mama and me.

Preparing for our day at the park had become a ritual. We would rise early, pack a lunch, and leave the house no less than an hour before the start. On our way over to the park each year, Thomas would recount with increasingly greater detail how he'd left the office early that day, picked up Mama and me, and then walked with us to the game along this very street.

He'd say, "Your mama was holding your left hand and I your right. You loved it so much when we'd lift you into the air. You'd churn your legs and giggle uncontrollably. . . . When we got to the park, we found a shady spot under that old elm where you and I sit every year. Such a great spot isn't it? On the third-base side right up close. But you couldn't sit still, so we let you run around nearby. We didn't know what to expect. Your mama and I knew nothing about baseball. Your Uncle Aaron had recommended we go; said it was all the rage back East.

"The Reds were playing the Indianapolis Blues of the Alliance League. I only remember a handful of our players, Doc Kennedy from Brooklyn, Billy Redmond from Saint Louis, and Johnny Shoup from West Virginia. Funny how you remember the smallest detail when you really care. . . . After the game, you got to talk to practically the whole team. I teased your mother, who was so beautiful. I said the Reds were like flies to honey. They'd come over to flirt with her under the pretense of seeing you, Lil' Jim. Back then the boys played barehanded; only a few had fingerless gloves. And the bats? They were anything imaginable: flat, long, short, thick, thin. The last inning that day was a doozy! Redmond singled, then stole second; and with two men out, Kennedy drove one up the middle scoring Redmond with the winning run. The final score: Reds five and the Blues four."

It was uncanny. It was as if Thomas had an inner clock ticking in his head. He'd time our walk so that he'd be announcing that all-important final score just as we walked into the shadow of that time-honored elm between third and home. I loved hearing that old story. It didn't matter how many times Thomas told me. I soaked it up every time. I wanted to know everything I could about my mama.

Our third special place was always the last we visited before Thomas returned home. We'd hitch up the wagon and drive out to Evergreen Cemetery where Mama and Grandpa are buried. We'd pass through the wrought-iron gates, cross a rustic bridge, and stop at a small gothic cottage to visit with Little Grace. That's what Thomas called the old caretaker's daughter even though the last time we visited she was married and holding an infant in her arms. Every time we dropped by, Thomas and Little Grace would talk about the wave of fever epidemics that had killed thousands here when she was a little girl. And then as if trying to preserve a memory, Thomas would always ask, "You still recording the names in your ledger? Still tolling the bell?" To which she would simply reply, "Yes, of course. . . . Yes."

After our brief visit with Little Grace, we'd drive up the rise toward the family plot. As with our trips to watch the Reds play ball, Thomas and I reacted differently to this special place. Where I saw flowering meadows, he remembered the heroes' trench where thousands of caskets lay buried side by side and end to end. Ministers, priests, nuns, and nurses—volunteers who'd come to help and landed here. Where I saw rolling fields, he recalled the hundreds of unmarked graves of Negroes, freed and slave, still separated from their masters in death as they were in life. Where I sensed the beauty of the knolls, vistas, monuments, and trees, he relived the searing pain of watching fever patients die and then be stacked out here awaiting an unceremonious burial.

When we reached the Taylor plot, we'd always jump down, hitch the mare to a low-hanging branch, and walk over to the graves. We'd stand there side by side staring at the headstones and reminiscing. This year, my sixteenth, was no different.

"One of the first things I remember was the promise you made."

"Promise?"

"When Uncle Aaron was taking me away to Nashville after the fire."

"What'd I promise you, Lil' Jim?"

"That you'd see me in the summer and we'd go see the Memphis Reds again."

"And you know I kept my promise. We went to see the Reds play that following August."

"But up until now I only thought you kept part of your word."

"How's that?"

"You recall what I asked you after you said we'd go see the Reds again?"

"Ah . . . sorry, Lil' Jim, it's been a long time."

"I asked you, 'Mama too?' Remember what you said?"

"Not exactly."

"You said, 'Yes, Lil' Jim. Yes. Mama too.'"

"You were a child. Christmas was coming. How could I have said anything else? But you know, Lil' Jim, I wasn't really lying. I meant what I said. I was speaking metaphorically. . . ."

"I know. I know now. It hit me the other day at the park while we were watching the game. Maybe it's because I'm getting older now, but, for the first time, I felt Mama was there with us. She was everywhere—in the smiles of fans, the hustle of our heroes, and the shade of that old elm halfway between third and home."

"It's always been the same for me. I see her everywhere I go. Someone's smile or slightest gesture will evoke warm memories of your mother. My only regret is you didn't have a chance to really know how special she was. Hannah was the most beautiful belle in Memphis. And that beauty seeped into her soul. We all loved her. She was special. A remarkable combination of beauty and raw courage. It was her valor—yes, that's the right word, because we were fighting a battle against the scourge. It was your mother's valor that steeled me to leave my clerical post and join her on the front lines. . . . I'm sorry, Lil' Jim. It's your sixteenth birthday. Enough of my memories."

"It's okay. I don't mind. I love your stories. You're telling me things about Mama I've never heard before, things that make me proud."

"And there are so many more tales to tell now that you're older. But why don't we go sit on the bench over there? I've got a present for you in my knapsack."

After taking a seat and briefly admiring the view, Thomas unbuttoned the canvas flap and slowly pulled out the gift he'd wrapped in burlap. He smiled proudly as he handed me the small lumpy present and said teasingly, "Pay attention now how ya open it, Lil' Jim; it just might bite."

I placed the package on my lap and carefully began unrolling the multiple layers of cloth. "Ah, what have we here? . . . Something leather. . . . No, no. Wait. . . . There's more."

I smiled broadly as I held up my new knife sheathed in a handmade scabbard—a classic bowie with a foot-long blade; chipped, double-edged point; brass mounted and wooden grips. "My God, Thomas, where'd you find it?"

"Had it packed away at home. Has a lot of history behind it. Belonged to my grandfather, who later gave it to my older brother, Robert. As a junior officer, Grandpa had carried that bowie from the battles of Monterrey and Buena Vista, to the siege of Vera Cruz, and finally to Chapultepec Castle, where Grandpa later lost a leg topping the castle wall. After getting back home, Grandpa used that very knife to whittle himself a wooden leg out of barrel staves.

"Grandpa passed this bowie on down to my brother, Robert, when he was leaving to fight in the War Between the States. . . . Yes, sir, your knife there's seen a lot of fighting."

"What'd your brother do after the war?"

"Didn't make it home, Lil' Jim. Killed near the end of it."

"What happened?"

"He and his men were trapped in a box canyon by Union troops who just happened to be passing through. Tried fighting their way out. Just too many bluecoats. Robert and half his men were killed, the other half captured. Surviving members of Robert's Raiders were later granted permission to bury him not too far from where I live now, at Grave's Bend on the Duck River. When you come visit, I'll take you out there to see the spot."

"The knife's a great gift, Thomas."

"I thought you should have something from your . . . ah . . . old friend here."

"It'll always remind me of you and all the good times we've shared. But there's another reason it's ideal. It's got you talking some about your family. You've never spoken much about 'em. I'd love to hear more stories."

"Let's save 'em for another day, Lil' Jim. It's getting late now, and Uncle Aaron will be getting home from work soon with your birthday dinner."

4

UNCLE AARON DIDN'T notice we'd entered the room. He was sitting at the dining table writing feverishly. Thomas knocked softly on the door frame and said, "Something smells awfully good around here."

Uncle Aaron looked up long enough to respond distractedly, "Dinner's in the bowls on the stove. Just give me a couple more minutes and I'll clear all this away so we can eat."

Thomas turned, winked, and motioned toward the kitchen. I knew what he meant—"Let's get out of Uncle Aaron's hair, see what Mrs. Tibbett's cooked up for dinner, and sample the menu." Since Aunt Jane and her boys left town for Thomas's visits, they missed my birthday every year. But the one good thing coming out of all of it was the incomparable Mrs. Tibbett always served as my birthday cook.

I nodded and quickly led the way back toward the stove. "What do you think Uncle Aaron's working on?" I asked.

Thomas shrugged. "Had he mentioned working on anything special?"

"Not that I recall."

"Well, he's just probably trying to meet this week's deadline. You know there's always a lot of pressure getting things to press."

"I know. He spends way too many hours at the office. Causes problems here at home with Aunt Jane. She says he's neglecting us. So this kinda makes me feel guilty."

"About what?"

"Having him leave the office early and drop by Mrs. Tibbett's to buy my birthday dinner."

"Don't take it that way, Lil' Jim. By his actions he's saying he cares about you."

"I know; but I've never liked putting people out or being the center of attention."

"Nonsense. Take my word for it. If he didn't want to be here, he wouldn't be." Thomas smiled, handed me a fork, and said, "Now let's get on with the job at hand."

After sampling the pork chops and fresh pole beans, we moved on to the target we'd saved for last—Mrs. Tibbett's legendary mashed potatoes with gravy. Honestly, it was the only reason a white man would ever venture into South Memphis alone anymore. Some give her restaurant and specifically her potatoes credit for helping heal the city's wounds. While there's been a lot of friction between the classes and the races, there's one thing about which Negroes, the Irish, and whites can agree—no one since their own mother's passing has ever produced such smooth, buttery, and comforting Tennessee cuisine.

Just as Thomas and I were about to plunge our forks into the brimming bowl, Aaron leaned through the doorway and announced, "I've reached a stopping point. Why don't you two put your pitchforks down and bring the bowls on in the dining room. I'll fetch some plates out of the cabinet."

We settled in at the table, and Uncle Aaron raised his glass of sweet tea. "Happy sixteenth birthday, Lil' Jim." He smiled and added, "And since your Aunt Jane isn't here, I guess we can dispense with the thanks and just get to digging in."

Uncle Aaron's faint smile with his birthday wish was the last we'd see all night. He seemed distant, distracted, all of the energy drained out of him. So after several long, awkward pauses during dinner, Thomas cautiously offered our help. "Something you want to talk about?"

Uncle Aaron stared into his plate twirling his fork in his first and only serving of Mrs. Tibbett's potatoes. "I'm sorry. I know it's your birthday, Lil' Jim, and it's your last night here, Thomas. There's just so much going on around Memphis."

"You want to talk about it, Aaron? We're here to listen."

I added my encouragement. "It's okay, Uncle Aaron. Tell us what's troubling you."

"Something that happened today. . . . And, I know this may sound strange to y'all, but it's about my vision for the future."

"Vision?" Thomas asked.

"The one I laid out in the *Planet* a decade ago: 'Casting Off the Yoke and Standing Firm.'"

"The article you gave me the first year I came back to visit?"

"Yes. That's it."

"I think it's one of the most thoughtful and well-researched arguments I've ever read," Thomas responded. "You accurately predicted what would happen after Reconstruction and Redemption. The white elite would use elections, new laws, and violence to set new boundaries for the Negro. And that's exactly what's happening. I remember you wrote politics wouldn't be the answer, at least not in the short term. Progress would depend on the Negro getting an effective education, starting his own business, becoming wealthy, and then exercising political clout."

"But the solution's not working out as I'd expected."

"Maybe you haven't given it enough time to work. A decade's not all that long in political terms. I know the elites have regained control, passed some onerous legislation, and remained silent as vigilantes intimidate the Negro into submission. On the other hand, more Negro children are going to school, staying there, and getting a useful education; more Negro entrepreneurs are starting their own businesses; and we're now hearing that even some of them are becoming wealthy. So it's only a matter of time before these fellows start throwing their weight around politically."

Uncle Aaron put his head in his hands, sighed, and said dejectedly, "It's so frustrating. . . . You're right to a point. While our schools could be much better, at least more of our children are getting educated, more starting their own businesses, some even getting into brokerage, banking, and insurance. More are making good money, but that's where it ends. Republicans aren't winning elections anymore, the laws are going in the wrong direction, and the violence is only getting worse. As I predicted in the piece, the elite were hell-bent on putting us back in our place and keeping us there.

"It's like I've wasted ten years of my life writing article after article encouraging our folk to work within the elites' rigged system. One thing's for sure: they're not playing by the rules. If they can't accomplish their goals legally, they just step outside—trump up charges, drag our people out of jails, and summarily beat them. None of these vigilantes are ever prosecuted for their crimes. The town folk won't come right out and say it, but it's what they want—sending the message for Negroes to get back in their place and stay there."

Thomas shook his head and objected mildly. "Not so much here in Memphis, though. Much more likely across the border in Mississippi, Arkansas, and Louisiana. After the '66 riot here, I understand things pretty much settled down."

"I'd have agreed with you up until this year; but the violence has picked up. Mostly beatings and torching Negro properties. Since other newspapers aren't reporting the crimes, the horror remains hidden beneath the veneer. You see, half of Memphis is direct descendant from slave stock; and over a couple of centuries, we'd learned our lessons well. It didn't take the white folk long to begin resetting the boundaries after rebel soldiers and Confederate sympathizers regained their right to vote. The unspoken message is becoming clear to all of us: be humble like a slave and everything will be just fine. I was a lonely voice crying out in the wilderness. But I honestly don't think anyone's been paying much attention to what I've been writing. Whose gonna care what one misguided mulatto's having to say? But now that there are two of us . . ."

"Two of you?"

"Yes. Ida Wells. She bought an interest in the *Free Speech and Headlight*, along with the Reverend Nightingale of Beale

Street Baptist and J. L. Fleming, who'd brought the paper here from Arkansas. Ida's turning that church paper into a political journal. All of a sudden the big boys have begun taking notice and rebutting our articles on their editorial pages."

"But in a way, isn't that good news?" Thomas asked. "The two of you engaging the editors in a citywide debate. . . ."

"If I were approaching the situation academically, I'd agree. But the editors are using threats of Negro domination to instill fear in the elites while refusing to investigate alleged crimes around South Memphis. Over the last six months or so I've begun hearing the whispers, mostly about beatings and fires. And that's what I've been investigating the last few months. Was going to publish an article to expose the violence before it turned deadly. But now it's happened, and it's hit close to home. That's what I was working on when you two got back this evening."

"What's happened?" Thomas asked.

"Well, let me start at the beginning. When Jane and I moved the family back here from Nashville, I discovered things were a lot different from when I was growing up. Remember how you and I could go anywhere? If we wanted to go up to the markets around Court Square, there was nothing stopping us. But our first week back, Jane came home with disturbing news: white folk were telling her she could find everything she needed in South Memphis, among her own kind. So that's what she did. She found a fellow running a small market who'd sell her fresh meats and produce—for a price. Kept the quality food hidden behind a curtain in the residence adjoining the business.

"Their arrangement worked out pretty well for I guess two years or so, until the grocer announced he and everyone else were being driven out of business by a white fellow who'd opened a market on the outskirts offering fresh food at cut-throat prices. So for the next six years or so, Jane had little choice but to buy from this white man who'd run everybody else out of town.

"And then it happened just as I'd described in the 'Standing Firm' article. After attending a freedman's school, a couple of brothers opened a market in the outskirts, just up the road from the white fellow who'd been running his grocery monopoly. They opened up about two years ago. The surrounding neighborhood was almost all Negroes. The Percy brothers called their grocery 'A Market of Our Own.'

"They were well known and popular; and since they'd been schooled in the food business, they'd made the proper connections to allow them to offer quality food at competitive prices. So market forces went to work. A majority of our folk, including Jane, tried the new grocery and began defecting from the white shopkeeper's business, breaking his stranglehold on the neighborhood."

"You ever met the men?" Thomas asked.

"Proud to say I have, on several occasions. One evening at dinner Jane explained she'd found a new grocery run by a couple Negro brothers offering fresh produce and meats at a reasonable price. She said the business was growing incredibly fast. Her comments piqued my curiosity, so I went with her on her next shopping trip. Met the brothers, who agreed to an interview, which ran in the *Planet* the following week. I began the article by reminding readers of the 'Standing Firm' article and then declared the brothers living examples of what I had proposed in theory some ten years ago. I still remember the catchy phrases I drafted introducing the interview—educate, incorporate, accumulate, and then legislate."

"Sounds like it was a win-win for you and the brothers."

"I honestly wasn't thinking in those terms when I published the piece; but now that you suggest it, I guess the interview did help promote my solution and their business. But at the time I was just trying to demonstrate how the brothers on their own initiative saved their money, found ten additional Negro investors to join them as stockholders, and then successfully launched their enterprise. Their story just fit my theory perfectly."

"How's their business now? Did your solution work over time?"

"They did remarkably well. Quickly turned a profit."

"What about the white fellow's store?"

"Has been rumored to be on the cusp of going under for the last sixth months."

"Have you talked to the brothers recently?"

"As a matter of fact, just last week . . . at the jail."

"At the jail?" Thomas exclaimed. "What happened?"

"The brothers said a county sheriff accompanied by the white shopkeeper came in to the store asking the whereabouts of a Negro who lived in the neighborhood. The officer said he had a warrant for the Negro's arrest. When the brothers explained they had no idea where the fellow was, the white shopkeeper barged in and accused the brothers of lying and harboring the fugitive."

"The shopkeeper? Not the sheriff?"

"That's right. The rival shopkeeper. And that's not all he did. He whipped out his pistol and slashed it across the elder brother's face!"

"Right in front of the officer?"

"Right in front of him. And the cop didn't say or do anything. But the older brother reacted impulsively. He ripped the pistol from the shopkeeper's hand, knocked him to the floor, and gave his accuser a real good whupping."

"Did the sheriff jump in to help the shopkeeper?"

"Couldn't. The younger brother was holding the officer at bay."

"So that's how the Percy brothers ended up in jail?"

"Not exactly. The shopkeeper went immediately into town and swore out a warrant for the brothers' arrest. Charges of assault and battery."

"Did the brothers comply with the subpoena?"

"Absolutely. Played exactly by the rules. They went before the criminal court, quickly posted bond, and then hurried back out to their store. You see, after taking the beating, the white shopkeeper had threatened to clean out their business, lock, stock, and barrel. And since they took the shopkeeper at his word, the brothers consulted an attorney to understand their rights if the white fellow attacked."

"What'd the lawyer say?" Thomas asked.

"He explained that since the brothers were beyond the city limits and Memphis police protection, they had every right to defend themselves if attacked. So they recruited several friends, armed them with the few guns they had, and positioned the men in the grocery to help defend the property against an expected Saturday night assault."

"Did the shopkeeper show up and attack, Uncle?" I asked.

"Yes and no. Yes, he showed up; but according to the reports, he didn't attack."

I looked over at Thomas quizzically and then interrupted Uncle Aaron again. "Well, what happened then?"

"The brothers told me the shopkeeper appeared at the front entrance around midnight just as they expected. But that's not all. They heard a commotion at the rear of the store, turned, and saw six or seven white men racing into the room. Believing the attack was on, the brothers and their friends opened fire, wounding four of the intruders."

"Well, according to their lawyer they had every right," Thomas said.

"That's where things got complicated. You see, the fellows dressed in civilian clothes entering at the back of the store were supposedly deputies claiming to have a warrant for another Negro's arrest. They weren't there to ransack the property. When the brothers and their friends realized the alleged mistake, they lay down their guns and submitted to arrest. The men were convinced they could prove their innocence—that they had no intention of shooting deputies trying to enforce the law."

"Released on bail again?" Thomas asked.

"No. Not this time. Not after the morning newspapers published fiery headlines condemning the brothers and their friends for their barbarous acts. Things began to spin out of control. Deputies returned to the brothers' neighborhood, forcibly searched a number of houses, and arrested upward of thirty Negroes, charging them with conspiracy. The judge ruled there would be no bail for any of the detainees. In the meantime the editorials ratcheted up the rhetoric recommending death for the Percy brothers if any of the wounded died."

Fearing what would happen to the brothers, I asked, "Did any of them die, Uncle?"

"No, thank goodness. Several days after the shooting, the newspapers reported the deputies were all out of danger and would fully recover. That's when I went to the jail to interview the brothers about what had happened."

"Well, that must have put an end to it," I said.

"That's what you'd think, especially if you were confident the rule of law would prevail. But the editorials had done their dirty work; had encouraged vigilantes to step outside the law and send a clear message that Negroes must never shoot white folk no matter what. So not long after the newspapers announced the wounded deputies would recover, a well-armed mob implemented a plan, to which I believe every well-heeled white citizen was privy."

"You really believe that?" Thomas exclaimed. "You believe everyone would know about a vigilante plan?"

"Absolutely. But hold on and I'll explain why."

"Okay. Go on. Tell us about the plan."

"So between two and three o'clock this morning, the vigilantes went to the jail, supposedly overpowered the guards, and dragged the brothers out of their cells. Put them on a switchyard engine conveniently waiting behind the sheriff's office and drove them just outside the city limits. As they yanked them down off the engine, the older brother grasped one of the lyncher's guns. And while the mob tried wresting it from him, the gun went off, fatally wounding one of the conspirators. Several in the crowd then pulled out their weapons and fired at the elder brother, tearing away the lower part of his face and shattering his wrist. The lynchers threw the men down and encircled them. The younger man knelt beside his brother, who was lying on his side with his knees drawn up to his chest. He was moaning loudly and shaking uncontrollably. The younger brother looked up toward the gang leader and begged for his life for the sake of his wife, his daughter, and an unborn child. The boss shook his head and then signaled the engineer to blow the whistle to deaden the sound of the fusillade. The younger brother shouted, 'If you will kill us, turn our faces to the west.' And after honoring his wish, the circle flared into a deadly arc and fired repeatedly."

"My God! How'd you find all this out so quickly?" Thomas asked.

"Well, that gets us back to my assertion that everyone knew what would happen before it happened."

"So how'd you find out so fast?"

"I read it in the morning newspapers."

"The morning newspapers!" Thomas exclaimed. "They go to press sometime around four in the morning."

"You've just proved my point. Most of it was already written. All they had to do was add a few lines of detail. Two columns wide, and the only explanation? It was planned, and everyone knew. And I learned several other things today while you and Lil' Jim were gone. First, that one of the local policemen just up and died today—suddenly—of 'undetermined' causes. It doesn't take a Pinkerton to figure that one out. The officer had to be the fellow who was accidentally shot while trying to wrest the gun from the older brother.

"Next, when the folk in the neighborhood found out what had happened, they stormed the Tennessee Rifles armory looking for guns only to find out the criminal court judge had already ordered the armory emptied a day or so before the lynching. Is there any doubt this was all planned?

"And third, when the white authorities heard the Negroes were massing to retaliate, they rushed a hundred armed men to the neighborhood. And once they'd dispersed the unarmed crowd, they broke into the brothers' store and stole all the wine, cigars, and the money from the cash drawer."

Thomas shook his head in disbelief. "My God, Aaron, what were they thinking? Don't any of these people remember the yellow fever just over ten years ago? You weren't here, Aaron, but everyone hailed the Negroes as heroes. They stayed behind in Memphis while most of the white folk fled the city, including many in the police force. The Negroes stepped in as policemen and protected all these white folks' houses. And they did most of the nursing and grave digging to boot. Times have sure changed. . . ."

"Or maybe they're just taking us back to the way it was before emancipation, suffrage, and the war. And if that's true, then it's pretty easy to predict how this row will all play out. Creditors will attach the remaining grocery stock in the brothers' store, sell it to the white shopkeeper for pennies on the dollar, and help the white man restore the monopoly he'd previously enjoyed.

"No one will be arrested, tried, or convicted. There will be no compensation for the brothers' wives or children. They'll be left to fend for themselves. And only by the grace of God and the kindness of strangers will they keep the roofs over their heads.

"And if the message wasn't clear before in Memphis, it is now. The protection we'd enjoyed under the law is no longer there. All confidence in justice has been destroyed in a single night. When we awoke this morning and learned our innocents had been handed over to the mob, we became angry and swore vengeance. We looked for guns, but our masters had already removed that threat. What were we to do? Attack with sticks and stones? In a word, no. As the editorials reminded us today, it'd be sheer folly to resist. It would mean certain death for our wives, our children, and us. The power of the state, the law, and the military is now squarely aligned with the lawless mob. The unspoken truth here—despite our achievements, our standing, or our character, Tennessee law will no longer protect us. Sad to say, white supremacy's back."

"What will you do now, Uncle?" I asked.

"The only thing I know to do, Lil' Jim. I'll fight."

"But you said it'd be crazy. Hopeless. They have torches. They have guns. What do you have, Uncle?"

He reached into the inside pocket of his jacket and pulled out a pencil and several pieces of paper. He held them up shaking his fist resolutely. "I have these, Lil' Jim! I have these!"

5

WHEN I WAS a small boy, before I said my prayers Mama, Thomas, and I would stand at my bedroom window and watch the flashes of light. Mama said it was the angels setting off fireworks celebrating my birthday. It was one of my first and last memories of her. After my mother died, Thomas and I carried on the tradition each August when he came to visit. We never said much. We would just stand there, staring out into the constellations, lost in our own memories, patiently waiting for the next meteor to arc the summer sky.

This brief silence every year was when I felt closest to Thomas and the distant recollection of a mother's love. It's ironic and bittersweet. While Thomas was there with me sharing the angels' celebration, I knew that in a few minutes he would leave the room and I would lie there alone watching the last of their fading show. I'd hear every excruciating chiming of the mantle clock counting down the hours until Thomas disappeared and I began another journey across vast stretches of loneliness.

For as long as I could remember, we followed a convenient ritual the day after my birthday. Uncle Aaron would rise early and cook Thomas a substantial breakfast. We'd drive him over to the depot, say our farewells, and see him onto the train. Once he'd departed, we'd take a seat in the concourse and wait the hour or so until Aunt Jane's train rolled in from Nashville. And the year I turned sixteen wasn't any different. When the station manager announced the eleven o'clock's arrival, we walked back out onto the platform to greet Aunt Jane, Marcus, Daniel, and Lil' John. As they stepped down from their car, I assumed my customary position off to the side watching Uncle Aaron reunite with his family.

While the comings and goings of Aunt Jane and Thomas had remained routine, everything else had been turned upside down. Uncle Aaron was right about the lynching. It had shaken the Negro community's confidence in the justice system and in the elite's ability to act with a modicum of good faith. Venom had been injected into the city's bloodstream again, raising racial tensions to levels not seen since the riot in '66. Negro patience and faith in the future had deteriorated into a toxic blend of cold cynicism and seething resentment for anyone white.

But I never sensed their antipathy while traveling around South Memphis with either Uncle Aaron or Aunt Jane. Adults wouldn't be so blatant nor children so bold as to insult me in my guardians' presence. It was different at school. Whenever I was on the playground or walking to school with Marcus, Daniel, and Lil' John, our classmates would launch their vicious attacks. But ironically, they didn't always aim them directly at me. They'd taunt my cousins, deriding them for dealing with the devil. And they based their attacks not so much on who I was but what I was—a perceived white elite. I can still hear their mocking chant in an exaggerated dialect:

Do, please, marster, don't ketch me,
Ketch dose fellars behin' dat tree;
They stole money en we stole none,
Put 'em in the calaboose des for fun!

And the ridicule took its toll. It wasn't long before my cousins wouldn't have anything to do with me in public. They refused to walk with me to school, leaving me to run the verbal gauntlet alone. Despite Uncle Aaron's repeated reprimands, the boys would blurt out the most hurtful things students were saying about me behind my back. It was clear I'd quickly become a source of friction at home, pitting the children against their stepfather and me. So many a night I cried myself to sleep, until I realized my tears wouldn't change a thing. I slowly learned to stow my feelings and pursue my love of ideas rather than relationships with other people.

But my color wasn't the only reason for the mounting tension in the household. Not long after the brothers' lynching, Uncle Aaron published his promised broadside, "Blood on Our Hands," attacking mob rule and the alarming retreat toward white supremacy. The local newspapers immediately returned fire, denying Uncle Aaron's allegations that the whole town knew of the murderous plot in advance and was thus complicit in the criminal conspiracy.

Day after day the editors ratcheted up the rhetoric, using code to incite violence: "Why should we allow such an impostor to live among us?" and "Is there no way to silence this scandalous press?" Uncle Aaron rightly feared for his life, his family, and his newspaper office. And God only knows what would have happened if Uncle Aaron's mentor, Mr. Shaw, the former *Planet* editor and politician extraordinaire, hadn't stepped in, convincing the mayor to provide round-the-clock protection until the acrimony died down.

None of us really adjusted well to the pressure. We tried pushing it to the back of our minds; but it was always there, just in another form. What had been acute pain had become over time a throbbing ache, which could fray even the strongest nerves. And it was during such unscripted moments that Uncle Aaron and Aunt Jane would scream their frustrations, vulnerabilities, and the truth.

Toward the end of November while home recuperating from the flu, I overheard one of their more heated exchanges. I was running a fever and had come downstairs to get some water. As I walked down the hallway toward the kitchen, I heard their raised voices. I warily peered around the corner into the parlor. Aunt Jane was clearly agitated. She was pacing, rubbing her temples, and stridently demanding answers. "How much longer can this go on? The papers just keep at it, day after day, week after week. They're trying to get us killed or drive us out of town."

"I promise you it won't happen, Jane."

"All it takes is a lunatic with a gun."

"Oh no, that's not what I meant. They might kill us, but they'll never push us out of Memphis. My roots are too deep here for them to do that."

"What in God's name were you thinking, Aaron? Declaring every white man here has blood on his hands! You should have at least told me what you were planning. You had to have known you were stirring up a hornet's nest."

"But it's the truth, Jane. They're determined to rule and lock us down in chains again."

"A spoken truth that could get us all killed. Is it really worth it?"

"Is it really worth living, if we cower, afraid to speak the truth? Despite the risks, I still think it was the right thing to do. Everything's moving in the wrong direction. If we're not going to speak out, we might as well just extend our wrists and let them apply the shackles."

"Honestly, Aaron, how much longer you think Mr. Shaw can hold sway over the mayor? If we lose the guards, they'll burn the house for sure, or worse!" Aunt Jane collapsed back onto the settee and broke into tears. "I just don't know how much more of this I can take. I pray every hour they'll spare the children."

Uncle Aaron sat down beside Aunt Jane and slipped his arm around her shoulder. "I've been thinking. You could take the children to Nashville and stay there until the anger dies down. It'd be good for you and the boys. It's okay. I can make do here as long as you promise to write."

Aunt Jane looked up and smiled through the tears. "I could never leave you here alone. I told you from the start we're a team. But even if I wanted to go, I couldn't take him."

"Who?"

"Lil' Jim. My folks just wouldn't stand for it. They've visited here. I'm embarrassed to— In a nutshell, Aaron, they don't like him much. They say he's different."

"Different? How so? Because he looks white?"

"Not just that. It makes me uncomfortable to say it. . . . They imagine there's just not enough man…not enough Negro in him."

"My God, Jane. Are your folks any different than the white—" Uncle Aaron stopped midsentence and changed direction. "If Lil' Jim's the real reason you're not going, then he could stay here with me. We get along just fine when you and the boys are—" Again, he caught himself and veered away from danger. "So if it'd help, what do you think of going to Nashville without him?"

"I meant what I said, Aaron. We're a team. But if only . . . You know. It's so hard on the boys, getting ridiculed in the streets and at school. Please don't take this the wrong way. I know he's family to you, your sister's boy. Please don't be angry, but sometimes I just wish he wasn't here."

"My God, Jane! Don't ever let him hear you say—"

"I wouldn't. . . . But the truth's the truth."

I turned away from the door, climbed the stairs, and curled up under the covers. I'd lost my thirst and heard enough truth for one day.

6

WHEN I GOT wind Aunt Jane's relatives were coming for Christmas, I decided to make my move. For weeks I'd sat on the fence, fearing to leave and loathing to stay. But I remembered their prior visits. Every time we'd get together, they'd shut me out of their conversations; and if I tried barging in, they'd look askance, prompting Aunt Jane to scold me. Throughout my childhood, I innocently blamed myself for their behavior. After all, I was violating one of the grownups' cardinal rules: "children should be seen, not heard." But once I'd learned their hostility was rooted more in prejudice than my immaturity, I quickly developed a callous disrespect for them, which now drove my decision to pull up stakes and see the world.

So it was no longer a matter of if but when I'd leave. And thanks to Uncle Aaron's grousing about the in-laws arriving on Christmas Eve night, I then knew precisely the day and time I'd have to be out of the house for good. It was dreamlike sitting at the dinner table every evening hearing the family eagerly anticipating Christmas while I was uneasily counting down the days until I stepped out into the night never to see them again. I must admit every now and then I wavered; but then I'd return to my room, pull my suitcase out from under the bed, and steel my resolve by rummaging through the memories I'd packed to take along: Uncle Aaron's articles "Casting Off the Yoke" and "Blood on Our Hands," Thomas's bowie knife, and a small bag of money I'd saved up from birthday gifts.

On Christmas Eve night I feigned a sick headache forcing me to stay home while the family drove over to fetch the in-laws. This gave me a chance to finish packing and write a brief note thanking Aunt Jane and Uncle Aaron for their love and support and explaining diplomatically I was leaving because I wanted to find my own way in the world. When I heard the back door slam shut, I knew that was my cue to strap the scabbard to my belt, don my winter coat and hat, grab my valise, and never look back again.

Since my limited funds would have to go for food, I chose to head down to the rail yard and hop a freight. Walking along through the empty streets, I remembered wistfully standing at the window in years past gazing out at scenes like this and thinking, "What a beautiful sight—clear, starry, and a full moon casting a silver spell over the landscape." But the stiff, cold wind now piercing my jacket and numbing my cheeks quickly stripped away any romanticized notion of beauty on this Christmas Eve night.

A left, a right, and then another left brought me to the no-man's-land between McCreary's woods and a steep ridge overlooking the roundhouse and switching yard. A half dozen shadows huddled near a roaring fire projecting gargoyles onto the evergreens. There was no spotter on the ridge tonight; it was Christmas Eve. Nothing would be moving on the main line for another day or two. Thomas had told me about this place. He said the fellows here reminded him of all the hobos he'd met growing up who'd stop by the farm and devour his mother's cooking on his granddad's back steps. He also mentioned coming down here every other Sunday or so, bringing food and medicine for the sick. He said he loved spending time here with his "sojourners," meeting all types—the old, the young, the sinner, the saint, the playwright, the poet, the hustler, and the priest. And I recall him saying, "Yes, sir, they're all types from every imaginable place, but they share a trait, Lil' Jim—they're all dreamers with an unshakable belief that their luck will change."

I walked over to where the men were sitting, found a break in the circle, and eased myself down close to the fire. No one acknowledged my joining the group but continued staring silently into the flames. Thomas had failed to mention several other features hobos share either by choice or necessity. All the fellows were thin, wore their hair long, sported unkempt beards, and somehow managed to find old rebel-issued blankets—the gray woolen ones with the distinctive yellow accent stripes—to sleep on or wrap around themselves. The irony didn't escape me; the lone Negro here had wrapped himself in Confederate gear. Ironic but understandable. How could anyone despise a thick blanket on such a cold night?

A strong blast of wind roared down the corridor between the ridgeline and the trees, driving fiery tongues high into the stars. The fellow to my left flinched and blurted, "I think Jerusalem Slim's trying to tell us something, Sky Pilot. It's pay me now or pay me later. Perhaps a prayer or a song celebrating the birth will do. . . . Happened again just like last year. Remember how Bindle ridiculed my idea then? Well, he ain't with us anymore, is he? I hear he's in the bone orchard. Tried flippin' a hot shot and greased the tracks east of Jackson. Probably no candy mountain for him."

Staring straight ahead into the fire, the hobo to my right responded, "If it's okay with the rest of you 'bos, let's take Spider's advice this time—say a few words, read a little scripture. It's fittin', and we can't afford losin' another brother from our annual convention."

After the other fellows chattered their cold approval, Sky Pilot pulled a dog-eared gospel from under his blanket, flipped briefly through the pages, and read a few verses from Luke's account of the birth: "And the angel said unto them, fear not: for, behold, I bring you good tidings of great joy. . . . For unto you is born this day in the city of David a Savior, which is Christ the Lord."

He closed his Bible and continued, "That's enough about the birth; let's talk about the grown-up Slim and what he means to all of us. In between summer sermons, I work a farm, mostly driving a jolt wagon. Well, from time to time this clover kicker and I will share the sacrament, some dago red. Isn't the oil of joy but it's still a tin roof. Every time after a few swills, and I mean every time, he says, 'Frank'—he always calls me by my given name; never calls me Reverend. He says, 'All you tourists are goin' from nothin' to nowhere.' And I reply, 'Beg to differ, sir. I'd say we're goin' from somewhere to somewhere. Not just us road hogs, but every one of us, you plow jockeys included. Everyone's on the move. No one's ever really home. We're all searchin' for somethin'—love, happiness, a companion.' The chief and I are oil and water, never agree on much, but he always gets me thinkin'. And come to think of it, none of us here ever spends much time in the jungle. All us cinder sifters are single O's. I admit it, 'bos, sometimes I get real lonely. Wish I had a partner sharin' the space between somewhere and somewhere. . . . How about you boys?"

The silent, reluctant nods began with the hobo to Sky Pilot's right and traveled counterclockwise in a wavelike motion, finally crashing up against me.

Sky Pilot then hopped back on the cannonball. "But come to think of it, Slim's always there ready to grab an armful of boxcars with you. Never refuses if you ask. Never lets you down. He's a blowed-in-the-glass stiff, I tell you."

A deep baritone objected, "He'd never flag a dicer with the likes of us, Sky Pilot!" The rest of our unholy flock murmured in agreement.

"Why, Dr. Bates?" Sky Pilot asked.

"Slim's just not anything like us."

"I disagree, Doctor; I'd say he's more like us than anyone else movin' to and fro."

"How so?" another skeptic asked.

"Slim was a 'bo like us, Flannel Mouth."

"You say he carried the banner?"

"Every day, Glims, until he caught the westbound home."

"A Weary Willy? You sure of this, Sky Pilot?" Spider asked.

"I'll bet my road stake on it. Let's see what the good news

has to say." Sky Pilot opened his Bible and began reading again from Luke: "'And it came to pass in those days, that there went out a decree from Caesar Augustus that all the world should be taxed. And all went to be taxed, everyone into his own city. And Joseph also went up from Galilee unto the city of David, which is called Bethlehem, to be taxed with Mary his espoused wife, being great with child. And so it was, that, while they were there, the days were accomplished that she should be delivered. And she brought forth her firstborn son, and wrapped him in swaddling clothes, and laid him in a manger because there was no room in the inn.'

"So you see, 'bos, Slim was born on the road in a stable. And what about later on while he was teaching? Matthew explains, 'And a certain scribe came, and said unto him, Master, I will follow thee whithersoever thou goest. And Jesus saith unto him, thc foxes have holes, and the birds of the air have nests; but the Son of man hath not where to lay his head.'

"So I'm tellin' all you Boxcar Willies he's one of us. And to put the icing on this cake, where'd they bury Slim? Well, Matthew tells us, 'There came a rich man of Arimathaea, named Joseph, who went to Pilate and begged the body of Jesus. Then Pilate commanded the body to be delivered. And when Joseph had taken the body, he wrapped it in a clean linen cloth, and laid it in his own new tomb.' So you see, boys, Slim was a travelin' from the beginning 'til the very end. He was buried in a borrowed grave!

"But those ain't the only reasons I know he was a breezer. Listen to his own words, and you tell me. . . .Slim's speakin' to us in a tongue we all understand, a lingo he learned on the road. 'Therefore I say unto you, take no thought for your life, what ye shall eat, or what ye shall drink; nor yet for your body, what ye shall put on. . . . Behold the fowls of the air: for they sow not, neither do they reap, nor gather into barns; yet your heavenly Father feeds them. Are ye not much better than they? . . . And why take ye thought for raiment? Consider the lilies of the field, how they grow; they toil not, neither do they spin. . . . Wherefore, if God so clothe the grass of the field, which today is, and tomorrow is cast into the oven, shall he not much more clothe you, O ye of little faith? …

"'Therefore take no thought, saying, what shall we eat? or, what shall we drink? or, wherewithal shall we be clothed? For your heavenly Father knows that ye have need of all these things. But seek ye first the kingdom of God and his righteousness; and all these things shall be given unto you.'" And as Sky Pilot closed his Bible and lowered his head in prayer, an "Amen" began to the preacher's right and echoed counterclockwise around our circle.

After a respectful silence, Spider spoke up lightheartedly. "Speakin' of eatin', we need to plot out our Christmas stew, especially if Slim's joinin' our pot gang tomorrow. We'll have to put everybody to work takin' the whiskers off and shacklin' up. My grandpa used to quote the Bible a lot, Sky Pilot. One of the verses he drilled into me—from Saint Paul—he said, 'The one who is unwilling to work shall not eat.'

"So how about we keep it simple. Breakfast and dinner went off last Christmas without a hitch. Everyone up for taking on the jobs they had last year? Worked real well."

After all the jungle veterans nodded their acceptance,

Spider reviewed their previous assignments and continued speaking in their baffling lingo: "Let's first work on breakfast. Last year we had pig's vest, cackleberries, saddle blankets, and black strap. You 'bos all right with that?"

Everyone nodded his approval.

"For dinner we had Irish turkey, gump, forty-fives, and punk and plaster. You boys okay with that?"

Everyone again nodded his acceptance.

"Let's see now . . . Sky Pilot, you're in tight with that butcher, Walters. So we'll leave you in charge of the block scrapings. Remember you're goin' again for gump, pig's vest, and the Irish turkey. Glims, you've got the cackleberries and the flour for the saddle blankets. Dr. Bates, you're the master of the black strap, and Flannel Mouth, you're bringin' home the forty-fives and the punk and plaster. So, you 'bos, put on your glad rags in the mornin', scoot on down to the Main Stem. Don't spear any biscuits, but slam a gate or two. Find some angels. Hittin' a lick tomorrow will be like shootin' fish in a barrel. It's Christmas—they'll all go easy on us."

"What about these new fellows here?" Glims asked. "What are they goin' to do?"

Sky Pilot jumped in. "Let's first learn a little about you fellows before we put you to work. It's only right." He then turned to me and asked, "What's your moniker, lamb?"

"Moniker?"

Sky Pilot surveyed the circle, smiling. "Your road name, boy."

"Lil' Jim, sir."

"Lil' Jim, huh? Well, Lil' Jim, where's home?"

"Right here in Memphis, sir."

"Where you headed, Lil' Jim?"

"Everywhere, sir."

Flannel Mouth chimed in, "Everyone here's heard that one before."

"How old are you, Lil' Jim?" Sky Pilot asked.

"Going on seventeen, sir."

"Shouldn't you be home celebratin' Christmas with your folks? Do they know you're here? They have any idea where you're goin'?"

"No, sir. My mama's dead. Died of the fever years ago. And never knew my father. Want to leave Memphis and travel out East."

"Pretty much an orphan then, huh, Lil' Jim? Well, 'bos, how about we take this lamb under wing and help him nail an eastbound rattler?"

The circle nodded its approval.

"Well then, Lil' Jim, welcome to our annual convention here in the Memphis jungle."

"Thank you, sir. I'll help any way I can."

Spider then turned to the Negro, who appeared to be in his mid- to late forties. "Well, sir, you came walkin' up out of the woods and sat down here not long before Lil' Jim showed up. What's your name, brother?"

"Brutus."

"Where's home, Brutus."

"These woods right now. Just waiting for the trains to pick up again."

"Where'd you live before comin' here?"

"Across the line in Corinth."

Flannel Mouth jumped in. "My pappy was wounded there fightin' under Maury."

"So where you headed, Brutus?" Spider asked.

"Harpers Ferry. Got a sister up that way."

"Goin' up to the John Brown Division, huh?"

"John Brown Division?"

"Uh-huh, the main freight yard of the B&O outside Harpers Ferry. Sounds like you're a first of May. . . ."

"First of May?"

Spider took his turn surveying the circle and smiling. "Uh-huh, no offense, Brutus. Just means you're new at this ramblin' thing."

"That's true enough. Never had to think about leaving Corinth until the business went under. Lost everything."

"Your line of work?"

"Undertaker. Joined my daddy in '66. Had everything: real estate, horses, a carriage. Mercantile agents said my credit was excellent. Made good money, especially after gettin' appointed recorder of births, marriages, and deeds. Yes, sir, made good money, that is, until I took sides in politics. Folks turned on me. And here I am, sitting out here freezing my fanny on Christmas Eve. No offense."

"Well, let's drive a bargain, Brutus. You help us out with the stew buildin', and we'll get you pointed in the right direction headed north. Whaddaya say?"

"Okay by me."

"Well, 'bos, while all of you're in the big town rustlin' up the victuals, Lil' Jim and Brutus here'll help me get the wood in. We'll have a big fire blazin' by the time y'all get back."

Sky Pilot slapped his thigh, slowly stood up, and said, "Looks like the fire's dyin' down a bit. Ain't a night to be cov-erin' with the moon. Better get over to the woods, hunker down in the fleabags, and pound the ear." Everyone groaned as they struggled to their feet and began walking toward the trees. Sky Pilot jokingly admonished us. "Sleep fast, you hear? Christmas mornin' will be here 'fore you know it."

As I marched toward the woods with the men, Brutus tapped my arm and signaled I should follow him. At the first fork in the path, the others veered left as Brutus and I turned to the right. We continued along this branch until we reached a sturdy lean-to Brutus had constructed out of some old boards while waiting for the freight yard to reopen.

"Come on in. Put your suitcase over there. You can take a seat if you like. You got something to wrap up in?"

I nodded. "I've got a small blanket in my bag there."

"You'll need it. The lean-to blocks the wind, but it still gets cold out here. Especially your feet. They'll be blocks of ice when you wake up in the mornin'. So tell me, Lil' Jim, you say you're headed everywhere, but where you headin' first? There's got to be a first stop."

"Probably lay over in Warfield for a spell."

"What's there?"

"An old friend I've known all my life. A real good guy. Used to teach in my grandpa's school. Left there to become a doctor. Treated folk during the fever. Left Memphis after our house burned down and moved east to Warfield. Wanted to start over."

"Well, I got a pretty good ear, Lil' Jim. Not for all that lingo those fellows were throwing around but . . ."

"That's for sure. Me too. I thought I was the only one tangled up in their words."

"So with my pretty good ear, I hear what folk are saying and what they're not. I read between the lines. Sky Pilot asked, but you didn't really answer about the folk you're running from. Where were you staying before coming down here?"

I hesitated and then replied, embarrassed, "With my Aunt Jane and Uncle Aaron."

"Why you running away from them?"

"Just didn't fit in. I really tried. Surrounded by a lot of folk but felt like I was living on the edges, separated from everyone, so lonely fifty-one weeks out of the year."

"So I guess the next question is, 'What was different about that other week?'"

"That's when my friend, Thomas, came back to Memphis."

"Thomas? Is he the doctor in Warfield?"

I nodded.

"Well, it makes every sense to pay him back with a surprise visit."

When the questions slowed, I jumped in to return the favor. "My Uncle Aaron's a newspaperman. Not the day-to-day news; writes opinion pieces. One of the themes he comes back to again and again is what you just said."

"What's that?"

"Running. He says we're all running—running away from something or running toward it. You running away from Corinth or running toward a new start with your sister in Harpers Ferry?"

"I like you, Lil' Jim. We'll make a good team hopping a freight together. . . . So I wanna be straight-up honest with you. Your uncle's a smart man. It's true, we're all running to or from something. But in my case it has nothing to do with Corinth or Harpers Ferry." Brutus paused and stared down at his hands. "I made all that up."

"Made it up? I don't understand."

"I never lived in Corinth. My pappy wasn't an undertaker. I never had a carriage. Never recorded deeds, births, and deaths. Don't have a sister in Harpers Ferry either. Like you, Lil' Jim, I'm headed everywhere."

"Why all the cock and bull, Brutus?"

"Maybe I should just start over with you from the beginning. My mama and pappy were slaves. Sold out of South Carolina into Tennessee. I was born well before the war. Worked the fields beside them. My given name is indeed Brutus, but my private name is Jobah. We all have private names, you know. Our way of telling the master he ain't got complete control. So I'm Brutus around the hobos here. But when they're not around, it's okay to call me Jobah."

"Okay, Jobah." I had never heard of someone having a private name. I was flattered Jobah was trusting me with his. "Go on."

"Joined the US Colored Troops—the Thirteenth. Patrolled the tracks up near Camden. Fought at Johnsonville and Nashville. Took Overton Hill. Drove Hood's rebels south toward Alabama. Let's see. . . it was twenty-six years ago to the day we battled Bedford Forrest's cavalry at Anthony's Hill.

"When the war ended, I came here looking for my folks. Seems every one of us slaves ended up in Memphis after the Proclamation. Found my mama and pappy. We lived in two rooms above a barbershop in South Memphis near the old fort. We did odd jobs until the fever hit in '73. My mama did the nursing, and pappy and I dug the graves. . . . I got into carpentry later on. My folks weren't so lucky in '78—the jack got both of 'em. I dug their graves too. Married that Christmas, but the fever took Mima in '79. Went back to building houses. But white folk had me arrested for 'serious breaches of social etiquette.' No offense, Lil' Jim. Said I refused to yield the sidewalk to a white man; said I talked back to him and was 'impolite' to his wife. Sent to state prison. The warden then leased me out to a bastard farmer. Convict leasing—just another name for slavery." He shook his head. "Couldn't see ever gettin' out from under it. Finally risked it all: ran away and here I am.

"Ya see now why I made up that story about Corinth and Harpers Ferry? If I told 'em the truth, these fellows would be hot to collect the bounty. I'd end up back on the farm, in the prison, or even worse—dancing at the end of a lyncher's rope. So I'm doing both, Lil' Jim, running from the law and running toward the freedom we'd all been promised years ago."

7

LONG BEFORE SUNRISE Spider marched through the woods waking the dead. He was banging on a pan with his fork and spoon and shouting, "Rise and shine! It's Christmas Day!" I rolled over onto my back, stretched, and slowly sensed the painful numbness in my feet. Brutus was snoring. I turned back again on my side and slid my legs up toward my belly. I didn't really mind the blocks of ice because a warm surge of triumph coursed through me. I had survived my first night on the road away from the family.

I finally crawled out from under the lean-to and walked back to the clearing. Spider was now busy building a small fire to fortify the men with the last of the coffee before launching them on their missions. One after another Brutus and the rest of the hobos stumbled out of the woods carrying their tin cups and greeting everyone with an obligatory "Good mornin'" and a "Merry Christmas, y'all." Everyone pretty much kept to himself until the coffee began percolating and filling the air with the most alluring aroma. Slowly our disparate group coalesced and began circling the fire in an increasingly smaller orbit.

"Smells larapin, Spider, but if that java's mud, I'll be usin' toothpicks to hold my eyes open all day," Glims said jokingly.

Spider looked up from the fire and responded, "Keep those picks for your pickets, Glims; this here's a pile driver, I tell ya. With a cup or two of this lightnin' in ya and your new shroud there, you'll dazzle all the mumbly pegs."

"Looks like ol' Glims here's been glomming the grapevine," Flannel Mouth said teasingly.

"Don't accuse me of gooseberryin'. I'm a respectable discard artist. This is a genuine snapper rig."

"Probably off a canned heater," Dr. Bates chimed in.

Sky Pilot stepped into the verbal jousting before things got out of hand. "Listen up now. I don't care where you 'bos got your duds, I think y'all look real good. I just hope they're all boiled up or at least you've read your shirts. Don't want any crotch crickets leapin' over on any of our angels.

"Before we have our java, let's gather 'round, grab a hand on either side, and offer up a short request. Bow your heads now and let's get to askin'. Slim, we seek a modest lump today. We're not moochers. And we're not wantin' to live off the fat of the land. Not askin' for alligator bait. Just some hopins. Don't let the biscuits hang high. Lead us to the real marks and help us make the riffle today. In your name, Slim, we pray. Amen." After a half dozen "Amens" circled the fire, Spider poured the brew, inspected every hat and jacket, and then sent the hobos off on their assignments.

Spider, Brutus, and I kept our promise and had the fire roaring by the time the fellows began reporting back with their Memphis bounty. Glims was the first to return.

"Whaddya have in the poke there, Glims?" Spider asked.

"Good news and bad news, Spider."

"Let's go with the bad news first. The good news'll then take the stinger out of my ass."

"Musta slammed a dozen gates, Spider. No one in the givin' spirit. No flour for the saddle blankets."

"The good news then?"

"Remember how Sky Pilot says sometimes you can't wait for Slim to act on your behalf? You have to do for yourself on your own? Well, when I saw I was gettin' nowhere fast, I spotted a cacklin' shack and borrowed a dozen and a half—not hen berries mind you, but duck berries—the size of melons. Enough here for all us 'bos."

After Dr. Bates appeared carrying two large bags of freshly ground coffee, Flannel Mouth returned triumphantly with at least a week's supply of beans, bread, and butter. As Spider then took possession of the city's largesse from the three, I heard him whisper prayerfully, "Well, now it's up to Sky Pilot, Walters, and Slim to make Christmas a real success." And fifteen minutes later the "Master of the Block Scrapings" returned smiling with a large sack flung over his shoulder. "Close but no cigar, Spider. Walters shared his Irish turkey and the sow's vest with buttons. Only had a coupl'a gumps. Graciously accepted 'em, though. Thought you might use 'em to whip up a jungle stew. And Walters's young wife even offered up a spud or two for good measure."

"Well, let's praise Slim for hearin' us out, 'bos. In our line of work we can't be choosers. But we'll still have a fine Yuletide feast. You can count on it. You 'bos go sit a spell and chew your cuds. Brutus and Lil' Jim here will be my cookees. We'll first whip up breakfast. How's this sound? Thick crispy slices of pig's vest with Adam and Eve on a raft. So how many of you in for wreckin' 'em? Okay then, three. So I suspect the rest of ya want your duck berries with their eyes wide open."

The jungle breakfast we shared that morning was the start of the best Christmas I could remember since Grandpa held me on his lap and read aloud Irving's stories of spending the holidays in the English countryside.

But early the next morning the mood changed dramatically. Caution and anticipation replaced our Christmas banter when Dr. Bates suddenly stood up, signaled silence, and pointed up the steep ridge to our right. Over the years he had earned the nickname "Screech" because it was said his hearing rivaled that of barn owls haunting lofts and steeples throughout the South.

"Whaddya hearin', Doc?" Spider whispered.

"Ashcat cleaning the firebox 'fore stokin' the yard donkey."

"Glims, why don't ya take a look over the hill and report back," Sky Pilot said.

When Glims turned to begin climbing the ridge, I spontaneously leapt from my birch stump and scrambled up the hill behind him. As we neared the crest, he dove onto his stomach and crawled the rest of the way to the top. I followed his lead, got on my belly, and inched up beside him.

"Boy, this is serious business. You gotta keep still. I dunno. This could be a hot yard. I don't see any yard bulls. But we sure as hell don't wanna get ossified."

"What are you saying, Glims? I don't understand your lingo."

"Ya gotta keep quiet up here, boy. Could be yard police.

Not that I have the bull horrors, ya know. Look. Look over there. It's the fireman I heard clearin' out the goat. Gonna get the fire buildin'. Get the eagle eye and the car knockers to start assemblin' the freight. Looks like he's gonna couple those cow cages, those three oil cans there, and those four whale bellies and put 'em back by the doghouse. Then I bet he humps those side-door Pullmans there. Gotta keep a keen eye on those; they're our accommodations. We'll be lookin' out for the one-eyed bandits. They'll probably be right up there at the head end, next to the hog and the tender."

"One-eyed bandits?"

"Sorry. it's habit. Boxcars with one door open and one shut. Want the door on this side open. Understand?"

"Yes, sir."

"I suspect the yard master'll sign off on this bull local today and we'll be pullin' out tonight. That's good. It'll be hard to see us, and it'll give us 'nough time to jungle up one last time 'fore splittin' for another year. One thing, boy, be sure you board with one of us 'bos. Train'll be movin'. It'll be dark. Gotta keep an eye out for the midnight creeps when you're crossin' the tracks."

"Midnight creeps?"

"Humped freight cars rollin' through the yard. Make no sound. They'll kill you. I've known three 'bos smashed under 'em."

We slid around on our bellies, got up, and then scurried down the hill to relay the news.

Not long after dark on that moonless night, Sky Pilot gathered us around the campfire to give us the plan and to say his good-byes. "Gentlemen, Dr. Bates says he hears the steam hog backin' into place. Not long now. Was good seein' y'all again. Good meetin' ya, Brutus. Good seein' ya, Lil' Jim. Everyone got their belongin's? Everyone got their spike? . . . Here's one for you, Brutus. And one for you, Lil' Jim. Jam it in the lock on the open door so the knockers can't lock ya in. Here's the plan now: we'll climb the hill together, spot some bandits, and when ya hear the highball, we'll make a run for it. And last of all, 'bos, Godspeed to y'all until next year."

After scrambling up the hill, we didn't have to wait very long. The engineer blasted the highball whistle, and the train began slowly moving out along the departure track toward the main line. We all ran down the ridge into the yard, grabbed hold of a boxcar, and swung ourselves safely inside. I peered into the dark trying to figure out if anyone had climbed aboard with me.

"Anyone there?" I whispered.

"Me. Is that you, Lil' Jim?"

"Yeah. That you, Brutus?"

"Yep."

"Anybody else here? . . . Anybody else?"

"Looks like it's just you and me, Li' Jim. Just you and me."

The train rumbled on, and when our freight reached the main line, the engineer gave two blasts on the whistle and opened the throttle to full speed. Brutus and I sat side by side with our backs against the wall opposite the open door. We didn't see any need just yet to close it and jam the lock with a spike. We had agreed it would help pass the time seeing the landscape speed by between one town and the next. I also found it reassuring watching the miles grow between old Memphis and me. But I couldn't begin to close my eyes and sleep. My heart was still racing not so much from fear but the sheer excitement of the adventure I had undertaken and so far survived.

We were steaming along at a fast clip until I did what I had done so many times before in my life; I jinxed us. Just as soon as I imagined we'd be nearing Hollow Rock at dawn, our train began slowing and gradually came to a complete stop. And then it got even worse. Not long after hearing trainmen shouting unintelligible instructions up and down the line, we began moving in reverse.

"What do you think they're up to, Brutus?"

"Looks like we're backing onto a siding. We'd better slide the door shut for now. Leave it cracked for air."

"Does this mean we're stuck here?"

"I don't know for sure, Lil' Jim. As long as we can hear the locomotive chuffing, I guess we're all right. But if it gets quiet, that means we're uncoupled, and Lord knows when we'll get on again."

"What will we do then, Brutus?"

"Guess we'll find the other boys and figure something out."

About fifteen minutes later, we heard banging near our car, which was followed closely by two long whistle blasts that signaled the engine was about to begin moving again. Next came the successive clanging of the couplers engaging up the line. And then within another minute, all we heard was the winter dawn.

I started moving toward the thin line of pale light across the car. "I'll crack the door to see what's going on."

"No! Let's wait and listen up for trainmen. Won't hurt to wait a minute. Then we'll go lookin' for the hobos."

After ten or so minutes of silence punctuated occasionally by a distant hound and rooster, I began moving again toward the door. "I can't stand it anymore, Brutus. The suspense is killing me."

"Okay. But go easy with it."

I slowly pulled the door back just enough to poke my head out. I looked to my left. All the hoppers, tankers, and empty cattle cars were still there. I then turned to the right, and my heart sank. There were only two boxcars in front of us. The locomotive, the tender, and the rest of the boxcars were gone.

"What do you see?"

"Nothing you want to hear about. The engine's gone. Could be up around the curve there, but I don't hear anything."

"See anybody stirring?"

"Nobody."

"Well, if you don't see any trainmen, let's grab our things and go looking for Sky Pilot and Spider. They're probably laying low the way we are a dozen or so cars up toward the head."

"There's not a dozen up there anymore, Brutus. If they aren't in the two cars right next to us, they're long gone."

"What do you mean two cars?" A tone of incredulity had crept into Brutus's voice.

"There are only two up there ahead of us. No joking. There are only two, Brutus."

"Here, grab your suitcase, and let's go check them out."

Brutus and I jumped down and ran up to the boxcar next to ours. The door was shut tight. I tapped lightly. “Anybody there?” Silence. “Anybody in there?” Again, no response.

We moved on up to what had become the lead car. I tapped. “Sky Pilot? Spider?” No response. “Anybody there?” Again, silence.

“Looks like they’re all gone, Lil’ Jim.”

“But how did they know to avoid the last three boxcars? They told us to run for any of the one-eyed bandits. What did they know?”

“Well, I guess we’ll never find out now, will we? But there’s no use cryin’ over spilt milk. Looks like God has something else in mind for us, Lil’ Jim.”

“Think we ought to just stay here and wait? Something’s got to come back to pick us up.”

“I don’t know. Could be days or weeks before anyone claims us. Let’s cross the main line and check out the cornfield there. Believe that’s the direction we heard the hound barking and the cock crowing. I know it sounded a way off; but if our luck changes, we might get something to eat and get out of this damned cold.”

I had my reservations leaving the one thing we knew—the freighter—but I was willing to follow Brutus for the time being. We crossed the tracks, climbed over a split-rail fence, and headed north. After trudging through several acres of frozen farmland, we came to a stand of timber. We turned east and walked along the edge of the woods for several minutes. Suddenly Brutus stopped and pointed. “Look! Up ahead! A path. Let’s see where it goes.”

We had only walked into the forest about a quarter of a mile when we could already see daylight beyond the woods. Brutus slowed and began looking from side to side, scouring the forest floor.

"What do you need?" I asked.

"A thick stick."

"What for?"

"That dog we heard a while ago sounded pretty mean to me. Don't want him gnawin' on our bones, do we? You look for a club too, you hear. If he charges us, we'll burn his hide on both ends. Not going to let a hound get between us and a hot meal."

But just as we exited the woods, we discovered there probably wouldn't be any hot food today. The path ended at the front step of a small abandoned cabin.

"Probably some of my brothers lived and died here," Brutus said. "Coulda been slave or tenant. . . . All the same, isn't it? Well, it looks like we're on our own for eatin', but at least we can get in out of the cold and listen for the trains. Let's see the accommodations we've got in there."

The cabin was so dilapidated, I didn't have high hopes that it would contain much of anything, much less something useful. But I was wrong.

"I'm surprised there's anything left," I said.

"Yeah, ain't life sweet? We've got a tolerable table and chairs but no food."

"The fireplace looks solid, though. We can build a fire and stay warm while we're waiting. You got some matches?"

"In my pack there," Brutus replied. "Let's go out and

scrounge up some wood. After that we can start dreaming about food again. I still haven't stopped thinking about that farmhouse with the hound dog and the rooster. Must be around here somewhere."

Within a half hour, we road amateurs had proudly managed to find some dry wood and get a decent fire going. Brutus looked over and said, "Hate to bring up a sore subject again, but I'm gettin' mighty hungry." He immediately turned and gazed at my valise sitting over by the door. "What do you have in your suitcase there?"

"Some clothes, some souvenirs, my traveling money, and a hunk of cheddar and hardtack."

Brutus grinned broadly. "You mind sharin' some of your cheese and biscuits? I'll pay you back in kind with interest . . . promise you that, Lil' Jim."

I swept the dust off the table, retrieved the cheese and crackers, and set them down over by Brutus's chair. "Well, let's take our coats off and stay a while. Enjoy some fine food and bask in the heat."

After savoring a few bites of cheese and crackers, Brutus looked up toward the ceiling and slowly scanned our small room and sleeping loft. He sighed as his smile eased away. "You know, Lil' Jim, this ain't a happy place. Negroes who lived and died here musta suffered—musta suffered *a lot*. Grew up in quarters like these. All my family squeezed into a space no bigger than this three-hundred-square-foot shack. In a strange way it was good to go out to the fields to work all spring and summer. It was hot, but at least you could stretch your legs and breathe. Probably the real reason I left to join the Thirteenth Coloreds after the Proclamation. Escapin' the squeezin'. After the war, I went back looking for my mama and pappy. And I'll be damned—we all ended up in two rooms. But ain't life sweet? The two rooms together were no bigger than the one-room slave cabin we'd shared before. Something just wanted to keep us down. After the jack killed both of 'em, I had more space for a little while. Then the white bastard lied and I ended up in a state cell no bigger than half this room. Ain't no denying it now, Lil' Jim. Life is sweet. Wasn't long 'til the warden leased me out to the plantation. Back to living like a slave, sharing one-room quarters with four other cutthroats. So I began to pray, to pray every day. And what does the silence say? 'Run and breathe freely again.' So I ran, and what happened? I first meet up with some hobos; I end up on a freight to nowhere; and then I find myself right here . . . right back in a slave quarters starin' across the table—no offense, Lil' Jim, don't mean anything personal—starin' into the blue eyes of the next generation determined to keep us down. Now I say, ain't life sweet?"

I didn't know what to say or how to react to the anger simmering just beneath his flawless ebony skin. I must admit he'd cut me to the quick. I pushed back from the table and said as calmly as I could, "I don't know about you, Brutus, but I'm really tired. I'm runnin' out of steam. Think I'll try getting a little sleep over by the fire."

"Hope I didn't hurt you, boy. I wasn't talkin' directly about you. Just frustratin', workin' hard time and time again and still end up where I began—an old slave quarter in the middle of nowhere."

"No offense, Brutus, no offense."

He pushed back from the table. "Well, while you're nappin', I'll keep an ear out for the freight and scout around for something more to eat."

8

After Brutus pulled his jacket on and left, I moved over to the hearth, lay down facing the fire, and draped my coat over me. I quickly fell asleep and began dreaming about going to a baseball game—walking between my mama and Thomas; holding their hands; kicking my legs out and laughing as they lifted me off the ground.

I don't know how long I had been asleep when a whistle blasting two longs, a short, and then another long dragged me away from the diamond. I rolled over on my back and groggily surveyed the room. Brutus was standing at the table. He looked over and said, "Not to worry, boy. It's a through train signaling for the road crossin' above the sidin'. Go back to sleep now. Get your rest."

I turned back over toward the fire and lay there now wide-awake until I heard Brutus leave again. As soon as the door shut, I jumped up and quickly opened my valise. Was I dreaming? Or was Brutus standing at the table rummaging through my suitcase when the freight went by? Nothing seemed to be out of place. Aaron's newspaper articles, my clothes, and my bag of money were all there. But something said check your savings. I untied the bag and poured the contents on the table. The Indian head pennies and the Morgan dollars were there;

but small flat stones had replaced all my gold Coronet pieces. My heart began to race. I put the bag of coins in my pocket, returned the suitcase to the corner, and began rehearsing what I'd say when he returned.

It wasn't long before Brutus pushed the door open with his foot. He was carrying an armload of wood. "You awake again?" he asked.

"I couldn't get back to sleep."

"Got to thinking I'd better bring in a few more logs just in case we're stuck here for another day or two. If you're feeling better now, we can try finding that farmhouse with the hound before it gets dark. What do you say?"

I didn't respond. I just stood there staring at him.

"Something wrong, Lil' Jim?"

"I don't know, Brutus. Could be."

"What do you mean 'could be'?"

"What were you doing with my suitcase on the table when the freight went through?"

He laughed nervously but then coolly replied, "You caught me dead to rights, Lil' Jim. I confess. I was still hungry. Thought you might have a little more grub stored away for safe keepin'."

"Borrow anything, Brutus?" I probed.

"You find anything missin', boy?"

I pulled my savings from my pocket, untied the bag, and poured the contents on the table. "Looks like all my gold pieces turned to stone, Brutus."

First fear and then hatred flashed in his eyes. He bolted toward me swinging his fists. I managed to block the first few punches, but his momentum drove me back against the wall. He continued attacking, pummeling me with lefts and rights from all directions. Knowing I had to move away from the corner, I drove my knee into his crotch, allowing me to escape toward the center of the room. He turned and lunged, driving both of us onto the table where he first pinned my arms and then slid his hands up around my neck. I instinctively slipped my hand to my waist, grasped the handle, and thrust my bowie into his belly once and then again. I could feel the pain loosening his grip. He collapsed onto me, coughed, and whispered, "Just like all the rest. Just like . . ." When I rolled him off of me, he slid down onto the floor faceup, staring blankly into the rafters.

I was shaking. I didn't think. I just acted. I changed my bloody shirt, cleaned my knife, retrieved the gold coins from the lining of his coat, grabbed my suitcase and jacket, and then quickly retraced my steps back to the main road running beside the railroad tracks. When I reached the highway, I turned eastward and began walking. I didn't know exactly where I was. I just knew I was on the road somewhere past Humboldt on my way to Warfield. The wind had picked up. It was already midafternoon and cloudy. I knew it would be dark by five o'clock. I had to find a place to spend the night out of the cold. Even a barn or a shed would keep me from freezing.

Thirty minutes into my trek I heard the most welcoming sounds—a horse and wagon headed east approaching from the rear. I turned and flagged the driver down. "Excuse me, sir, I was wondering if I might catch a ride with you."

"Where you headed, son?"

"Warfield, sir."

"Whatcha doin' out here walkin' along with your suitcase?"

"Long story, sir."

"Well, I'm not goin' as far as Warfield. Stoppin' off in Camden."

"How far's Warfield from there, sir?"

"Oh, some fifteen miles or so as the crow flies, on the other side of the Duck River."

"If I might ask, sir, where you staying?"

"Above a tavern with friends. Ain't no place for young'uns. But hop on up and let me think if there's someplace suitable in Camden."

"Thanks so much, sir. You don't know what this means."

I climbed up onto the bench beside the driver, and he snapped the reins.

"How far to Camden, sir?"

"Right now, uh, less than four miles. We'll surely be there before dark." The driver extended his hand. "My name's Armstrong, son. And yours?"

"Taylor, sir. But my family's always called me Lil' Jim."

After shaking his hand, I slid toward the edge of the bench. Mr. Armstrong must have been hard of hearing. He'd been shouting ever since driving up behind me.

"Now tell me, Lil' Jim, what in the Sam Hill are you doin' out here?"

"Leaving home to get on with life, sir."

"How old are you, boy?"

"Sixteen and a half, sir."

"Mighty tall order for a lad your age don't you think? . . .

So where's home?"

"Memphis, sir."

"I hate pryin', but you havin' trouble with your mama and papa?"

"No, sir. Mama died of the fever and I never knew my father."

"Where were you stayin' in Memphis then?"

"With my aunt and uncle. But don't get me wrong, sir, they've always been kind. I just felt it was my time to move on."

"So whatcha doin' out here walkin' along with your suitcase?"

"Took the train, sir."

"The train?" He turned toward me and smiled. "Ain't no depots around here, Lil' Jim, and I didn't see any Pullmans broken down along the main line. What kind of train you travelin' on?"

"To be honest, sir, a freight."

"You been minglin' with the tramps, boy?"

"Yes, sir. Can't lie."

"Dangerous proposition, Lil' Jim. Criminals. Perverts. Roustabouts. Is that where you got that scratch on your cheek? Someone try hurtin' ya?"

I spontaneously reached up and touched the fresh scab. "No . . . no, sir. After getting stranded on a siding by myself, I followed a path into a woods looking for help. Must've been some brambles or a low limb. Never felt a thing."

"Well, the fact you weren't harmed this time doesn't mean you'll always go scot-free. I tell you, young'uns shouldn't be communicatin' with the likes of these vagabonds."

Spider and Sky Pilot ne'er-do-wells? I started to object, but the violence I had just suffered at the hands of a fugitive trumped my inclination. I acquiesced. "Yes, sir. I'm sure you're right. You've lived a lot longer than I have."

I wanted to move on beyond his admonitions, so I turned the conversation to him. "Speaking of a long life, sir, how about telling me a little about yourself." The tactic worked. And Colonel Armstrong filled the rest of the time between nowhere and Camden with compelling descriptions of fierce battles in both the Mexican-American and Civil Wars.

After reaching the town center, the colonel looked over and said, "I think I know just the right place for you, Lil' Jim."

"Where's that, sir?"

"Just up here a way on the left."

And within five minutes we were pulling up in front of a large, three-story brick building. The sign above the door read, "Camden Youth Asylum." The colonel jumped down, hitched the mare, and said, "Grab your suitcase, boy, I think these folks'll let you spend the night."

As we walked up onto the porch, I had a strange but impossible feeling that I'd been there before. Probably thinking of some place similar in Memphis. The colonel knocked, and a lady answered almost immediately. "May I help you, sir?"

"Hope so, ma'am. This lad here has nowhere to stay tonight. Hopin' you folks could help him out."

The woman stepped aside and motioned for us to enter. "Come on in. . . . Follow me. We'll go down the hall to my office on the right."

When we reached the entrance she turned to me and said, "Why don't you go on in and take a seat there. Let me speak with this gentleman for a minute, and then I'll be right in."

I went into the room and sat down. Colonel Armstrong and the lady were standing out of sight just beyond the threshold. But because of his partial deafness, I could hear everything the colonel shouted describing my situation.

"We got a runaway here, miss. Said he hopped a freight. Found him walkin' along the main road between Huntingdon and Camden. Scratches on his face. I'm not buyin' his story about brambles or limbs. Says he's orphaned, living with relatives. Says everything was fine at home, just wanted to travel. Thought perhaps you could contact his folks, let 'em know. Or if you thought better, keep him here for a while."

I couldn't make out what the lady said, but the colonel ended their conversation with "Thank you very much, ma'am. I'll be gettin' along now."

The lady entered and sat down behind her large oak desk. She opened a drawer and pulled out a blank file. Before she could launch her interview, I fired a preemptive strike. "I can tell you before we get started I don't mind spending the night. But I'm not staying any longer. No offense, ma'am, but I've heard stories about your places."

She looked up from her papers and smiled warmly. She was perhaps in her forties and still beautiful: blue-gray almond-shaped eyes and long chestnut-brown curls lightly streaked with silver. "I don't plan on keeping you against your will. No obligations on your part. You're free to leave in the morning right after you have a good breakfast. I promise you that." She pointed to the empty file and continued, "But the state requires me to collect information on anyone who stays here on the premises. So I'll ask you a few questions; and when we're done, I'll get you down to the dining hall in time for supper. How's that?"

"Okay by me, ma'am."

"It's all right to call me Miss Emmett, if you like. . . . So let's begin. What's your family name, boy?"

"Taylor, ma'am."

"Your given name?"

"James."

"Where's your home?"

"Memphis."

"Mr. Armstrong said your parents are dead. Is that right, James?"

"Not exactly, ma'am. Never knew my father. Mama died of the fever."

"He said you lived with relatives."

"Yes, ma'am. My aunt and uncle."

"Where were you going when Mr. Armstrong picked you up?"

"Warfield."

"Why Warfield? You know someone there?"

"Yes, ma'am. Thomas. He's a friend; known him all my life. Left Memphis after the fire—that is, the fire that killed my family. Went to live in Warfield. He's a doctor. Been seeing him once a year since he left. Thought I'd surprise him."

Miss Emmett stopped writing and put her pencil down.

"I'm sorry, ma'am. Did I say something wrong? Is something the matter?"

She shook her head and gazed into my eyes. "Would you do me a favor, James?"

"Yes, ma'am."

"Would you please take your coat off?"

I looked at her quizzically. "If you want."

"Okay. Now do me one more favor. Roll up your right sleeve, and let me see your forearm."

I thought it strange, but I did as she requested.

"Looks like God marked you with a heart-shaped symbol, didn't he, Lil' Jim?"

"Lil' Jim? How'd . . . how'd you know my familiar name?"

"You probably don't remember, but we've met before. In fact, you've been in this very room sitting in that very chair."

"I don't understand."

"During the '79 fever, Memphis got hit really hard. A lot of parents died, and our Memphis orphanage was overwhelmed with children. They sent many of their orphans out here to Camden. You were among the last of the children to arrive. You were special. You showed up here with bandages on both of your hands. I asked you how you hurt yourself. You told me you'd been in a fire with your mama. One of the Memphis workers who chaperoned your group here said a fellow found you wandering alone in the streets and took you to our Memphis asylum.

"Since your bandages were awfully dirty, I took you to our medical area and applied new ointment and clean bandages. While rolling up your sleeves, I discovered the heart-shaped birthmark on your right forearm. I'd heard about your birthmark before, Lil' Jim."

I jumped in. "Heard? Who told you about it?"

"Thomas."

"Thomas?"

She smiled coyly. "Yes, Thomas is a good friend of mine too, Lil' Jim. He came out here to treat the children with the fever. And as you said, he later moved out this way."

"Well, how'd I end up back in Memphis?"

"I went to my supervisor and told her I knew who you were and where you lived. I offered to get you back to Memphis. You and I took the train and then a coach over to your granddad's place. But we got a real surprise when we pulled up in front of the house. There were a lot of workmen clearing debris, but no signs of Thomas. That's when your Uncle Aaron showed up and asked if he could help. He recognized you and said he was going to rebuild your granddad's place even though the fire had practically leveled it. I asked your uncle if he knew how to get in touch with Thomas. He said he'd drive us over to Thomas's office.

"Lil' Jim, I want you to know how happy everyone was to see you. They all thought you'd died in the fire with your granddad, your mother, and your aunt. I believe her name was Amanda. And everyone was also mistaken about your mother having died in the fire. They found her in a hospital where she did indeed die of the fever a little later on."

"I . . . I don't know what to say. No one ever told me any of this. I have some foggy memories of riding the train and the burned-up house, but I was never sure if they were real or from a dream. Thank you. Thanks for telling me, Miss Emmett."

She smiled, looked over at the clock, and said, "I'm sure you're hungry. Let's get you down to the dining hall. After dinner, we'll find you a place to sleep. You'll need a good night's rest because . . . you know why?"

"No, ma'am. Why?"

"Tomorrow you and I are going to go track down our old friend, Thomas."

While the other hundred children ate supper at long tables running the length of the hall, I got to join the asylum staff at the grown-up table. After introducing me and explaining my connection to the orphanage, Miss Emmett began reminiscing about the scary times here during the '79 fever. "If Lil' Jim's friend, Dr. Thomas, hadn't come up here from Memphis, we might have lost all the children and the workers."

"God bless him," the administrator said. "He was a saint, I tell you. And don't forget the other physician who volunteered to come here. Ah. . . ah. I think it was Reagan. No, no. Riggan. Dr. Edward Riggan from Virginia."

One of the staff spoke up. "Dr. Edward Riggan? From Virginia? You know where in Virginia?"

Another of the workers answered, "Yeah, Joe. It was Boydton, in Mecklenburg County near the North Carolina border. I remember him well. The doctor and I used to correspond the first year or so after he went back home. But you know how it is—you get busy, forget to write, and the letters die out. But it was Boydton for sure."

Joe picked up the folded newspaper beside his plate and opened it to the front page. "I think I've got some bad news for y'all. Why does everything always seem to happen around the holidays?"

The administrator broke in, "For God's sake, Joe, what happened?"

"From the front-page right-hand corner, 'Dateline: Petersburg. December 24. (Special). Reports received here tonight say that five unidentified Negroes were arrested and lodged in the Mecklenburg County jail for the murder of Dr. E. Riggan. The Negroes were taken from their cells last night by a mob and lynched. Dr. Riggan was fifty years old.'"

The administrator gasped. "My God! Dr. Riggan was in his late thirties or early forties when he was here, so he would be around fifty now. That's got to be our Dr. Riggan. It's horrible. . . . Well, those Negroes got what they deserved. As the apostle said, 'Seeing it's a righteous thing with God to recompense tribulation to them that trouble you.' This is the Word of the Lord. Amen."

As I bit down on my lip, I thought to myself, "A righteous thing to drag these nameless innocents from their cells and slaughter them without fair trials?"

After dinner Miss Emmett showed me to my room. "We have a nice place for you here, Lil' Jim. It's reserved for prospective parents." She paused and then added ironically, "It's like new. Sad to say, it doesn't get much use. Well, get to bed now. Get a good night's rest. You and I have a big day ahead of us tomorrow."

The room was clean but cold. Since the staff hadn't expected guests, there was no fire blazing on the hearth. I sat down on the edge of the bed, opened my suitcase, and retrieved my blanket. I took a deep breath and relived the last few days. Why did my color drive my family away? Why did the white folk lie about Brutus? Why did the warden lease him to the farm? Why did we both run away on what should be a joyous holiday? Why were we separated from the others? Why did the freight drop us off at the siding? Why did the hound bark and the rooster crow? Why was there an empty cabin at the end of the path? Why did Brutus take my gold? Why did I confront him? Why did he attack me? Why did Miss Emmett know Thomas? Why did she remember me? Why did my mama die of the fever? Why was I rescued and brought here? Why did Miss Emmett take me home? Why did my uncle take me in?

I removed the scabbard from my belt and slipped my deadly bowie beneath Uncle Aaron's newspapers. I read aloud the title of his broadside about the Percy brothers' lynching, "Blood on My Hands." What I'd heard at supper was repulsive. The reporter never even bothered getting their names. "Five unidentified Negroes were arrested and lodged in the Mecklenburg County jail. . . ." The mob became judge and jury. And the folks here quoted the scriptures to condone the mob's behavior. Don't they realize they've now got blood on their hands too?

I stowed my valise, turned down the lamp, and crawled in under the covers. I was back in the cabin lying there beside Brutus, staring up into the night. "I felt the sting, Jobah, when you spoke of the squeezing. The cruel running from the slave quarter to the plantation and then back again. Back here, as you said, to this unhappy place where Negroes suffered. You said you were just following your prayers. But something wanted to keep you down, keep squeezing until the very life drained out of you here and mingled with the earth. And it used my whiteness, Jobah, to perform its ritual—to sacrifice a blood brother on its altar. I did its bidding. No judge. No jury. I became your lyncher. Oh, I'll stand before the multitude declaring 'I am innocent of the blood of this just person, see ye to it,' but, brother, you and I know I have blood on my hands. Stains that won't wash away. Stains that will keep on squeezing."

9

"I'LL BET YOU a fat man to a biscuit we'll find him here at the office," Miss Emmett said as we pulled up in front of a two-story frame building in the center of Warfield. "Our friend Thomas lives to work. But I guess it's a good thing. His patients love him, and they seem to live longer than other folk around here. My husband, Reverend Emmett, jokingly says Doc's doing a good thing keeping people alive 'cause dead Christians don't drop coins in the collection baskets on Sundays."

She pointed toward a granite post and said, "Lil' Jim, would you mind hopping off and hitching the mare." I jumped down, tied the horse, and quickly moved over to Miss Emmett's side. I gallantly extended my hand to help her step down. She smiled and responded lightheartedly to my gesture in a syrupy, Southern-belle drawl, "Well, now, aren't you the gentleman."

As we walked up toward the front door, Miss Emmett grabbed my arm to stop me. "I know Thomas has a sense of humor and loves pulling surprises. So let's pull one on him. You stand off to the side where he can't see you. I'll knock and start the conversation. When I say 'surprise,' you step out beside me. How's that?"

I laughed and fired off a saying of my own, "That'll put pepper in his gumbo!"

We conspirators chuckled and continued on up the walkway to the door. She motioned me off to the left, knocked, and shouted, "Doc, you there? You in there?" After a minute or so, we heard someone fumbling with the lock. When the door swung open, I heard Thomas murmur, "Am I still dreaming? Is that you, Clara? What . . ."

"Sorry, Doc. Did I wake you?"

"I was just catching a few winks on the cot before heading off on my rounds."

"We've got to stop this, Doc."

"What do you mean?"

"It was almost eleven years ago now to the day Aaron and I came calling with Lil' Jim in Memphis. It was just like today. You'd been sleeping, still caring for the folk with the jack. You stumbled to the door and said you must be dreaming. You touched all three of us to see if we were real. Remember?"

"I'll never forget, Clara. It was one of my happiest days, seeing you and him. Remember? We brought Lil' Jim into the office and let him sleep on the cot. He'd been through so much—the fire, the orphanage, five years old. And he still didn't know his grandpa, his mama, and his Aunt Amanda were all dead." He paused and exclaimed, "What in the world am I thinking having you standing out there! Come on now. Get on in here out of the cold."

Miss Emmett laughed and raised her hands in mock protest. "No. No. Now you wait just a minute. I brought you a belated Christmas present just like before."

"Present?"

"Well, more a surprise."

When I heard my cue, I stepped out beside Miss Emmett. Thomas's lips began moving, but nothing was getting out. He quickly stepped to the side and motioned us to come on in out of the cold. He grasped my shoulders, gazed into my eyes, and gave me a big hug. He then turned toward Miss Emmett, embraced her, and whispered, "You know, Clara, you have some explaining to do . . . just like last time."

Thomas quickly cleared some medical journals from the chairs near his desk. "Y'all take a seat here." As he turned to fetch another chair, he pointed to the makeshift bed directly behind us. "You see that cot there, Lil' Jim. That's where you slept last time you came to my office, in Memphis. You were five years old. Time sure flies, doesn't it, Clara?"

She teasingly deflected the question. "Doc, tell me that's not the same cot you had back in Memphis."

"Afraid to say it is, Clara. But why throw away something that still works?"

She shook her head. "That's just like you, Doc. You never seem to get rid of anything."

He smiled warmly and said wistfully, "Especially memories of lost loves. . . ."

Miss Emmett didn't respond; she quickly reached over and tousled my hair, signaling she wanted to move on to another topic. "Well, Lil' Jim, I guess you'll have to describe the first part of your adventure for Doc. I can only explain what happened after you showed up at our door again."

"So tell me, boy, how'd you end up in Warfield?"

"Just coming to visit you . . . to return the favor for all those years you came to Memphis."

"Your Uncle Aaron and Aunt Jane know you're here?"

"Not yet. But I plan on telling 'em."

"How'd you get here? Take the train?"

"Yeah."

Miss Emmett looked over and frowned at my dissembling.

"Okay, okay. I packed up and left. Don't get angry now. I wrote 'em a nice note explaining I was leaving to see the world. Didn't have much money, so I hopped a freight. Ended up stuck on a siding; started walking. A fellow picked me up on the highway, took me to Miss Emmett's asylum. I was just gonna spend the night there and leave. Try hitching rides from Camden to here."

"How'd you get that nasty scratch on your cheek, boy?"

"Probably brambles or a low limb when I went looking for food before setting out on the highway."

"So, Clara, how'd you know who he was? You hadn't seen him in over ten years."

"The same way as before, Doc—the heart-shaped birthmark on his forearm. Remember? You'd told me about it not too long after he was born. So when I saw it again, I knew this had to be your Lil' Jim. I asked him where he was headed, and he said he was on his way over here to find you. And since yesterday was my last day working this week, I offered to give him a ride this morning."

"My God, what are the chances?"

"The Reverend and I keep telling you the Lord works in mysterious ways. And here's living proof."

"Well, let's celebrate my belated Christmas surprise with some good strong coffee."

Miss Emmett looked over at the mantel clock. "I'd love to, Doc, but the Reverend's expecting me home, and I don't want to have him worrying."

"I'd love to have you stay, Clara, but I understand. Come on, Lil' Jim, let's see Clara out to her carriage."

After giving us both big hugs, Clara climbed up onto the bench and took the reins. "Now, Lil' Jim, you enjoy your stay. And as for you, Thomas, I hope we'll be seeing you at Sunday services this week. There are really no good excuses anymore. It's so easy now that you built your place out near Hurricane Creek. And perhaps you can persuade Lil' Jim here to come along. It could set him off on the right path for a lifetime."

"I'll be there, Clara, if there are no emergencies. And I promise I'll work real hard on getting Lil' Jim there too."

We waited until Miss Emmett's carriage turned the corner before walking back up the path to the office. Thomas moved directly toward the potbelly stove. "I'm still gonna have that coffee. How about you?"

"If you're having some, I'll have some too."

After settling in with our steaming cups, Thomas sighed and returned to our earlier conversation. "I want you to be honest with me, Lil' Jim. It's pretty clear to Clara and me you didn't come to visit. You ran away and took a risk riding the freights. Why? You seem to have had a comfortable home in Memphis and had caring relatives to boot. So tell me straight, boy. Why'd you leave?"

"*Seem* can be a tricky word, Thomas. To everyone on the

outside looking in, everything seemed just fine. But I was living in a no-man's-land. I gradually became aware I could go uptown to the markets where my family couldn't. On the other hand, I couldn't go into South Memphis without Uncle Aaron or Aunt Jane's protection. And it wasn't just South Memphis; it was school and home as well. Teachers wouldn't call on me, and the playground bullies made my life hell. And at home . . . well, I knew Uncle Aaron and Aunt Jane meant well. But they'd spend most of dinner ignoring me and asking the other boys questions about their progress in school. And since the bullies teased the others about associating with me, the resentment and distance built up at home. You could tell. The boys even stopped inviting me to their rooms to talk and play.

"So I didn't live from day to day but from year to year when you'd come to Memphis and we'd visit our special places. So much joy anticipating your arrival. So much pain watching your train disappear around the bend again for another year. All because my features and skin color resembled a white elite and theirs didn't. It's a problem can't be solved, Thomas, especially with the way the city's divided now. So I'm never going back . . . and I hope you'll find a way to take me in."

Thomas didn't hesitate. He leaned forward and said, "You're welcome to stay as long as you want, Lil' Jim. But there'll be some conditions. You'll finish your schooling, you'll work the family farm up the road, and you'll please Clara by showing up for services this coming Sunday morning." He gave me a wink.

I extended my hand excitedly and asked, "For as long as I want?"

"Of course, for as long as you want."

"It's a deal, Thomas. The school, the farm, and Miss Emmett's church. I'll make you proud."

When Sunday morning rolled around, I kept the first of my promises. I washed up, put on my cleanest clothes, and accompanied Thomas to Reverend Emmett's church in Hurricane Creek proper. We found a space toward the rear of the crowded sanctuary. While I had only been to church a handful of times, mostly between Christmas and New Year's Day, I had worshipped enough to know what to expect at the Christian services. And to be honest, the opening acts that day were pretty standard fare—two hymns, "The Old Year Now Hath Passed Away" and "Another Year Is Dawning," and prayers laced with themes of rebirth and new journeys.

But when Reverend Emmett stepped up into the pulpit, he, as Sky Pilot would say, began "bending the iron." The Reverend first pared the usual ten to twelve verses of scripture to only one curious line from Deuteronomy, "Thy shoes shall be iron and brass; and as thy days, so shall thy strength be." And when he launched his homily, he became more narrator than holy man.

"One day a fellow from the Pharaoh's court went out to watch the Hebrew slaves hard at labor," he began. "He hadn't been there long when he observed an Egyptian overseer brutally beating a defenseless worker. The courtier looked around; and discovering there was no one else near the two, he rushed the supervisor, killed him in a rage, and buried him among the dunes.

"When the courtier returned the next day to observe the slaves, he found two Hebrew workers going at it tooth and nail. He stepped between the combatants and reprimanded the aggressor, 'Why are you pummeling your brother?' The Hebrew retorted, 'Who made thee a prince and judge over us? Do you intend to kill me the way you slew the supervisor yesterday?' Learning there were witnesses to his murder of the Egyptian the day before, the courtier now knew he would have to leave the court and even worse, flee Egypt for good. There were no longer any prospects of enjoying a comfortable bureaucratic life in the Pharaoh's service.

"Well, our courtier-killer managed to avoid capture and fled east to the land of Midian to start a new life. When he arrived in his new homeland, he sat down at a well to rest. He hadn't been there long when the seven daughters of Jethro, a shepherd priest, came to water their flock. As they were exchanging social pleasantries, some rival shepherds appeared and tried to drive the women's flock away from the well. And just as he had in Egypt, our courtier stepped in to defend the helpless from an unprovoked attack. Once the hostile shepherds had backed away, this caring stranger helped the women water their flock and then sent them on their way.

"When the daughters returned home, their father asked why they'd come back so soon. They explained how they'd been threatened and how an Egyptian had delivered them out of the hands of the shepherds and watered their flock. And Jethro said unto his daughters, 'And where is he? Why is it that ye have left the man? Call him so we may break bread.' So the daughters happily fetched their hero, and the Egyptian and Midianite sat down to dinner. And you'd have to say it was a very productive meal for our courtier. When all was said and done, he had a place to live, a field to farm, and a woman to marry. I'd say not too bad for a day's work."

The Reverend rolled his head to the right in an exaggerated fashion, encouraging the congregants to share a laugh in the midst of his serious tale. He then raised his arms to reclaim the reverent silence and continued. "So the courtier's wife bore him a son; and remembering his refugee status, he named the boy Gershom, which means 'stranger,' because the courtier was a stranger in a foreign land.

"After settling into this quiet life of farming, our Egyptian newlywed led his flock into the remote 'backside of the desert' near Mount Horeb. Well, he hadn't been there very long when the Lord appeared in a flame of fire, changing our courtier's life and altering history. The booming voice said, 'I am the God of thy father, the God of Abraham, the God of Isaac, and the God of Jacob.' And our courtier did what most of us would have done. He hid his face because he was afraid to look upon the Lord.

"And God explained why he'd come. 'I have surely seen the affliction of my people in Egypt and have heard their cry. I know their sorrows; and I've come to deliver them from the hands of the Egyptians and bring them to a land flowing with milk and honey. So come along now, and I will send you unto the Pharaoh so you can free my people, free the children of Israel.'"

Reverend Emmett paused again and asked the attendees, "Now can you imagine what our courtier-killer must have been thinking? 'My God, here I am having dodged the law living the quiet life of a farmer, and along comes the Lord asking me to return to the scene of my crime and confront the very ruler who has a bounty on my head for murder.'"

This time the Reverend rolled his head broadly to the left encouraging us to enjoy another good laugh before shepherding us back again into his serious tale.

"And just as any of us would do, our Egyptian courtier objected, saying, 'Who am I to go to the Pharaoh and explain I've come to take his slaves out of Egypt?' But God reassured him, 'Certainly I will be with you; and when you've brought the people up out of Egypt, you will serve me on this very mountain.'

"So, my friends in Christ, what lessons should we draw from our New Year's story of the Egyptian murderer, Moses? First, God forgives those who seek redemption. Second, we experience many dawns in our lives. And finally, if any of you are called to greatness, remember that while the journey may be long and rugged, 'Thy shoes shall be iron and brass; and as thy days, so shall thy strength be.'"

I lay in my new bed near Hurricane Creek that evening, Reverend Emmett's words reverberating off the memories and dreams. "Strange," I whispered to myself. "I meet an obligation and replace the morning guilt with the shimmer of midday redemption. Not the elite's political grail sustained through intimidation, assault, and lynching, but the forty-year redemption Moses earned climbing Nebo to see the

Promised Land. The Reverend said we'll all witness untold daybreaks. And I can affirm his assertion even if we limit the horizon to only the last few weeks. There are indeed so many opportunities to fall and rise again. . . . I pray only one thing, Slim. If you ever call on me to serve, you'll grant me the courage to don those iron shoes and demand of Pharaoh, 'Let my brothers go.'"

10

MOST OF THOMAS'S gifts came with histories, but this year's belated Christmas present also came with a surprise. When he returned from his rounds, he rushed into the house wearing a broad smile. "Hurry up, boy! Get your boots on. I have something to show you out in the barn."

"What've you done now, Thomas? I know you're up to something."

He just laughed and replied, "Get a move on before he disappears."

Thomas hurriedly led the way out to the barn and to the far stall on the left. He opened the gate and introduced me to a large black gelding with reddish markings on the mane, the tail, and the belly. "Merry Christmas, Lil' Jim. This is Black Widow."

"Ah . . . thanks, Thomas," I replied.

"What's the matter, boy? You don't like him? He's a beauty."

"It's not that, Thomas. Grandpa always said, 'Don't look a gift horse in the mouth.' But you know I've never ridden. What am I going to do with a big horse like this?"

"I'll have you riding in no time. I promise. I know he looks scary, but he's gentle and is used to being ridden."

"Where'd you find him?"

"One of my patients, Mrs. McCord. She rode him to church and to market every week unless the weather was really bad. She's getting on up in years now, and her brothers have insisted she give up the riding. They promised to drive her to town every week. So when she was in the office yesterday, she asked me if I knew anyone in need of a good riding horse, someone who would provide a good shelter. So I dropped by her place on the way home from the office, found Black Widow healthy, and bought him on the spot for a fair price."

"That's a pretty ominous name, don't you think?"

Thomas laughed and replied, "Kneel down. You see that reddish marking on his belly there?"

"Yes."

"What do you see?"

"If I cock my head to the right, it looks a little like . . . ah . . . what do you call it? An hourglass."

"And what does the female black widow have on her abdomen?"

I laughed. "Ah, I see. The black widow has the reddish hourglass on the stomach. Mrs. McCord probably didn't know the female's the only one with the marking. . . . I was sure getting worried there. I thought maybe the horse had an ugly streak or a checkered past."

"Well, I might as well tell you there's more to the story than the hourglass, Lil' Jim. And you'd eventually hear about it anyway."

I nervously continued stroking Black Widow's muzzle. "So what would I hear anyway, Thomas?"

"Mrs. McCord . . . ah . . . she's what they call 'Black Dutch.'"

"Black Dutch?"

"It means she's mixed. Has Creek blood in her. Well, she married Mr. McCord, a Scotsman, who owned a fairly large farm between here and Hollow Rock. He bought this fifteen-hands stallion at auction for Mrs. McCord and nicknamed him 'Black Dutch' in honor of his new bride. And according to the newspapers, while Mr. McCord was breaking him in—in fact, riding him for the first time, riding him bareback—someone fired off a round near the corral and spooked Black Dutch. When he reared up and lost his balance, Mr. McCord lost his grip and fell off. And Black Dutch came crashing down on him, killing Mr. McCord instantly.

"As the rumors go, Mrs. McCord's brothers wanted to shoot the stallion, but she refused, saying it was a gift and it really wasn't the horse's fault that someone fired a shot so close to her husband. The brothers then worked a deal with their stubborn sister. Since the plan all along was for Black Dutch to be Mrs. McCord's riding horse, the brothers persuaded her to let them castrate the stallion to calm him down and make him easier to handle. But just between you and me, having seen these fellows operating in the Warfield saloon, I tell you it was their way of getting back at the horse. Castration was revenge pure and simple."

"Goodness, Thomas. So he does have a checkered past! How'd his name get changed from 'Dutch' to 'Widow'?"

"I don't know for sure, but if I had to bet, I'd suspect her wag brothers had something to do with it. Just another dose of their dark humor. They probably started using 'Black Widow' when they saw Mrs. McCord riding into Warfield. The town folk got the play on words and began using the name to perpetuate the gallows humor. Mrs. McCord's the only one I know of around here who still calls the horse Black Dutch."

"So every time someone calls the horse 'Black Widow' they're in so many words saying 'here's the horse that made this Black Dutch woman a widow?'"

"Yes, I believe that's exactly what the brothers were up to. And they were very clever about it. There was deniability built into the horse."

"How's that?"

"They could always point to the gelding's belly and declare the hourglass is all they really had in mind." We both chuckled at the brothers' cleverness.

So now I had a horse. The next step was going to be learning how to ride it.

"When can we get started with the riding, Thomas?"

"We'll begin right away. You'll need to be up and on your own by next week."

And it was at this point in the conversation the present with a history became the gift with a past and a surprise. "Why next week?" I asked.

"Remember our agreement the day you arrived? I said you were welcome to stay, but there were conditions—you'd finish your schooling and you'd work the family farm up the road. You see, when my father died, my grandpa's younger brother, Uncle Billy, came over to run the farm. In fact, he ended up inheriting the property when my grandma died.

There was no one left on our side of the family—my mother, father, sister, and older brother were all dead—so my grandma willed the place to Uncle Billy to at least keep the farm in the family. When Uncle Billy could no longer manage, he asked his eldest son, David Lee, and his daughter-in-law, Theresa Anne, to take over the reins. Uncle Billy's other sons had no interest in farming and scattered to the wind. I think one's in Sacramento and the other's in Kansas City. So David Lee's been in charge ever since. In fact, Uncle Billy passed the place on down to him when he died.

"David Lee and Theresa Anne must be pushing sixty by now. But you have to admire them. They played it straight up, Lil' Jim. After the war, it was hard getting folk to come work the farm. David Lee paid fair wages to the few freedmen who signed on; and he proudly refused to lease any of the Negro inmates from the state prison. Said it was an abomination—like putting the Negroes back in chains. So he relied a lot on neighbors and church folk to get things planted and harvested. Been like that for a number of years now, hanging on by a thread. And if you haven't already guessed, that's where I think you have a calling."

"To help them out with the farming? But if I'm spending a lot of time there, how can I keep my other promise—finishing my schooling here in Hurricane Creek?"

"I've given that some thought too. You can follow in my footsteps, boy. There's a one-room school at the eastern end of the property. I'm sure there's some smart, dedicated folk doing the teaching. Don't believe it held me back one bit. So you can meet both commitments—finishing your schooling and helping out with the farming—right there on the property."

"That's well and good, Thomas, but when will I ever get to spend time with you? To be honest, that's a great part of the reason I stopped off in Warfield."

"No need to worry, Lil' Jim; there'll be plenty of time for visiting. Since winters are slow on the farm, you can ride down here on weekends. And besides, I'll be going out there to help with the planting and the harvesting. Will be out there on some of the Saturdays after doing my rounds. You see, boy? I'm not going to let you down. Sound like a plan?"

We stepped out of the stall and closed the gate. I half-smiled and replied reluctantly, "Sounds like a plan. . . ."

While Thomas was at his office the following Saturday morning, I packed my belongings; and when he returned, we saddled our horses and headed east on the Nashville highway. We had ridden a little over five miles when Thomas pulled up on the reins, stood up in the saddle, and pointed toward a split-rail fence on the right. "This is where the four hundred acres begin. Those are David Lee's cattle feeding on the hay there."

He tapped his heels into the mare's side and said, "Let's head on down toward the main gate so I can give you a better lay of the land. The fence running north-south here separates the far grazing field from the near field, which David Lee usually plants in feed corn. And that's his land across the tracks there too—a forage field bounded on two sides by Trace Creek and on another by his peach and apple orchards. There's an old Indian trail running north-south through there. Ancient hunters encamped on both sides of the path for thousands of years. My brother and I would spend hours searching for their arrowheads, spear points, and square-back knives. . . . Beyond the gate to the east is the family garden and on past that there's another hayfield butting up against the school property. That's the Miss Owings School down there at the far end of the farm. The dirt road running through the hayfield there is a right-of-way leading back up the hill toward the Anderson farm. They've been neighbors for as long as I can remember."

We turned in through the open gate and rode up toward a white, two-story farmhouse with black shutters sitting on a hill at the end of the entry road. At the bottom of the rise to the left was an old slave quarter, a well house, and a large buckeye tree about forty feet tall with a short gray trunk, scaly bark, and low-hanging branches. Thomas smiled and reminisced, "My grandpa planted that buckeye before heading off to the Mexican War. In the autumn we'd collect the fallen nuts and put some in our pockets because Grandpa said buckeyes would bring us good luck. When we crushed the leaves, they'd stink; I guess it was nature's way of warning us that every part of our tree was poisonous."

Thomas dismounted and said, "Here, give me the reins. Now hop off, and we'll tie the horses on these branches for now."

We climbed the short rise leading to the front steps, but instead of going up onto the porch we turned the corner between the house and the out buildings.

"They're probably around back," Thomas explained. "Let's see if we can raise them. Watch your step on that big rock there. That's where my grandma used to feed the hobos. A lot of fellows down on their luck. God, the stories they could spin. . . ."

The nostalgia in Thomas's voice was palpable and I wondered what more he wasn't telling me, but my questions would have to wait.

"David Lee!" Thomas shouted. "David Lee! Theresa Anne! You in there?"

A deep baritone responded. "Comin'. Hold your horses! Is that you, Doc?"

"Sure is, and brought some company with me."

A large muscular arm pushed the heavy door back. "Hurry. Get on in here out of the cold."

David Lee appeared to be in his early sixties. He was a battlefield of fiery red and placid gray from head to foot—an unmanageable shock of bright red hair graying at the temples; a bulbous red nose and jowls peeking out from behind a silvery beard; a red-and-gray-checkered shirt; and scarlet suspenders lifting his gray trousers up snugly beneath his substantial belly.

He motioned for us to follow him into the house. "Let's go in the dinin' room and sit you boys down near the stove. I'll get Theresa Anne to fire up a fresh pot of coffee." He turned away toward the hall door and roared, "Theresa Anne! . . . Theresa Anne! Come on down here quick and see what the cat's dragged in."

Within seconds a tall, thin woman, at least a head taller than her husband, rushed into the room and extended her arms toward Thomas. "It's good to see you, Doc. It's been a while."

"I know. You've been playing hooky from church too. And don't think Reverend Emmett and the elders haven't noticed. I got an earful last Sunday. Won't be long before they'll be sending a posse out here rounding y'all up too."

"You just tell 'em I'm doin' the Lord's work. Goin' over to relieve John Anderson so he can attend Mass. His wife, Mary, she's failin'. Her doc in McEwen tells John she hasn't got much longer. Nothin' seems to work. Really sad. But John will have his boys and daughters-in-law to see him through the tough times." She paused and then turned toward me. "And who might this handsome young man be?"

I extended my hand. "Lil' Jim, ma'am. Lil' Jim Taylor from Memphis."

Thomas stepped in. "I've known Lil' Jim all his life. I taught at his grandfather's academy before becoming a physician, and I lived with Lil' Jim's family through all the yellow fever epidemics. I migrated out here after his grandpa's house burned down. But I've paid visits back to Memphis each summer ever since, and now Lil' Jim's returning the favor. He's been living with his Uncle Aaron but felt it was time to move on. Now he's looking for work while finishing his schooling. I knew y'all were always looking for an extra hand. . . . He's got his own horse for errands and can do odd jobs around here before the big push with the planting and harvesting. I also figured he could finish up his schooling at Miss Owings before heading off to college. What do you think?"

David Lee looked over at me sternly and asked, "You willing to work, boy?"

"Yes, sir."

"Long, hard hours?"

"Yes, sir."

"Thomas, you know how hard it is. You think he's up to the task?"

"I'll stake my reputation on it, David Lee."

"Whaddaya think, Theresa Anne? Should we give Lil' Jim here a shot?"

She looked toward me and smiled. "I've got a feelin' this boy can help us out and has the pluck to do whatever he sets out to do."

David Lee thrust his hand out and said, "Okay by me then. It's a deal, Lil' Jim. I'll pay you a small stipend plus provide you room and board."

"Can you put him upstairs in my old room?" Thomas asked.

"Afraid there's no room left in the house, Doc," Theresa Anne replied. "My brother, Howard, whose been our foreman for umpteen years, sleeps downstairs here in the second bedroom; and the schoolmistress, Miss Sallie, and Margaret, her assistant, occupy your old room upstairs and the one across the hall. I'd call 'em in to introduce you but they're both up at the school gettin' ready for classes to start up again next week."

"Where you think you'll put him then?" Thomas asked.

"Bella's cabin is free," David Lee responded. "It's still in pretty good shape, and the furniture's still there. It's just the way Bella left it when she and Sergeant Basanater left for Nashville."

"May need a little dustin'," Theresa Anne offered.

"Yes, and I'll need to get some wood in for the stove," David Lee added.

"Where are your things, boy?" Theresa Anne asked.

"Stuffed in the saddlebags outside, ma'am."

"Well, we'll get you settled in; but first you boys have to have some coffee and pie to warm you up." She then raced off to the kitchen, fetched the coffee and dessert, and returned declaring, "I guarantee you, this is going to satisfy your sweet tooth!"

After devouring second helpings of Theresa Anne's apple-currant pie, we stopped off to retrieve the saddlebags and then headed over to the old slave cabin. Since there was only one small window, David Lee lit a lamp and led the way in. He immediately pointed to the slick dirt floor. "As I said, we've kept it pretty much the way it was when Bella left."

Despite the single window and the primitive floor, the cabin held some pleasant surprises. There was much more furniture than I'd ever imagined. I now had at my disposal two cots, a pine table with two chairs, and an old chest of drawers. David Lee pointed toward the dresser, laughed, and said, "From time to time Anderson comes around and offers to buy it back. Twice he's offered me ten dollars. That's ten times what Grandpa said he paid him for it. Anderson said it's sentimental; was the first piece of furniture he ever made for himself." David Lee laughed and added, "I guess the Christian thing to do would be to give it back, but I just keep forgettin' about it."

After dusting off the furniture and starting a fire in the stove, David Lee and his wife invited me for dinner and then returned to the farmhouse. Since Thomas would be leaving before the evening meal to get back to his patients, he pointed to the saddlebags and said, "You better unpack your things; I'll need to take a pair of those back with me. While you're doing that, I'll run out and grab a few more armloads of logs from the woodpile. You really don't want to let the fire burn out."

As soon as Thomas left to fetch the wood, I started transferring my few belongings from the saddlebags to the chest of drawers. But I didn't get very far before I discovered two carved figures pushed to the back of the top drawer. I sat down on one of the cots and inspected them. The one appeared to be a child wrapped in a sheet or blanket; the other a bearded fellow whose torso and moveable arms were carved from walnut. His lower body was cattle bone, and his turban and robe had been woven from fine horsehair.

Just as I was getting up to continue unpacking, Thomas returned with his load. "This plus the rest I stacked outside ought to hold you over until tomorrow afternoon. Get more in tomorrow, you hear." He dropped the logs in a box near the stove, turned, and immediately focused on my right fist. "What do you have there?"

"I don't know, Thomas. I found them in the drawer."

"Here, let me see."

I walked over and handed him the carved figures. He didn't say anything; he just stood there staring at them and turning them over again and again.

"You ever seen these before?" I asked.

"Sure have, Lil' Jim. God, they bring back memories. . . ."

"Hope they're good ones or I wouldn't have wanted you seeing them."

"A mixed bag, boy. Some good and some not so good. But I'm glad you showed them to me and happy David Lee didn't sell the chest of drawers back to Mr. Anderson just yet."

"Looks to me like the baby Jesus and maybe a wise man."

"Very good, Lil' Jim. That's exactly who they are. Belonged to Bella. She once explained they're Jesus and Balthazar, the only two pieces she had left from a nativity set whittled by an early slave and passed down to her as a child. She gave Balthazar here to my brother, Robert. Gave it to him for good luck beneath the buckeye tree out there when he was heading off to the war."

"That's an unusual gift for a soldier. I wonder what made her choose it."

"You might think she gave it to him because she treasured it. That might be, but I've always thought there was more to it than that. You see, Bella was very smart. She must have known Balthazar had offered up frankincense to Jesus and the smell of frankincense represents life to many Christians. I think she must have known its trees survive in the most unforgiving places too. So to Bella this Balthazar figurine was a symbol of life and survival. But things sure didn't work out the way we all hoped. Robert died toward the end of the war."

Thomas pushed the moveable arms down to Balthazar's side. "Funny thing here."

"What's that?"

"I distinctly remember the arms were down at Balthazar's side when Bella gave him the carving. But when one of Robert's Raiders returned his effects, the king's arms were fully stretched above his head—perhaps Robert's way of praying for the war, for the pain to end."

I could see the anguish in Thomas's face. I also sensed he had more he wanted to share, and I was ready to listen. "What about the other carving?" I asked. "Is there a story behind the baby Jesus too?"

"Almost too painful to remember or tell. . . . Bella had a son, Israel. Had a child's mind locked in a man's body. Could follow orders and do physical labor, but not much more. We all loved him. He and Bella were family to us. Well, this all started so innocently. I remember exactly where I was and what I was doing. I was sitting at my garret window reading Wordsworth. Something caused me to look up, and I saw a Union officer running up the entryway with his gun drawn. It took some doing, but David Lee's father, Uncle Billy, and I captured the fellow and took him in the house for questioning. I'll never forget it. He said his name was Burns and he was a Confederate spy who'd been on the run from Union troops for several days. I tell you, Burns could spin a fine tale. . . . So Uncle Billy bought his story and allowed him to stay with us while he hid out from the Feds. As I said, he was so smooth. He could sell religion to the pope. But long story short, he stayed on for several months and my sister, Rachel, fell in love with him.

"The following spring Israel and I went out in the fields to repair fences. On our way back, we discovered my half-dressed sister and Burns embracing just off the path. In his childhood innocence Israel thought Burns was attacking Rachel. He charged Burns from behind and cracked his neck, killing him instantly. It happened so quickly; there was nothing I could have done to stop him. I panicked, and . . . I'm not proud of what we did. Israel and I retrieved Burns's belongings from the farmhouse, dragged his body up into the woods, and buried him in a shallow grave.

"A month after Burns's death, a white lieutenant showed up with a detail of Negro cavalrymen. They told Uncle Billy they wanted to buy thousands of railroad ties for the new Nashville & Northwestern Railroad running between Nashville and the Tennessee River. As the Feds surveyed the timber, they discovered Burns's shallow grave and dug him up. Well, there was one thing Israel and I had missed: the soldiers found Burns's pocket watch with the engraving, "James Albert Parker," who had been reported missing in action after he and his Federal troops were attacked by rebels just south of Warfield.

"Well, they marched our whole family into the house, interrogated us, and came to suspect Israel had murdered this Federal soldier. Lincoln's boys then held a brief trial in the dining room where you and I just had our coffee and pie. Of all things, a black officer argued they must execute the freed slave to send a message of fairness to the locals and retribution to the Union troops. They hanged Israel later that day . . . hanged him from our "good luck tree," the buckeye out front there. Before leaving, the Feds said they'd return the next day and negotiate a deal for the railroad ties. Just imagine, Lil' Jim, how many passengers have passed over those very cross-ties and never known a thing about our Israel.

"This baby Jesus here. Bella gave it to her son just before he walked out to face the executioner. Maybe she thought it would comfort him in some way, perhaps give him good luck. Maybe the branch would break, the noose slip, or the Negro soldiers would have mercy on him at the last minute. I don't know. But once the hanging was over, I retrieved the baby Jesus and returned it to Bella. I told her he'd clutched it until the very end."

"Why you think she'd forget and leave something like this behind?"

"I don't think she forgot, Lil' Jim. She left them here because they belong here. They're part of the past she was leaving behind. She was going to Nashville with the Sergeant to start a new life. And besides, the carvings were steeped in excruciating memories and bad luck rather than in mystical powers to save either my brother or her beloved son."

"What do you think we should do with them, Thomas?"

"Let's just put them back where Bella buried them—at the back of the drawer."

"Well, I'm gonna finish stowing my things, but I'll leave the top drawer free— you know—out of respect."

"You're a good fellow, Lil' Jim. Finish unpacking and we'll walk up to the school before I leave. I want to show you around."

11

WHEN I HAD finished stowing my belongings in the chest of drawers, Thomas and I followed a path bordering the family garden and the forage field on one side and hugging the timberline on the other. We didn't say much along the way. Thomas appeared to be lost in his memories, and I wasn't about to ask any questions. Based on his earlier narrative and the actual lay of the land out here, I concluded we were walking the very trail where Thomas discovered Burns with his sister and the Feds pulled Parker from his shallow grave. As we walked along, I remember thinking, why would anyone choose this cursed path over the more direct route along the highway? I suspected it had everything to do with Thomas's demons—his attempt to cleanse his long-held guilt and perhaps achieve a scrap of redemption.

While climbing the front steps to the school, we could hear hammering inside. Thomas knocked loudly and shouted, "Miss Sallie!" "Miss Margaret!" The banging stopped, the plank door opened slowly, and an attractive brunette appeared. The young woman was wearing a pale yellow high-neck blouse and a long navy skirt. Her dark hair was parted in the middle and pulled back in a bun, except for several unruly curls, which were flowing down over her forehead. She was a paragon of femininity, except for the incongruous hammer she was holding in her left hand. "May I help you, sir?" she asked.

"Hello, miss. I'm Thomas and this is Lil' Jim. He's moving out to the farm here and will be going to your school starting Monday. We walked over here so he could get his feet wet before his first day. I'm really glad you're here this afternoon. Do you mind if we have a quick look around inside?"

The young lady turned and called, "Miss Sallie! There's a gentleman out here with a new student. They'd like a little tour of the premises."

A voice responded, "By all means, Margaret, show 'em in."

I followed Margaret and Thomas into the building and quickly scanned the place. I was pleasantly surprised. Even with the winter overcast the large room was bright and warm. A woodstove stood at the center of the space. It was the focal point for the teacher's podium, an upright piano, and four rows of student desks. There were blackboards on the front and side walls, which were decorated with several still lifes and photographs of state political figures.

Thomas approached the matronly schoolmistress standing on the riser and extended his hand. "Thank you for inviting us in. Miss Sallie, I presume?"

"Yes, and you're . . . ?"

"Thomas, ma'am. And this here is Lil' Jim, a new student who's moving out here to the farm."

I stepped forward and thrust my hand out confidently. "Nice to meet you, ma'am."

Miss Sallie looked over at Thomas and said, "So this here's got to be your son or younger brother. I'm good at reading features, and I suspect the two of you must be related." She then turned to Margaret asking for confirmation. "Don't they just look alike, Margaret? Striking. I mean the eyes, the square chin, and the hair."

Margaret looked back and forth at Thomas and me and replied, "I didn't see it before, Miss Sallie, but come to think of it they do share a chin, the hair, and especially the eyes."

I looked over at Thomas for his reaction to Miss Sallie's unusual observation. But Thomas chose to ignore it and quickly changed the subject. "I went here during the war, Miss Sallie. My grandfather donated the property here for the Sugar Grove School, the one that burned down and was replaced by the Miss Owings."

Miss Sallie smiled slyly and responded inexplicably, "All right, boys and girls, stand up; put your arms out straight from your sides—straight like the highway out front. Turn your hands palms up, and cup 'em. You're now a balance scale. Your body's the fulcrum, your outstretched arms the beam, and your palms the weighing pans."

It was as if Miss Sallie and Thomas had begun speaking in tongues. Thomas continued where Miss Sallie had left off. "So using our balance scale as an example and saying Trace Creek here is the fulcrum and our Nashville-Memphis road is the beam, which weighing pan is up and which is down?"

On cue, Miss Sallie started again. "The Nashville weighing pan is up in the air and the Memphis pan is down. So is Nashville lighter than Memphis? But why? Why would Nashville be lighter?"

Miss Sallie paused, and Thomas answered, "Well, when I arrived in Nashville, I was struck by how light, how bright everything appeared: the buildings, the ladies' silk dresses, the flowers, the smells, the smiles, the civility, the willingness to converse. Everyone and everything appeared to float in a timeless paradise void of pain."

Miss Sallie probed again, "But why was Memphis heavier?"

And Thomas concluded the mysterious dialogue: "When I visited there, it was much more difficult to live; Memphis was forty years younger than Nashville and less elegant. Many citizens struggled to make a living, and social life hadn't yet developed to Nashville's level."

They began laughing uncontrollably as Margaret and I stared quizzically.

"Is that you, Sallie Cummings?" Thomas asked.

"Sure is, Thomas. With a few more pounds and wrinkles."

"Wasn't Master Hudson the best?"

"I wish I'd been half the teacher."

The laughter subsided as the dialogue continued. "You know, Sallie, we were really lucky missing the fire that Friday. I was playing hooky to help tend the garden, and I believe you were sick."

"I know, Thomas," Miss Sallie responded. "I didn't think I was so lucky at the time. I still remember feeling so sick and wondering why I had to be the one getting that horrible flu."

"I'm sure all the students felt that way, even Master Hudson. But ironically, Miss Owings and five of our other classmates must've felt the opposite. Through some blind luck they'd escaped the high fever and vomiting going on all around them."

"I couldn't attend their funeral. I was still too sick. Did you go?"

"Yes. In Warfield," Thomas replied. "Since the Feds had requisitioned the church, they provided a large tent in case it stormed. It was the least they could do. Don't remember much about the singing, the sermon, or the prayers. One picture was burned in my mind, though. It was at the very end of the joint services. Pastor Reed raising his arm, offering the benediction, and then watching those six wagons beginning six journeys to where six families would continue the suffering in their own way." Thomas looked down and continued, "I'm sorry to be reliving all this with y'all."

"It's okay," Miss Sallie said. "I'm sure Margaret and Lil' Jim don't mind our remembering the past and the friends we lost."

Thomas pulled out his pocket watch and said, "It's getting on toward three o'clock. Won't be long until dark. I'll have to be leaving soon. I've got to get back to Warfield to check on patients."

"So, Thomas, you became a doctor?"

"Well, not at first. Taught at an academy for several years. Then the yellow jack drew me into medicine. . . .You ever get into Warfield or Hurricane Creek?"

"Once in a blue moon. Usually go into McEwen for church and shopping."

"Well one way or another I'm sure we'll find time to catch up."

"Absolutely. I'd like that." She stepped down off the platform, embraced Thomas, and said, "It's been really good seeing you. It's like finding a part of your life you thought you'd lost for good."

"I feel the same, Sallie. I feel the same way."

Miss Sallie extended her hand toward me and explained, "Classes will begin here again on Monday at nine o'clock, Lil' Jim. Try to come at least a half hour early so Margaret and I can learn a little about the schooling you've had down in Memphis."

"I'll come early for sure, Miss Sallie. See y'all Monday."

For our return trip Thomas chose the more direct route. As we walked along the highway, I broached the subject of his classroom dialogue with Miss Sallie. "Don't want to offend, but Margaret and I didn't understand half of what y'all were saying. I really like hearing your stories and learning more about you. So you mind filling me in about Miss Owings, the fire, and the funeral?"

Thomas looked over and nodded. "Only for you, boy. No one else. So where to begin? . . . You remember when we were talking earlier today about the white lieutenant and his Negro detail showing up and wanting to buy thousands of railroad ties for the new Nashville & Northwestern Line?"

I nodded. "Yes, of course."

"Well, that new railroad became a critical supply line for the Feds. They'd bring arms and materials up and down the Mississippi River to Memphis, offload the supplies onto boxcars, and ship the goods to Nashville, which quickly became a major supply depot for the Union army pushing ever farther into the South. You see, Tennessee fell early during the war. There were few major battles after '62. So the state witnessed a different kind of fighting: forty thousand Federal troops trying to protect depots, telegraph wires, and supply lines from attacks by mostly small bands of rebel insurgents. This is what my brother, Robert, was doing during the war, wreaking havoc on the 'occupiers,' as he called them, on their communications, munitions, food, and the like. So railroads were always rich targets and especially that new Nashville & Northwestern Railroad running between Nashville and the Tennessee River. And once the rebel attacks on the railroad began, the Feds countered by deploying troops to guard the trains, the depots, and the tracks. But the soldiers couldn't possibly guard everything between Memphis and Nashville. So every day we'd hear about more burned bridges, damaged trestles, and lightning strikes on the trains themselves."

"How could they attack the speeding trains, Thomas?"

"Oh, the rebels were very clever. They'd capture Union track repairers, order them to draw the spikes from a rail, and remove the fastenings from the end to make it loose. The guerrillas would then lie in wait in the bramble on the sides of the track bed. A locomotive would come roaring through, hit the loosened track, derail, and slide over on its side. The rebels would then swarm the train, kill the crew, chop holes in the engine boilers, and torch the brimming boxcars headed for Nashville.

"And it was just about there, right there in the family garden, I saw one of these raids firsthand. I was alone, pulling weeds. Uncle Billy was in the far western field tending the cattle. It was about eleven o'clock on a Friday morning. First, I heard the sharp whistle blasts and then the loud clanging of the engine bell. But something was different that day. I sensed the locomotive was slowing; and then I heard the loud screeching of the driving wheels spinning into reverse. As the engine sounds faded, the gunshots began. *Pop, pop, pop,* silence, echo, *pop, pop,* silence, echo, echo, *pop, pop*; and then the shouting began. I ducked down and scrambled over to the fence there to take cover and try to see what was going on."

"Were you scared?"

Thomas smiled and said, "Let's just say it got my attention. Anyway, I crept along the fence line there until I could see the train. But I couldn't believe what I was seeing. The engine was sitting sideways across the tracks and bellowing thick, gray smoke out of its stack. At first, I didn't see a soul, but then I picked up three men running across the highway onto our property. The rifle and pistol shots rang out again. The three men stopped, squeezed off several rounds from their Navy Colts, and then resumed running across our hayfield between Anderson's road and Sugar Grove School. When the gunfire stopped, I saw another two men, this time armed with rifles, run out from between the burning boxcars, cross the highway, and crawl over our split-rail fence onto the property.

"Well, the first three men stopped, began shooting again at their pursuers, and then split up. While one went running toward the tree line, the other two headed straight for the Sugar Grove School and went inside. The two Federal guards advanced cautiously through the field toward the school, firing randomly into the frame building. That's when my heart sank. I realized the bluecoats didn't know the structure was a schoolhouse. There were no signs on the property or the building itself saying 'Sugar Grove School.' But as my level of concern grew, I heard the welcome hoofbeats of Federal troops riding up the highway behind me.

"They hitched their horses to our fence, climbed over, and began advancing en masse toward the building. When they got within fifteen yards, the Feds fanned out into a semicircle partially ringing the exterior. The officer raised his arm and waved the troops into deadly action. The fusillade ripped into the thin walls; and I could see large, smoking chunks of wood flying off the surface. I jumped up and thought to scream, but something told me to stop. I could immediately become a new target, and if I started running toward them, they'd probably shoot me on the spot."

My eyes widened as he spoke. "What did you do, Thomas?"

"Things went from bad to worse. I saw several Negro soldiers run over to our woods and return to the officer's position with armloads of dry brush. If they couldn't shoot their way in, they were gonna burn the rebels out. The troops spread some old vine, sticks, and leaves beneath the building and lit them. As the flames licked up the front walls, my thoughts oscillated between hope and despair. Perhaps Master Hudson and the children weren't in the school that day; maybe they had taken one of their excursions down to Trace Creek. And then the pendulum would swing back the other way, and the burning structure would become Master Hudson and the children's fiery furnace.

"The door swung open; the rebels rushed down the steps with pistols blazing from both hands. When they turned to their left and started running toward our woods, Federal sharpshooters opened up, dropping both of them immediately. By now, the school was engulfed in flames; a section of the roof closest to the highway collapsed, sending dense smoke and intense sparks flying up into the evergreens. And then my deepest fears were confirmed: the light easterly breeze carried the unmistakable stench of burning flesh. People had died in the fire.

"As I reached for my handkerchief to cover my mouth and nose, I heard someone scrambling up behind me. It was Uncle Billy, who'd heard the shots and come running from the far field. I breathlessly explained what the Feds had done. Uncle Billy thought for a minute and then suggested a conservative approach—we'd quietly retreat through the garden, fetch the wagon, and ride up the road toward the scene, acting as if we had no idea what was going on."

"What happened next? Did the ploy work?"

"Well, a Negro soldier, standing in our field a relatively safe distance from the foul smell, watched us drive up, walked over to where we had hitched the wagon, and asked bluntly if we had any business in the neighborhood. Uncle Billy explained we owned the property; my grandpa had built the schoolhouse; that one of our part-time laborers taught at the school; and our neighbors on the next farm over had children attending every day. Uncle Billy then asked permission to approach the soldier's commanding officer to explain the demolished structure was a school, which was in session when his troops attacked."

Thomas's story had me riveted. "What did the officer say when you told him it was a school and children were inside?" I asked.

"He stared at us incredulously and immediately became defensive. He emphasized he and his men had no idea this was a schoolhouse. He said it didn't look like one and there was no signage declaring it a school. Uncle Billy paused and then broached our examining the smoldering ruins. The officer nodded his agreement."

"Did you and Uncle Billy go in?"

"Yes. I put my handkerchief over my face and followed the officer and Uncle Billy into the smoldering debris. At first we didn't see anyone and thought perhaps Master Hudson and the students had been completely consumed in the flames. But as we surveyed the room more carefully, we spotted a child's body in the southeast corner of the schoolhouse, which had been the least affected by the fire. And then we discovered two, three, four more children curled up asleep on the floor. And next to these innocents lay a partially charred adult, frozen in a final heroic act trying to protect the children."

"But where were Master Hudson and the rest of the students?" I asked. "Why weren't they consumed in the fire?"

"It was only much later in the day I learned Master Hudson and most of his students had become ill on Thursday from the flu and high fever. Ironically, only Master Hudson's assistant teacher, Miss Owings, and a few 'lucky' students had escaped the sickness and dutifully attended classes that fateful day."

"So when they rebuilt the school, they named it for Miss Owings in honor of her bravery?"

"Yes. And rightfully so. It was clear she was trying to save the students."

We reached the front gate and started back up the entry road toward the farmhouse. When we got to the buckeye tree, Thomas hesitated and suggested, "Before going back to say good-bye, let's walk up to the family plot for a few minutes. I haven't been up there since leaving home, and I think it'd be good for you to see it too."

We then took a path running beside an old washhouse, curved to the right past some leafless bushes, and climbed a slight rise to the cemetery gate. We didn't go in; we didn't have to. The cemetery was much smaller than I'd imagined, and we could read all the names from where we stood. We draped our arms across the top of the tall gate and stared in at the headstones rising out of the variegated ivy. "They're all there, Lil' Jim. There's Grandpa and Grandma. Over there, that's Mama, Father, and my sister Rachel. And that small marble marker there—the tapered headstone—that's Israel. Can you read the inscription?"

"I think so, yes. 'Israel has crossed over to the promised land.'"

"A play on words. A reference both to the innocent Israel buried here and to Joshua leading the children of Israel across the Jordan some five hundred years after God first made the promise." Thomas paused and sighed before continuing. "You know, I've read and taught Shakespeare's *Hamlet* at least a dozen times. And you think you've drilled down far enough to feel the characters' deepest emotions. But now I realize I'd never really grasped what Hamlet was sensing in the Yorick scene."

"The Yorick scene? I'm afraid we haven't gotten to *Hamlet* yet."

"Hamlet and his close friend, Horatio, were walking through a cemetery and came upon a sexton digging a grave. In those days you only got so long in the ground before someone else was laid in on top of you. So the two men stopped to speak with this digger who continued shoveling out the remains of earlier deceased onto the growing pile of dirt. During the conversation, the sexton exhumed a skull and said it had lain there for some twenty years. Hamlet asked to whom it belonged, and the fellow replied it was the former court jester's, Yorick's, skull. Hamlet asked to see it and explained to Horatio that Yorick had 'borne me on his back a thousand times and . . . here hung those lips that I have kissed I know not how oft.' Hamlet then questioned the skull: 'Where be your gibes now? Your gambols? Your songs? Your flashes of merriment that were wont to set the table on a roar?'

"Seeing these markers here now I realize I was merely reading Shakespeare's lines then, glossing over the emotion, never feeling what the playwright was trying to convey. You understand, boy?"

"I think so, Thomas. You're saying most of us have to live it to really feel it."

"Sad to say I believe it's true. But now I know, Lil' Jim. Now I know what Shakespeare was really saying. I look at these mossy headstones and realize my grandfather's bravery, my grandmother's insight, my father's trust, my mother's love, my sister's sacrifice, and Israel's innocence have all been reduced to these letters and numbers, fading symbols for the eyes of unknowing and uncaring strangers."

He put his arm around my shoulder and continued, "In the end, Lil' Jim, all we really have is one another. This delicate flesh and blood, enduring in the unsettling imperfection of now."

12

IT WAS THE only time I ever saw him come close to crying. Tears welled up in his eyes; but a deep sigh and reflexive smile stanched the flow. I'd kept my word. I'd spent two years helping David Lee and finishing my education at the Miss Owings School. But as Reverend Emmett would say on occasion, "When I was a child, I spake as a child, I understood as a child, I thought as a child; but when I became a man, I put away childish things." It was difficult explaining why I wasn't interested in following in his footsteps—attending his alma mater and becoming a teacher or a doctor.

"Why, Lil' Jim? Why leave Tennessee, commit ten years of your life, and risk everything?"

"It's hard explaining. It's a feeling, like when I knew it was time to leave Memphis and come here. But it's not what you think, Thomas. It's not a whim, not something I conjured yesterday. I'll grant you the seeds seem idealistic, but you can't argue with the determination and the follow-through over the last two years."

"The seeds, Lil' Jim?"

"Honestly?"

"Honestly."

"For one, the stories you've spun about your grandpa

and your older brother. For them it was more about honor, courage, duty, and sacrifice than anything else. Could there be a higher calling? Next, there was the Kipling collection you gave me for my eighteenth birthday. The *Barrack-Room Ballads* were all from a soldier's perspective. 'Danny Deever,' 'Gunga Din,' and 'Mandalay' run the gamut from military discipline to serving the realm in exotic places. And finally, there were the hobos you described passing through the Memphis rail yard, some of whom I met on my way out here. You said they reminded you of all the fellows you'd met growing up—men down on their luck stopping by your granddad's farm to enjoy your mother's home cooking on the back step. You even mentioned taking food and medicine to the freight yard every week or so. You said you loved spending time there meeting all types—'the old, the young, the sinners, the saints, the hustlers, and the priests.' And it was the same for me, Thomas. Spending Christmas with Spider, Sky Pilot, and the rest of the Boxcar Willies really got the ball rolling for me."

"I understand. But what was it about the hobos that influenced your decision?"

"It was really the same thread running through all the seeds, Thomas—through your stories, Kipling's poems, and the freight yard. It was the camaraderie. Remember? I told you how I felt growing up at Uncle Aaron's—feeling different and isolated from everyone. From my family, my schoolmates, my teachers. I never really belonged. I lived from year to year waiting for your arrival each summer around my birthday. A week of refuge from an oppressive year of loneliness. And while I was sharing my Christmas with Spider, Sky Pilot, and the boys, I realized my future lay in banding with others. Over time I refined my thinking to men undertaking missions far greater than themselves."

Before leaving that August only days after my birthday, I made the proper rounds saying good-bye to everyone from Miss Sallie, Margaret, and my classmates to the Reverend and Mrs. Emmett, David Lee, Theresa Anne, and several laborers on the farm. I then rode Black Widow over to Hurricane Creek and spent my last night home at Thomas's place. The next morning he drove me up to the Warfield depot, where we waited on the platform for the early eastbound train.

"You take good care of Black Widow for me, you hear."

"That should be the least of your worries, Lil' Jim. How many times have I seen you riding proudly into town over the last couple years?" Thomas smiled. "But he's another good reason to keep in touch. I mean, besides catching up on all the news back home and letting us know how you're doing."

He paused, looked down at his boots, and then gazed into my eyes. "No denying it, boy. It's gonna be different not having you around here." He sighed and smiled bravely. "But we'll just have to look forward to your letters and perhaps a return visit home from time to time."

"I'm gonna miss you too, Thomas. We go back a long way, don't we?"

Thomas chuckled at that. "Longer than you can imagine, Lil' Jim."

"I still hope I can count on your advice."

Thomas put his arm around my shoulder. "Of course you

can. And I promise to draft and post a response the same day I receive your letter." He pulled out his pocket watch. "Another five minutes and she'll be rounding the bend there. Early train starts in Memphis and runs pretty much like clockwork. Very few delays." He put his watch back in his vest pocket and said, "So how you feel this morning taking the big step, boy?"

"Can't say I'm not nervous. I'd be lying to you."

"Well, here's one piece of unsolicited advice before the train gets here. During his time in the military, Grandpa saw a lot of officers, some good and others only fair to middling. He pounded it into me that what separated the sheep and goats was their attitude toward their peers. While the mediocre viewed their fellow officers as rivals, the truly effective leaders focused solely on their own performance. Most of us spend a lot of time worrying about what the other fellow's doing rather than on how we can excel at our own jobs. Grandpa said if we're concerned about what others may or may not be thinking or may or may not be doing, then we just sap our own energy, insight, and likelihood of success. So listen to Grandpa, boy. Forget what your classmates are doing. Compete by getting the most out of yourself. You do that, Lil' Jim, and you'll sail through all your courses and rise quickly through the ranks."

"I'll try, Thomas. But it's hard unlearning what you've been doing most of your life. You know my light skin separated me from my family, my teachers, and my schoolmates. And when you grow up trying to belong, you spend most of your time paying close attention to what everyone else is saying, thinking, and doing. . . ."

"Things'll be different there."

"I know, and I'll give it my best shot. But I'm just saying lifelong habits are hard to break."

"You hear that? Two longs, a short, and another long. She's approaching the Walker Street crossing. She'll be rounding the curve there in less than a minute."

And then right on cue the train appeared and slowed to a stop.

"Grab your bags, boy. She won't stay long. You and that older fellow there are the only pickups this morning." Thomas gave me a big hug. "Stay safe. I love you, Lil' Jim."

"Love you too, Thomas. See you soon."

I boarded the train and quickly claimed a seat where I could see my old friend on the platform. I waved, and he waved back, letting me know he'd found me. The conductor walked over to where Thomas was standing on the platform, exchanged a few words with him, and then gave the engineer the "highball" sign. The engineer responded with two long whistle blasts. The brakes hissed and released. As my car began moving, Thomas saluted. I smiled and returned the gesture in kind.

13

DURING MY YEARS at West Point, I made a lot of trips by train. But most of them were up the Hudson to Fishkill Landing, where Troy's parents lived on an estate overlooking a sweeping bend in the river. Troy, the son of a rising politician, and I, "the frontiersman" as he called me, bonded as plebes during our freshman hazing and remained inseparable until receiving our orders following graduation. I grew to love Troy as a brother. We spent every Christmas and summer holiday together upriver strolling the village streets, hiking the wooded trails along Fishkill Creek, and climbing the circular staircase in the mansion turret to pore over the latest biographies of Sherman, Jackson, and Lee.

That didn't mean I forgot about the folks back home or had no intention of visiting them during the summer or the holidays. But the way our schedule worked out there was never enough time to make the roundtrip from New York to Tennessee and back again without missing classes and suffering the consequences. So I made do with correspondence—Margaret, Thomas, and David Lee keeping me up to date on births, deaths, and local politics, and I reciprocating with descriptions of campus life and the latest news from Fishkill Landing. Since I knew I was now well beyond his reach, I finally made amends with Uncle Aaron for having run away. I explained where I was and what I planned on doing. I thanked him again for his kindness and hoped he would keep in touch. I assured him I was really interested in his crusade and the progress he was making in changing minds.

As the semesters passed, I increasingly resigned myself to the likelihood of a single visit home between graduation and my first assignment. And by my senior year I had worked everything out in my mind—I saw myself stepping off the train at Warfield station proudly sporting my second lieutenant uniform, showing off my well-honed riding skills on Black Widow, and then, as a man of the world, describing East Coast living to folk who probably never left Magnolia County.

But even that highly anticipated homecoming never materialized. Only hours after taking the commissioning oath, I received my initial duty assignment and boarded a train headed west with an intermediate stop in Chicago five hundred miles north of Hurricane Creek. My final destination? Fort Assiniboine in north central Montana not far from the Saskatchewan border. My unlikely assignment? The young man who had never ridden until receiving his first mount as a gift had become a commissioned officer in the highly respected Negro Tenth Cavalry Regiment known throughout the military as the Buffalo Soldiers. Ironically, I had become a white leader of brothers who, because of their color, could serve but were not trusted to lead.

When I stepped off the train at the Havre depot, a tall, wiry Negro in his late forties saluted smartly. "First Sergeant

Blair, sir. Lieutenant Jack sent me to drive you back to the fort. Here, let me help you with your bags."

We climbed up onto the wagon bench and headed southwest toward a distant mountain range.

"How far is the fort from here?" I asked.

"A little over six miles. Pretty easy ride. Mostly plains, sir."

"How long you been in the regiment, Sergeant?"

"Ever since the beginning. I like to say my story's pretty much the regiment's. I enlisted in Fort Leavenworth, Kansas, after the war. Worked my way up over the years to noncom officer, sir."

I immediately became engaged. Perhaps the sergeant could relate firsthand accounts of the Indian Wars. "Well, if your service tracks with the regiment's, then you've seen some fighting in the Indian campaigns."

"Yes, sir, seen my share of the skirmishes. . . ." he responded with understated pride.

"I'm a student of military history. Think you can remember all the battles going back to the 1860s?"

"Not the little ones where you have the numbers with you, sir. But you never forget the big ones—the ones where your troopers are dying around you and you don't know whether you'll ride away alive. If anyone says they've never been scared, they're lying. I've seen veterans puking and pissing themselves when the tide turned." He smiled grimly. "You see, that's where you and I come in. You have to lead the fear out of them. You don't lose fighting from the front, sir." He raised his arms. "You see, I'm still kicking, and we've made very few widows."

"Absolutely right. Now, do you recall your first fighting, Sergeant?" I asked.

"Another thing you never forget, sir. Every detail burned in the memory. The weather, the time of day. The flow of battle. The fear. The officers, the tribes. We had just transferred over from Leavenworth to Fort Riley. It was a late August morning, 1867. Already scorching hot. Hadn't rained in quite a spell. The wind was whipping up parched eddies. We had been ordered over to Fort Hays to help track down hostile Cheyenne who had just massacred a railroad work crew.

"We rode out of Fort Hays heading northwest with the Thirty-eighth Infantry Regiment in tow. And about twenty-five miles out, our scouts spotted an active trail running along the Saline River. We had ridden a mile or so along the riverbank when four hundred Cheyenne warriors attacked. The captain ordered a defensive hollow square with the Thirty-eighth on the perimeter and our Tenth Cavalry in the middle. I thought we would make a stand right there along the river. It made sense. We were essentially surrounded with our backs to the water. But this is where I learned so much about leadership, tactics, and vision under fire. Seeking a more defensible position, the captain ordered us to move out while maintaining our square formation. Over the next eight hours we never stopped moving or laying down defensive fire, some two thousand rounds overall. And after engaging us in a running battle covering fifteen miles, the Cheyenne finally gave up the fight and withdrew.

"When we got back to Fort Hays, the captain had his wounds addressed and then spoke to the Tenth and the Thirty-eighth. 'Gentlemen,' he said, 'during your thirty-hour patrol, you covered over a hundred miles and fought off a fierce attack without reinforcements. You lost only one trooper in action. If teaching professionals were to introduce this action as a case study without revealing the outcome, I'm sure the students would rightly conclude the Battle of Saline River ended in your massacre. But your bravery and your officers' devotion to duty and coolness under fire would reverse the odds and prove them wrong. I'm proud of every one of you. You have my deepest respect.'"

Responding to his impressive tale, I said, "You must have been scared to death. Young. First fighting . . ."

"Was I afraid? Yes. Terrified? No. You see, that's where the experience comes in to play. I didn't know enough then to sense the real danger or terror. I figured if I listened to what the noncom was telling me, I'd be okay. I never felt the real terror until I became a noncom myself, responsible for a hundred troopers and knowing that my decisions and actions in battle would determine whether my men lived or died. That's when you begin to feel the pressure."

Wanting to glean as much as I could from this battle-tested veteran, I asked, "Did you see more fighting in Kansas? I've read some accounts but have yet to meet anyone actually there."

"Oh, it was mostly skirmishes, but our job was more than punishing the hostiles. Over the next eight years we moved from fort to fort in Kansas and the Oklahoma Territory, guarding railroad workers, stringing telegraph wires, building garrisons, and patrolling the various reservations. In '75 we left Kansas and the Indian Territory for good and headed down to Fort Concho in west Texas."

"More fighting there?" I probed expectantly.

"Again, mostly skirmishes, at least at the beginning. Sent there to protect the mail and travel routes from the Apaches and Mexican outlaws. . . . Scouted thousands of miles of unmapped lands and opened hundreds of miles of brand-new roads in some of the worst terrain you could imagine. But you know, it was probably the best thing ever happened to my men. No real comforts and always on the lookout for attack. Instilled discipline and toughened them up."

Sensing I was hanging on his every word, the sergeant smiled and continued, "But you wanted to hear more about the major battles. So in '79 and '80 we had a couple big ones with Chief Victorio and his band of Apaches. It was after they escaped their New Mexico reservation and headed south for Mexico, wreaking havoc along the way. Our objective: keeping him and his hostiles from returning to New Mexico and stirring up more trouble. Our plan was to guard all potential watering holes along the chief's likely route. Well, the plan worked. Desperate for water, they attacked us at a watering hole south of Sierra Blanca and then again at Rattlesnake Springs. Fierce battles but we blunted their attacks and forced them back toward Mexico. We gave chase, but they escaped over the border to live just a few more days."

"What happened?" I asked eagerly.

"Mexican troops ambushed them, killing Victorio and most of his warriors on the spot. Then for us it was back to patrolling, opening more roads, and stringing hundreds of miles of telegraph wires until the regiment was transferred to the Department of Arizona in '85."

Hoping for more riveting detail, I asked, "What did you do out there?"

"More of the same plus pursuing Geronimo and his hostile Apaches who had escaped their reservation. Even after the chief surrendered in '86, the Apaches continued to hit and run." He paused, looked over at me, and said proudly, "But we finally got the upper hand for good in '90."

Sensing we had reached the denouement, I probed reluctantly, "No more fighting then?"

"Nothing to speak of. And in fact, we were transferred up north to the Department of the Dakota the following year."

First Sergeant Blair stopped the wagon and pointed toward a large collection of redbrick buildings standing in a valley beneath a long, jagged range. "So after leaving Arizona, this is where we ended up. Fort Assiniboine. Those are the Bears Paw Mountains. That's the Milk River over there. And dead ahead is Beaver Creek."

"This is some setup. How long's the fort been here?"

"Started in '77, the year after Custer and the Little Big Horn. Took them four years to build. It's an offensive fort—no walls protecting the perimeter. Believe there are now over a hundred buildings. Pretty much everything you'd find in a small town including a library, a trading post, a hospital, a saw mill and the like. They say it's the largest post in the country."

"Really? How many men?"

"Thirty-six officers and over seven hundred noncom and enlisted."

Steeling myself for the challenges ahead, I responded, "A lot of men . . . a lot of responsibility."

He looked over again and smiled confidently. "That's why only the best and brightest are sent out here to serve."

We drove into the compound and stopped next to the quadrangle bordered by the enlisted men's barracks to the north and the officers' quarters to the south. First Sergeant Blair and I hopped down. He grabbed my bags out of the wagon bed and led the way onto the grounds. "That's the enlisted men's row to your right, and that's officers' row on the left. You've been assigned to the fifth building there." He pointed to small building on the left.

"Where are your noncom officer quarters, Sergeant?"

"Over that way, behind the shooting gallery and next to the stables." He gestured to a place far beyond officer row. "And by the way, once we get you settled into your quarters, I'm supposed to walk you around the fort to acquaint you with everything. But don't worry, we'll only be hitting the essentials like the post trader's store. It's where you can get a taste of the real world after spending months here hunkered down against the isolation, boredom, and the dreary winter months. There's liquor, smokes, colorful clothes . . . and the company's not all that bad either. The trader's witty and well-read, has a library and is willing to share." The sergeant smiled and then added, "Oh, and I almost forgot, there's a wife and daughter. The wife's got a real knack for books and the piano, and the daughter . . . well, the daughter's a sight for sore eyes. Long blond tresses, a full figure, blue eyes, and she's always smiling. But don't get your hopes up too high. She's pleasant to look at but rumor has it she's spoken for. Don't know for sure, but Lieutenant Jack sure spends all his free time over at the post."

I'd been settling in for little more than a day when First Sergeant Blair appeared and said Lieutenant Jack wanted to see us over at his office.

"You know what this is about?" I asked as we made our way across the compound.

"No idea, other than maybe giving you some of the usual assignments—recovering lost mounts, scouting and rounding up renegade Crees and burning their shacks. . . ."

It took just over five minutes to reach the lieutenant's office. We knocked on the door. The deep voice on the inside responded, "It's open. Come in."

As we entered the room, the handsome, lean, mustachioed officer rose from his chair, returned our crisp salute, and introduced himself. "First Lieutenant Pershing. Within the walls here you can call me Jack. Welcome to Fort Assiniboine." He sat back down and continued, "So Montana's your first assignment right out of the academy?"

"Yes, sir," I responded.

"Well, there'll be no routine duties for you, Lieutenant. We're going to throw you right into the fire. Something of an unpleasant nature, but it's got to be done. Just received the orders this morning. Gentlemen, take a seat and I'll give you the background. And then I'll want the two of you explaining this to the troopers who'll be riding with us.

"Over the last few years citizens have been clamoring to rid their towns of the homeless Cree. It's been in all the editorials. These folk put pressure on the local politicians who in turn lobbied the governor, who escalated the matter to Congress. Well, in May, the House and Senate passed and funded the Cree Deportation Act, which the president signed into law. Orders were quickly passed down through the chain of command and have now landed on my desk. The objective is to head over to Great Falls, round up the two hundred or so Cree, and ensure they end up back in Canada. I want the two of you to choose forty veterans to ride along on the mission. By the way, there'll be one other second lieutenant coming along who'll be returning from Missoula tomorrow. I plan on briefing him as soon as he gets back. Any questions?"

"No, sir."

"Dismissed."

It was a rough time for me, having just landed and already back out on the move, but by the thirteenth we had everything ready to go. We mustered at the eastern end of the quadrangle. "Boots and Saddles" rang out, and everyone said his good-byes. Lieutenant Pershing gave the signal to mount, turned his horse toward Great Falls Road, and waved us forward out of the fort.

Despite the rugged terrain, the first two days of the march went off like clockwork. But on the fifteenth we paid the piper. With all the spring rains, the Marias River had become a roaring torrent. Lieutenant Pershing stopped at the riverbank to weigh his options—either seek a calmer crossing upstream or risk plowing in here and saving a lot of time. He raised his gloved hand and shouted decisively, "We're crossing here!" He then rode back to speak with the teamsters driving our two wagons. "Cover the sides and bottoms of the wagon beds with tent flies. Collect all the lariats. Tie them end to end long enough to reach the other shore. We'll load the supplies into the beds and ferry them over using the rope line for steering. Then we'll swim the mules across."

I discovered a lot about leadership that day before and during the crossing. I first witnessed Pershing's creativity during his ad hoc planning and then watched him calmly react to every challenge thrown his way. And there were many setbacks that afternoon: the wagon beds partially awash; soldiers struggling to hold the cable; horses shying at the river's edge; and troopers and mounts floating off course downstream. But there was Pershing in the middle of the maelstrom barking orders one minute and shouting encouragement the next.

And toward the end of the ordeal I learned a third important lesson about leadership: maintaining discipline within the ranks. It was understood there would be no shirking by anyone during the crossing. Each man had a part to play to limit the risk and ensure success. Unfortunately, I observed a trooper from my platoon finding work at the water's edge only when Pershing was watching. Otherwise the private was standing around suggesting tasks for others to do. To his credit First Sergeant Blair detected the ruse and rode the fellow hard but with limited success. The soldier would start working when the sergeant screamed but would slack off once Sergeant Blair left to address the next emergency. It was about the third time the sergeant confronted the private that I realized Pershing was off to the side taking it all in. I expected him to ride up and take charge at any moment, but he didn't move. In fact, he turned to speak with a horseman beside him.

My first reaction was confusion. Why would Pershing ignore this blatant insubordination? Didn't he sense the sergeant needed help? Or was he weighing the sergeant's mettle? And then fear surged through me. Pershing's inaction had nothing to do with the sergeant; it had everything to do with me. Pershing was testing me. What would I do to maintain discipline within the ranks? I instinctively dismounted and started walking toward the noncom and the private without any idea what I would say or do. I just knew I had to do something and do it quickly.

When I strode up to the men, I swept the sergeant to one side with my forearm, clenched my left fist, and knocked the soldier several yards into the swirling waters. I turned away without saying a word, walked back calmly to my mount, and then rode off triumphantly to handle any further challenges coming my way. It was only at our encampment that evening that I learned what Pershing thought of my spontaneous action. He opened the flap of my tent, stuck his head in, and said, "Good work out there today, Lieutenant. It had to be done."

First Sergeant Blair delivered the final review the following morning. "I'm glad you did what you did yesterday, Lieutenant. I'd wanted to do it myself all day." He paused, fired an imaginary left hook, and smiled. "You sure knocked him silly, sir. Didn't you say you were from Tennessee, from Hurricane Creek?"

"Sure did, Sergeant."

"Well, you drove that boy like a hurricane, sir." And from that moment until his dying breath, First Sergeant Blair dropped my military rank and referred to me admiringly as "Hurricane Jim."

When we reached Great Falls on the seventeenth, we stopped overnight for updates from headquarters and then the next morning rode out to the Cree village on the outskirts near the municipal dump. Since Lieutenant Pershing had heard rumors the tribe could be hostile and resist arrest, he ordered his officers to distribute additional ammunition to all the troopers. As we neared the village, scouts returned with intelligence. They said the camp was comprised primarily of wall tents with a few tepees scattered about and estimated there were somewhere between a hundred and a hundred twenty-five men, women, and children living in the settlement.

Following Pershing's plan, we swooped down on the camp but met no resistance. We quickly located the chief, who graciously invited us into his large wall tent. As we entered, the chief pointed to the back wall, said "Ostumpetoge" (Come back inside), and blazed a trail through a host of women and children occupying the front half of the structure. While running the chief's gauntlet, I managed to survey most of the interior. The floor was a patchwork of hides, oilcloth, and pieces of old carpet. The family's clothes and sleeping blankets were neatly stacked against the side walls. The children's wet moccasins and several pieces of beef hung drying from support poles. At the center of the large room stood an old metal washtub with a stovepipe rising out through a hole in the roof.

Since we'd arrived just before mealtime, the chief insisted Lieutenant Pershing and I join his extended family for lunch before transacting any kind of business. We moved up to the center of the tent and sat down among the women and children encircling the makeshift stove. The chief's offspring ranged in age from a nine-month-old to two young braves in their late teens. Most of the family wore a mixture of traditional Cree and store-bought clothes. While the chief and his older sons sported Indian togs—leggings, breechcloths, blankets, and buckskin moccasins—his younger boys wore calico shirts, faded jeans, and leather shoes. The women and girls were uniformly dressed in calico smocks, blankets, and beaded moccasins.

After everyone was seated, the chief raised his hand for silence, offered up a Catholic prayer, and then signaled his mother to toss sweet grass in the stove as an offering to her pagan spirits. Just as the old woman finished her ancient ritual, the chief's infant began crying. His wife quickly leaned over, lifted the baby onto her back, and drew a blanket up tightly around her breasts. Within seconds the child stopped crying. The chief smiled lovingly at his wife and youngest son and ordered the meal to begin. Several of the women distributed tin plates around the circle and then served modest helpings of boiled calf's head, fried cornbread without butter, and small cups of tea.

When the meal ended, the chief, his two young sons, Lieutenant Pershing, and I retired to the back half of the tent to transact business. Lieutenant Pershing did his best to present the bad news in a humane way. He first explained the new US Deportation Act; he next assured the chief the "Great Mother of Canada" had absolved him and his tribe of any responsibility for the 1885 Riel's Rebellion; and then he described how the chief and the tribe would travel to Coutts Station on the international line, be handed over to Canadian authorities, receive amnesty, and live out their days peacefully in their homeland.

The following morning we got the Cree rounded up and moved into Great Falls for transport to Alberta. But once we got into town, our mission hit a major snag. A local lawyer got wind of what was happening and obtained a writ of habeas corpus demanding we show cause why the Cree should be detained. Lieutenant Pershing went before the court, cited the recent Deportation Act, and argued that federal law trumped state law and that the state had no jurisdiction over federal agents. So it now appeared the decision was in the hands of the local court. But Lieutenant Pershing left nothing to chance. Before the judge could accept Pershing's argument, the lieutenant had already ordered us to load the Cree onto cattle cars and send them packing to Canada. And by the time the judge had finally made his decision, the Cree were well out of his reach.

From Great Falls we rode over to Missoula where the Twenty-fifth Colored Infantry was garrisoned and used their fort for rest and relaxation during the first few days in July. But there's no rest for the weary. Lieutenant Pershing learned a large band of Cree had settled near Camas Prairie a hundred hard miles northwest of Fort Missoula. Fearing the tribe would get wind of us and flee into Idaho's nearby mountains, Lieutenant Pershing made another creative decision. Instead of traversing the difficult terrain on horseback, we would take the train to Horse Plains about ten miles southwest of Camas Prairie. So on the ninth our Troop D traveled by rail to its staging area, debarked, and then rode swiftly into town, arresting the Cree before they could escape to Idaho.

Sticking to Pershing's overall plan, we escorted the captives back to Fort Missoula, where the lieutenant began preparing for the next challenge—transporting this motley collection of families, horses, livestock, and personal possessions northward a hundred and fifty miles to Coutts Station at the Canadian border. The lieutenant's first objective now was mapping the easiest route possible; the next stocking spare rations and forage along the way; and finally fortifying the tribe's decrepit wagons, buggies, and travois so they would survive the difficult journey.

When he'd completed the planning, the lieutenant convened a meeting of his commissioned and noncommissioned officers to brief us on the details. He said we would be using old Indian and settler trails to lessen the rigors of the trip and mapped out the route for us. We were to travel along the Blackfoot River Bottom to Helmville, cross the Marysville Divide, hug the eastern slope of the Rockies, and finally meet up with the old McLeod Trail running north to Alberta. While realizing the lieutenant's proposed route would be strenuous, I agreed with his plan overall. It was the only viable way to move the tribe northward without tackling the almost impossible climbs through the Rockies.

On the twenty-second, only two days after the briefing, we saddled up and rode out of Fort Missoula headed east for Helmville. Despite our troopers' best efforts to keep the column moving, one thing after another slowed us down. First there were the usual impediments: wagons breaking and young braves committing mischief. Then there were the unexpected occurrences: a difficult birth and a measles epidemic. And last there were the truly alarming situations, including near drownings, which hurt Pershing's pride, and an Indian suicide, which ironically almost ended our young lieutenant's life.

The near drowning happened the night we reached the Marias River. Pershing had allowed everyone to camp along the riverbank before making the crossing the next morning. But without warning, the river rose during the night, sweeping men, women, children, troopers, horses, wagons, and livestock into the raging waters. And without the heroic actions of our Negro troopers, many lives would have been carried away downstream. Needless to say, our chastened leader realized he'd made a rare mistake and openly acknowledged he'd learned a simple but valuable lesson: always site your camp on high ground above a river.

But Lieutenant Pershing couldn't have foreseen or avoided a second serious incident, which nearly cost him his life. A veteran Cree warrior who had ridden with Big Bear at Frog Lake and Fort Pitt became despondent over the plight of his tribe. He raised a gun to his temple and pulled the trigger. The death bullet sped through the warrior's brain and lodged in a tree within inches of where Lieutenant Pershing was standing.

Despite the seriousness of the mission, I couldn't help but notice how breathtaking the scenery up the Blackfoot River valley and over the Rockies was. I'd never experienced anything like the grandeur of the snowcapped mountains, the roaring waterfalls, and the tall pines gracing the shores of glacial lakes. But once we'd crested the range and descended onto the eastern slopes, the landscape changed dramatically. We had entered a barren land void of water, signaling the rest of our journey would be less about sightseeing and more about endurance and survival.

Finally, in early August we reached Coutts Station and transferred our charges and their hundreds of horses to the Canadian Mounted Police. I remember First Sergeant Blair sitting down beside me by the campfire that night and assessing the mission. "If I must say so, I think we did a helluva job getting those folks up here without losing a soul."

I turned and looked at him quizzically. "I believe you forgot the suicide, Sergeant."

He smiled and responded respectfully but triumphantly, "I believe you forgot the birth early on there, Hurricane."

The following morning we pulled up stakes and headed back to Fort Assiniboine, where Lieutenant Pershing served only two more months while I endured two long years in the northwest wilderness. After the Cree roundup, we spent much of our time from spring through the fall patrolling the reservations and killing wolves before hunkering down in the barracks for a brutal winter. Boredom became the enemy, which I attacked with veracious reading from late November through the March thaw—everything from Caine's Icelandic novel, *The Bondman*, to Haggard's African adventure, *King Solomon's Mines*, and Stevenson's psychological novella, *Dr. Jekyll and Mr. Hyde*. When I wasn't reading, I was studying my lines or rehearsing for my next villainous roles in our latest repertory productions, La Frochard in *The Two Orphans*, Byke in *Under the Gaslight*, and Lawyer Cribbs in *The Drunkard*.

Ironically, in at least one way life imitated art. Since the post trader's daughter usually played the heroine and I the scoundrel, we never came close to sharing a kiss. An enlisted man's hero always came between us to perform the enviable act. And after Lieutenant Pershing left his "lady friend" behind, I became her latest suitor, spending hours on end at the wintry post sharing family meals and whispered innuendos. But piercing stares and arched brows from competitors and their wives always tempered our inclinations and kept us apart.

There was one ongoing activity, however, which transcended the seasons and provided the greatest joy: my probing conversations with First Sergeant Blair. I remember one exchange in particular not long after returning from Canada. "No matter what you say, Hurricane, I think we have every right to be proud. We were following orders, executing federal law, and we did it as humanely as we could under the circumstances."

"Let's be honest, Sergeant. The Washington hacks buckled to state pressure with the Deportation Act. It was as corrupt as the Hayes-Tilden compromise ending Reconstruction and suffocating Negro dreams. I studied Turner at West Point. He's declared the frontier over. You and all the other black troopers had done yeoman's work clearing the fields during the Indian Wars. And now America was complete with the white man in control. You see, the local politicians just followed Turner's lead and began pressuring the hacks back East to legislate the dregs out of their towns. They wanted to sweep the riffraff under the rug—those animals living out at the city dump feeding and clothing themselves with the white man's refuse. And extending the metaphor, we became the brooms to get that job done."

"Am I detecting a tinge of guilt, Hurricane?"

"Not so much guilt as regret. What about that old warrior who shot himself and almost killed Pershing? He would still be alive if we hadn't rounded up his tribe and marched them up to Canada. And how do you feel about stuffing all those folks in cattle cars there in Great Falls? I don't know about you, Sergeant, but it sure wasn't one of my finest hours."

"War is messy, Hurricane."

"This wasn't war. It was getting our hands dirty after the war ended."

"Forgive me, Hurricane, for saying so—you being white and everything—we Negroes in the troop, especially all of us older veterans, we have a different take on the Indian Wars and the flow of history between our peoples. Many of us Negroes were born in the so-called Indian Territory, you understand. And you know why? Because Indian masters dragged our parents and grandparents out West with them after trading away Indian lands to the politicians. We were their slaves; they've never been ours. And they fought with the rebels during the war. Fighting to keep us under thumb. Fighting to keep their property. So when it comes to the Indian Wars, I have to say we sided with Moses against them. 'And if any mischief follow, then thou shalt give life for life, eye for eye, tooth for tooth, hand for hand, foot for foot, burning for burning, wound for wound, stripe for stripe . . .'"

While the sergeant and I shared a heritage, I chose another tack. I didn't respond directly. I just quoted the Reverend Emmett. "And seeing the multitudes, he went up into a mountain and taught them, saying, 'Ye have heard it said, an eye for an eye, and a tooth for a tooth. But I say unto you, whosoever shall smite thee on thy right cheek, turn to him the other also. And whosoever shall compel thee to go a mile, go with him two.'"

"I know what you're driving at, Hurricane. But that's all history now. Water over the dam. Gone and done. We black troopers fought and died out here for thirty long years paving the way for the white folk. It's now high time to turn the page and think about ourselves. Seeing what happened to us after the war, I don't think we'll ever be respected, ever be free, if we don't start pushing before our good deeds are forgotten and all the goodwill's dried up."

"How you plan on doing that, Sergeant? Armed insurrection? Revolution? You and I both know they aren't just gonna hand it over to you."

"Then I guess we'll have to fight for it. Won't we?"

"Yes, Sergeant, we'll have to fight for it. Fight for it together. But hold your fire a little longer. When the time's right, we'll fight. We'll fight and win without firing a shot. You have my word on it. You'll see."

14

I WAS EMBARRASSED to write home about my adventures in Montana. What was there to talk about? The roundup of vanquished tribes? Killing wolves? Patrolling reservations? The severity of the winters? My reading list? The reception of our dramatic productions? The rowdy parties at the post trader's house? How could I compare to Annie Oakley or compete with Buffalo Bill's Wild West Show?

But in the dead of winter in '98 all that was about to change. I was polishing my boots when First Sergeant Blair rushed in. "Have you heard the news, Hurricane?"

"What's that?"

"I was over at the trading post just now. They blew up one of our battleships in Havana Harbor last night. Coming across the wires. Many dead and wounded."

"Who blew it up?"

"They're pointing fingers at Spain. It makes sense too. They haven't liked our meddling in their affairs. They've been trying to suppress the Cuban insurrection, and we roll into town with a battle fleet."

"What do you think McKinley will do?"

"I'm not a betting man or a seer; but if I had to guess, I think public pressure will push him to war. So if I'm sitting behind the mahogany desk there in Washington, I ask the War Department if they're prepared to retaliate. The secretary responds in the affirmative. Next question—are they prepared to drive Spain out of Cuba? The secretary again replies with a yes.

"Third question—what forces could carry out the mission? He responds quickly, 'For starters, the four colored regiments out West.' As president I ask, 'Why's that?' The secretary answers, 'They're battle-hardened, been the tip of the spear for thirty years. They've campaigned in west Texas, the Southern Plains, the Apache lands, and Sioux country too. And besides their history, they're naturally immune.'

"I interrupt, 'Naturally immune? Immune to what?' The secretary replies, 'To tropical diseases . . . and . . . and to the effects of moist air and high temperatures.' I turn to Vice President Hobart for his reaction. He lists the pros and cons. And then I approve the secretary's approach. I tell him to proceed with planning for war." First Sergeant Blair walked over, slapped me on the back, and asked, "How's that for a prediction?"

"So you really think we're about to leave purgatory?"

"If I were betting on it, Hurricane, I'd say we're headed from purgatory into hell."

"Exciting . . . but then again, scary too, if true."

And scary it was. Later that spring we mustered in the courtyard for our send-off to hell. The fort commander briefly described the travel plans and then turned the proceedings over to our eloquent brother of the cloth, Chaplain Tolland, who stressed Negro pride and manhood in his exhortation. "Once again fate has unleashed the hounds of hell and calls on you to right a wrong and defend your country's honor. I urge you to acquit yourselves like men. Remember, the world is watching. You have a chance again to prove the Negro will fight.

"When your fathers charged at Petersburg in '64, they yelled, 'No quarter. Remember Fort Pillow.' And I say to you now, when you're called on to take a hill, let the enemy know why you've come to fight, to 'Remember the Maine.'"

After a layover in northern Georgia, our Tenth Colored moved down to Tampa Bay to join the Ninth Cavalry and the Twenty-fourth and Twenty-fifth Colored Infantries. Since we were the last of the units to arrive, we were forced to encamp east of Tampa near Lakeland. The next six weeks in May and June of '98 were filled with tension—not so much from the anticipation of going to war but from the reception we received from the local citizenry. My soldiers had been out West for years, enjoyed many victories, and gained genuine respect from soldier and civilian alike. So when they shipped out to Florida, they expected to be treated as they had been in the West. They weren't prepared for the discrimination and bigotry they faced day in and day out.

First Sergeant Blair dropped by my tent and asked to speak privately. He was glum. "We've got a problem, sir."

I took a deep breath and asked, "What's up, Sergeant?"

"To keep up morale I've been allowing a squad or two at a time to head into town with strict orders to keep their noses clean. Well, two of our young privates ventured into a drugstore to buy some soda water. The druggist refused to sell it to 'em. Told 'em he didn't want their money and suggested they head over to where Negroes could buy drinks from their own kind. You know our soldiers have never been treated that way out West. The privates didn't know how to deal with the druggist's attitude, and they took exception. Words were exchanged. Things got pretty heated.

"About that time the barber next door walked in, got a flavor of what was happening, and barged into the argument. He told our men they'd better be gone by the time he got back. Pretty much threatened them. The barber went next door to retrieve his pistols. Three of the privates' buddies had been standing outside the drugstore all along and had heard the commotion inside. When they saw the barber returning with pistols cocked and loaded, they stepped between the barber and the doorway. Somehow, someway shots rang out. The barber was hit five times and apparently died on the spot."

"Where are our men now, Sergeant?"

"The sheriff's got them locked up in the county jail."

"You mean the three outside the drugstore?"

"No, I mean all of them—inside and out."

"See to it they get a good lawyer. If what you're saying is true, he can probably spring the privates who were inside asking for soda water. I'm afraid we'll have to leave the other fellows behind. Not enough time. Just got orders we're shipping out this weekend. Once you find the lawyer, write up an incident report. I'm gonna have to explain this up the chain . . . . Any questions, Sergeant?"

"No, sir."

"Dismissed."

The night before we broke camp, I learned I also was not immune to controversy. I knew the first sergeant was chagrined about the trouble that had erupted on his watch. But as I'd explained, I'd have done the same thing—allowing the men to go into town after warning them to keep their noses clean. How could he anticipate what was going to happen? So to demonstrate my sincerity, I invited the first sergeant to accompany me to the Breezewood Hotel for dinner.

"Sure looks like a swanky place, sir. You sure you want to do this? Spending your own money and everything?"

"If there's a right time to splurge, it's got to be just before shipping out. Hell, Sergeant, who knows when we'll have the next chance to dine in style."

When we entered the ornate lobby, the proprietor approached and extended his hand. "Welcome, Lieutenant. I suppose you're here to dine."

"Yes, sir. I've heard good things about your place here."

"Not my doing, sir. All the credit to Jean-Francois, our chef, sir."

Throughout our exchange the proprietor never addressed First Sergeant Blair or even looked his way. The sergeant had become invisible. "You dining alone this evening, sir?"

A wave of the past rushed through me. I'd seen this act before. I looked white. I could go uptown in Memphis; but because of their color, Uncle Aaron and Aunt Jane couldn't do the same without facing insults and veiled threats. But while I couldn't say anything as a child, I was now eager to right that wrong and take a firm stand. "No, sir. First Sergeant Blair here will be dining with me."

"No offense, Lieutenant, but my boarders and other clientele would object to eating with a colored man. Soldier or no soldier, I can't afford to accommodate him, sir. It'll ruin my business."

First Sergeant Blair calmly stepped into the fray. "I'm an American officer, sir. I've associated with white gentlemen most of my adult life. I don't propose to begin disgracing myself now eating at a side table or in a side room to accommodate a few of your white patrons."

You could have heard a pin drop. And while the owner gathered himself to respond, Major General Thompson rose from his table, walked over, and grabbed First Sergeant Blair by the arm. "Sergeant, you and the lieutenant there come on over and take a seat with me. And you, Mr. Proprietor, sir, get these soldiers some food and damned quick. I don't want to hear another word about it."

After we had settled in at the general's table, it quickly became clear he took a genuine interest in his soldiers' lives. The affable officer first asked us about our personal stories: where we were born, whether we were married, if we had children, and when and why we chose to join the army. He then moved on to our military experience: where we served, under whose command, and the battles we fought. It was at this point in the conversation I stepped back out of the spotlight and watched as the sergeant regaled the general with the same colorful accounts he had shared with me on the ride out to Fort Assiniboine, the battles of Saline River, Sierra Blanca, and Rattlesnake Springs and the capture of the Apache chief Geronimo in the Department of Arizona.

Long before dawn the next morning, we broke camp and headed off to war. Sailing from Tampa mid-June, our flotilla of thirty-two ships and seventeen thousand men landed east of Santiago on June 22. And it was only two days later I saw my first action at Las Guásimas. We had American and Cuban intelligence that a large Spanish force was lightly entrenched in the foothills west of us on the road to our key objective, Santiago. Former Confederate General Wheeler had deployed us in three columns: the First Volunteer Cavalry, the "Rough Riders," advancing on a bridle path partially obstructed by underbrush; the First Regular Cavalry, moving along a rough wagon trail north of the First Volunteer; and our Tenth Regular Cavalry (Colored) hacking our way through tall grass another mile or so north of the First Regulars. The general's plan was for our three columns to converge on the enemy's position simultaneously, but no one had taken into account the time it would take the Tenth Colored to blaze a trail through a century of thicket.

"You hear that, Sergeant? Sounds like they've started the party without us."

"Never seen anything like this. It's thicker than my papa's beard. Can you see anything?"

"Nothing. But that rifle fire's some distance southwest of here. Got to be the First Volunteers. . . . Tell the troopers to keep pushing ahead."

Several minutes later First Sergeant Blair turned and asked, "You hear that, Hurricane? That sounds a lot closer. Believe the First Regulars just arrived and engaged. Damn this grass. . . ."

Ten minutes later we reached the edge of the dense underbrush, swung our right flank around to the west, and began moving cautiously across an open field toward the first tier of some small hills. We had advanced about a hundred yards into the clearing when all hell broke loose. Thousands upon thousands of rounds cracked over our heads in quick succession.

"Everyone down! Everyone down!" I yelled. "See anything, Sergeant?"

"Nothing. No smoke, nothing. Sounds like the fire's coming from the right flank. We can't stay here. They'll zero in with the big guns. Wanna ease back toward the thicket?"

"Yes, we'll regroup and move southwest toward the Volunteers and Regulars."

Once we reached the underbrush, the fusillade let up. We collected the troopers and gave new orders. "Gentlemen, we're gonna skirt along the edges where you've got cover and not so much hacking to do. We've got to get down there to the battle quick. Can't let our boys think we let them down."

As we moved along through the thicket, I asked, "Did you ever pick out their position, Sergeant?"

"Never did, Hurricane. The Spaniards are trying something new, laying low, firing their Mausers, using smokeless powder. Really nothing to see. Our boys must be having a good time down there if the enemy's doing the same thing they were doing to us up here."

When we reached the main road, I ordered our troopers to stay hidden in the tall grass, form a line running north-south, advance toward the front line, and halt when they had gotten up to our Regulars' right flank.

As we neared the chaos, I located one of the Regulars' noncom officers.

"Where's your command, Sergeant?"

"Captain's shot, sir. Taken to the rear."

"Whose giving orders?"

"I am, sir."

"The Tenth's forming a picket over to your right, Sergeant. When I give you the signal, cease fire. When I give the second sign, open up again with everything you've got. We're gonna drive these fellows out of their comfort holes. Clear, Sergeant?"

"Yes, Lieutenant. Clear."

I scrambled back over to where First Sergeant Blair had assembled our troopers.

"Gentlemen, it's up to you to push the enemy back toward Santiago. And here's how we'll do it. First, we'll position you just to the north of here in the grass. When I give the first signal, the First Regulars are gonna cease fire. When I give the second, they'll begin laying down cover and you, gentlemen, will move out—bayonets fixed—and hit their left flank hard. Clear?"

"Yes, sir!" the troopers roared.

First Sergeant Blair looked over and winked, then turned back to the troopers and added, "Hit 'em like a hurricane, boys! I say hit 'em like a hurricane!"

"God bless you, gentlemen. Now move out to your positions and wait for the command."

I slumped back against a palm stump to collect myself

and to wait for the sergeant's return. I could feel my heart pounding in my chest. I spontaneously whispered a battlefield prayer for my men and me: "Please gods, protect us . . . steel our spirits . . . strengthen us with your power. Amen."

Five minutes later First Sergeant Blair scurried back. "The troopers are in position, sir." He paused and then whispered, "What are our chances?"

"Nothing about chances here, Sergeant. It's gonna work. It worked for Chamberlain at Round Top. These are the Buffalo Soldiers. Fought the Cheyenne, the Comanche, and the Apache. And with you and me out front leading the way? No, sir. There are no chances here. . . . Now after driving the Spaniards out of their holes, I'll meet you where the bridle path joins the main road. Clear?"

"Clear, sir. I'll see you on the main road."

"Ready to move out, Sergeant?"

"Ready, sir!"

"Godspeed."

I gave the First Regulars the signal to cease fire, and within minutes the Spaniards had reciprocated. We could still hear the First Volunteers mixing it up with the enemy some mile and a half away. But it had become as quiet as death where we crouched in the thicket preparing to spring on our prey. I waited for several minutes before giving the second command. Our troopers needed time to focus and make things right with lovers, gods, and wives.

I took a deep breath, scrambled over toward the First Regulars, and gave their noncom the thumbs-up. Within seconds their sergeant shouted, "Fire!" and we immediately sprang from our lair running and yelling like madmen. When we reached a prominent outcropping, I swung our troopers southward as a door on a hinge and slammed them into the enemy's left flank. The fusillade from the east and the bayonets from the north broke the Spaniards' will to fight. They leapt out of their trenches and began running westward toward Santiago. When our veterans felt the resistance snap, they thrust their Springfields into the air and gave out a mighty victory roar.

After pushing farther west on the main road, I met up with First Sergeant Blair as planned. We hugged in victory and then mustered our troopers under some palms directly across from the junction with the bridle path. I got a first read on potential losses from the platoon sergeants before stepping forward to thank our men for their bravery and outstanding success.

"Gentlemen, you Buffalo Soldiers, I studied your proud history at West Point. I know some of you here are veterans of the War Between the States and many of you served tirelessly throughout the Indian Wars. You've been tested time and time again and performed brilliantly. But reading about you and seeing you in action for the first time are two very different things.

"The printed page could never begin to capture what you achieved here today. But you veterans already know what you did. You know you saved the Regulars, the Volunteers, and the mission. The enemy had our boys pinned down along the bridle path and the road here. And in no time the Spaniards would have zeroed in and inflicted heavy casualties. But you were there for our men today. You accepted the challenge and saved our boys from sure defeat. Gentlemen, you did your country proud. Your exploits here will be written about and remembered. The nation owes you a debt of gratitude. Thank you for your courage and your service. It's an honor to serve in your regiment of heroes."

I moved over to First Sergeant Blair and said quietly, "Come along, Sergeant, we have other duties to perform."

"Before doing anything, Hurricane, you'd better get a doc to look at that hand. It looks awfully angry to me."

"I'll get one of the nurses to look at it later. It's more blood than anything. A bullet or shrapnel grazed the back of it. Never felt it. Don't know when it happened."

As leaders, we were duty bound to ensure our troops were well treated, so Blair and I walked back up the road past the enemy's trenches and found our field hospital—two large tents positioned off the road among a stand of old ferns. The walking wounded were resting in the shade up against boulders and tree trunks awaiting treatment. The image these fellows projected was deceptive. The true cost of battle lay hidden some twenty yards behind them within the walls of the hospital tents.

The sergeant and I walked over to the first tent on the left, pulled the flap back, and peered in. Two teams of doctors and nurses were working feverishly to save a couple of the First Volunteer Rough Riders. The bloodstained sheets, smocks, and inner walls contrasted starkly with the brilliant white exterior glistening in the intense afternoon sun.

We lowered the flap, moved over to the second tent, and gazed in. A half dozen or so nurses were crowded into the limited space attending four or five critically wounded troopers who had been transferred over from surgery. As we stepped back from the entrance, First Sergeant Blair reached into his pocket and pulled out two laguitos he had requisitioned after disembarking on Daiquiri Beach. He extended the slender cigars and said, "Wanna step back behind the tents there and enjoy a victory smoke?"

"I'm all for it, Sergeant, but let's visit with the wounded out front first."

"I don't recall seeing any of our men out there, do you, Hurricane?"

"I don't believe I did. But it won't hurt to visit for a while. Will help keep their spirits up.... You know, we're still gonna have to fight our way into Santiago, and we'll need every last one of these men to make it happen."

As First Sergeant Blair stuffed the cigars back into his coat pocket, he replied, "You're right, sir. Duty before pleasure. But promise me, once we've visited with the men, we'll step behind the tents there and enjoy a victory smoke."

"I promise, Sergeant. It'll be good to sit down, light up, and share our battle stories."

I honestly expected to keep my promise; but as it often happens in life and especially on the battlefield, an ugly truth or reality steps between us and our best intentions. After spending the better part of an hour visiting with the wounded Regulars and Volunteers, Blair and I returned to the field hospital area for that victory smoke. But as we turned the corner at the far end of the surgical tent, we confronted the brutality of war in its rawest form. A dozen or so bodies, including some of our own troopers, had been stacked there like cordwood.

"What the hell is this?" I asked.

"Looks like the surgeons are moving their failures out the back door, keeping these boys away from the wounded out front. I suspect the docs are well intentioned. Must be doing it to keep up morale."

And just as I was about to agree with the sergeant's theory, I heard a cough and then a low moan. "You hear that?"

"Sounds like it's coming from over there, beyond those bushes."

We moved through the thicket behind the hospital tent and discovered a Buffalo Soldier lying faceup on a blood-soaked blanket.

I reached down and placed two fingers on the corporal's neck. "He's still alive, but barely."

"Looks like the nurses gave him some morphine and then dragged him out here to cure all alone before tossing him over there on the woodpile."

"He's not gonna be alone anymore, Sergeant. We're staying here until it's over."

We sat down on the blanket beside the soldier to wait for his life to ease away. The young man was bloodied something awful and knocked unconscious by the morphine and the pain. After a few moments of silence, I asked the first sergeant something that had been weighing on me since the battle ended.

"Don't you imagine, Sergeant, this fellow prayed to make it out of here alive, to head home and pick up where he'd left off?"

"Looks like no one was listening to him up there today, Hurricane. You know, I've always wondered about that—why they hear one appeal and not another. We were all praying this morning before we charged the trenches, that's for damn sure. So you and I are here healthy and he's lying here swallowing his own blood. Why'd they hear us and not him? . . . And then again tomorrow they might not hear you or me. Ever think about that, Hurricane?"

The corporal made a faint gurgling noise and coughed. I could feel his hand instinctively tightening around mine. The soldier slowly opened his eyes and stared up into my face.

"Everything's gonna be okay, Corporal. We're staying here with you. You've got my word."

The soldier slid his left hand up toward his jacket pocket and began pulling on the button.

"Something in there, Corporal? Something you want me to see?"

He didn't react but continued gazing up into my face and pulling at the button.

I eased his hand away, unfastened the pocket flap, and pulled out a half sheet of paper. I held the note up with my left hand. "I suspect you want me to read this, don't you, Corporal?" I felt his right hand tighten again around mine. I then began reading what appeared to be his final requests. "Says here your name's Henry Hill. I'll be damned. Says you're from Hollow Rock. We're practically neighbors, Henry. I'm also on the east side of the Duck River near Hurricane Creek. You say here you have a wife, Caroline, and two sons, William and James. You want whoever finds you and this letter to swear they will let your family know what happened and do everything they can to help them."

I paused, gently squeezed his hand, and responded. "I swear, Henry, on my honor as a Buffalo Soldier, I'll do everything I can to help your family. I'll go visit them when I get back home from the war. But in the meantime, I'll write my friend, Thomas, and the Reverend Emmett at the local church. I'm sure they'll see your family's provided for."

Corporal Hill coughed. Dark blood oozed out of the corner of his mouth.

"It's okay to let go now, Henry. I swear I'll help them. Help them any way I can."

The corporal coughed again and closed his eyes. His breathing became more shallow and rapid. When I felt his grip begin to loosen, I looked down at our clasped hands. His rich, dark blood had mingled with mine. It had sought and found a brother.

15

NO. IT'S NOT apocryphal. I tell you it really happened. I was there at the base of Kettle Hill when the lieutenant made his request to lead the charge. But a lot had already happened before we got to the "alleged" conversation. A week to the day after our victory at Las Guásimas, we moved over to an old hacienda, El Poso, which would serve as the staging area for our next move westward. Late in the afternoon of the thirtieth, a fellow officer and friend, First Lieutenant Ord, invited First Sergeant Blair and me to climb to the top of the El Poso ridge and train our binoculars on the next day's objectives.

"Pan over to the northeast there," the lieutenant said. "See the stone fort and the blockhouses in the foothills?"

"Yes, I see them," I replied.

"According to my maps that's El Caney. Lawton's division left this afternoon and will strike there at daybreak. Once they've opened fire, we're supposed to move our two divisions in place at the base of San Juan Heights. Now pan over to the southwest. You see the two ridgelines there?"

"Running parallel north-south?" First Sergeant Blair asked.

"Yes. You've got them. The highest point on the ridge closest to us is Kettle Hill, and the other peak a little farther west is San Juan Hill. The two together make up the Heights. Lawton's attack tomorrow morning is primarily diversionary, but ours is the real deal. We've got to secure those hills before we can ever think about laying siege to Santiago. The general said it should take Lawton no more than two to three hours to overrun El Caney. Lawton's then supposed to move on over here and help us out with the Heights."

"But this isn't gonna be easy," I said. "There's the main road. And that's dense jungle on either side. And besides that, looks like we'll be advancing uphill most of the way even before getting to San Juan and the Kettle."

"And not to mention the water running through there," First Sergeant Blair added. "Any idea about the water, Lieutenant?"

"Not gonna lie to you. The maps are pretty sketchy. They show one river, the Aguadores, running east-west through the jungle and another, the San Juan, flowing north-south. I suspect the tributaries marked on the maps are guesses at best. The way I read it we're gonna have the biggest challenge with the rivers where they cross near the base of San Juan Hill. That's got to be a prime staging area for us before the attack."

"Reminds me of the Indian Wars," First Sergeant Blair said. "I guess we'll be using scouts rather than maps to get us where we're going."

First Lieutenant Ord continued, "But there's one good thing about the thicket down there in the basin. Enemy can't zero in on the scouts or our troops advancing on their positions."

"Yes, and I suspect we won't be seeing much of them either," Blair replied. "Looks like they're really dug in. I can barely make out some trenches branching off that blockhouse over there on San Juan Hill."

As we lowered our glasses, I said, "I guess we'd better start heading back before it gets dark and we have to stay out here all night."

The lieutenant smiled. "Yes, I'd hate to tackle the Spaniards and that jungle down there after spending the night up here fighting off the mosquitoes and the Cuban boas."

By five thirty the following morning, thousands of us were milling about waiting for the commands to "fall in" and "move out." But we knew we weren't going anywhere until we heard Lawton's men laying siege to the Spanish fort. We were all waiting for the starter's pistol to signal our race had begun. And when we finally heard the musket fire, we raised our Springfields in the air and gave out an enthusiastic roar.

We fell in and headed west on the main road toward the Aguadores ford. The path quickly became claustrophobic with dense jungle on both sides and a thick canopy overhead. The inside of our protective tube was hot and wet. The whistle of random incoming fire interrupted the annoying hum of giant mosquitoes.

"I'm gonna run on up ahead, Sergeant," I said. "I wanna see what we'll be dealing with once we get to the river. Looks like things are beginning to stack up here on the road."

"Stay safe, Hurricane. And don't worry, I'll keep our troopers moving toward the ford. See you at the river real soon."

For the next half hour, I weaved my way through one unit after another and finally reached the riverbank as a temporary member of the Seventy-first New York Volunteers. When the captain of the Seventy-first gave the order to begin the crossing, I went along to see what challenges lay ahead on the other side. But just as the Seventy-first reached midstream, the Spaniards opened up with a lethal fusillade. Men were falling around me everywhere. I quickly turned and raced back toward cover on the eastern bank. And when I safely reached the tree line, I turned, trained my binoculars on the far shore, and immediately began devising a plan to deploy our troopers once we had managed to ford the Aguadores.

Everything had now come to a halt. It was clear our field officers would have to find a way to counter their marksmen before our divisions could resume their advance. And to their credit, within fifteen minutes, they had developed an effective plan to neutralize the attacks: rush small groups of men across the river while other units laid down supporting fire. After supplying cover for the group ahead of them, that support team would then race across the river, while the next unit up would in turn supply suppression fire for them.

Needless to say, all this maneuvering caused the column to back up along the narrow road running through the jungle. In fact, it was more than two hours before First Sergeant Blair and our troopers reached the shoreline.

"What the hell's been going on up here, Hurricane? We heard the rifle shots."

"Enemy's been firing down from the trenches, taking our men out midstream. But we've found a way to deal with it—small units crossing while the follow-on groups supply cover. And while I was waiting for you, I surveyed the far shore and got the okay for our positioning. So once we get across the river, we're gonna swing northeast and find a creek running north-south into the Aguadores. We'll take cover along the creek in the woods there and await further orders. Clear, Sergeant?"

"Clear, Lieutenant."

"Choose your marksmen for the suppression fire, and then let's get over there. I'll see you in the woods on the other side."

"Yes, sir."

And no more than twenty minutes later, we'd all made it safely across the river to the woods running alongside the creek.

"Where now, Lieutenant?"

"We're moving out west through the thicket there. Our next objective is the San Juan River running along the base of Kettle Hill. Clear, Sergeant?"

"Clear, sir."

As we advanced toward the San Juan, the random incoming picked up. Our suppression fire at the Aguadores had ended, and the enemy was free to send his "Spanish hornets" whizzing by our heads again. When we reached a clearing near the riverbank, our battlefield commander ordered us to halt and wait for all the regiments to get into position. The plan was to form an arc stretching from the foot of San Juan Hill on the left to the base of Kettle Hill on the right. Our Tenth Cavalry had assumed a central position between the Thirteenth, Sixteenth, and Twenty-fourth Infantries to our left and the Third Cavalry and the Volunteer Rough Riders on our right.

The incoming fire became more intense and deadly as increasingly more of our troops moved into position. And after almost thirty minutes of sheer hell waiting for the command to attack the Heights, First Lieutenant Ord scrambled over from his unit.

"Where you headed, Lieutenant?" I shouted.

"Follow me, Taylor! You can vouch for me. If we don't move out, we're gonna all be chewed alive."

We took off running and ran stride for stride back to the junction of the wooded creek with the Aguadores where we found the brigadier general poring over some maps. First Lieutenant Ord approached the field commander and took the lead. "Excuse me, sir."

The general looked up. He appeared to be annoyed and snapped, "What is it, Lieutenant?"

"We're taking a lot of deadly incoming, sir. They've zeroed in on us, and we're exposed. Every regiment's taking casualties. Ah, General, sir, if . . . if you'll order a charge up the Heights, I'll lead it."

The general knitted his brow but didn't reply.

Lieutenant Ord persisted, "If you don't want to order a charge, sir, I'd like to volunteer. Lieutenant Taylor here will vouch that it's bad and getting worse. We can't stay there, sir. We won't have enough men left to take the Heights."

The general continued staring. But after an awkward silence, he responded, "I wouldn't ask anyone to volunteer, Lieutenant."

"If you won't forbid it, sir, I'll start the charge."

The general remained silent.

Lieutenant Ord then tried a slightly different tack. "I only ask you don't refuse permission to charge the Heights, sir."

I could tell the general was thinking long and hard about the lieutenant's proposal and how to respond to it. He finally replied, "Listen very carefully, Lieutenant. I want to make this very clear. I won't ask for volunteers. I won't give permission . . . and I won't refuse it. Clear, Lieutenant?"

"Clear, sir."

I thought we were doomed to failure because of the field general's reluctance to pull the trigger.

But then the commanding officer looked at each of us and ended the conversation. "God bless the two of you . . . and good luck."

We excitedly snapped to attention and saluted. Lieutenant Ord replied, "Thank you, sir. We'll see you on the Heights." We turned and began running toward the front line to give our troopers the good news that the Tenth Cavalry would be leading the charge up the San Juan Heights.

When we got back to our men, Lieutenant Ord's excitement was palpable. He said, "Taylor, tell the officers in the Twenty-fourth to pass it on to the Thirteenth and Sixteenth that the Buffalo Soldiers are moving out; that their regulars should fill in behind our men; and they should provide cover for us on the way up. Signal me once you've passed the word along. Meanwhile, I'll request the same of the Third Cavalry and the First Volunteers."

Fifteen minutes later Ord gave the command to attack the Spanish trenches. With his pistol in one hand and a sword in the other, he stood up, yelled "Remember the Maine," and began running up the initial slope between the two hills. Our Colored Tenth rose en masse, gave out a battle cry, and followed the lieutenant up the first rise. The Twenty-fourth Colored Infantry on our left and the Third Cavalry plus the Rough Riders on our right cheered loudly and followed on behind us.

But the easy jaunt up the hills we'd all imagined ended less than five minutes into the assault. We were walking one minute and scrambling the next. It was intensely hot, and the climb became steeper alternating between jagged outcroppings, prickly pineapple plants, and soft, plowed land. And when we finally reached the barbed-wire entanglements two hundred yards from the ridgeline, the Spaniards opened up with everything they had.

Not long after clearing the wire our Tenth Cavalry spontaneously split with half our troops veering off to the left with the Twenty-fourth Infantry headed toward the summit of San Juan Hill and the other half turning to the right with the Third Cavalry and the Rough Riders fighting their way to the crest of Kettle Hill. In the heat of battle First Sergeant Blair moved to the left with Lieutenant Ord as I branched off to the right with Colonel Roosevelt, the Third Cavalry, and the First Volunteers.

Under increasingly intense fire, our advance up Kettle Hill became bogged down. Troopers were collapsing in front of us with grievous wounds and heat exhaustion. Our forces began bunching up behind them. But just when it appeared the advance would stall, our Gatling guns opened up, enfilading the enemy's trenches. Our men yelled, "The Gatlings!

The Gatlings!" And within seconds the Spanish fire ceased, and our men rushed to the top. After briefly engaging the Spaniards in hand-to-hand combat, we forced them to beat a hasty retreat westward toward Santiago.

With our skirmish now over, we ran down the slope of Kettle Hill, raced past a small lagoon, and climbed the northern end of San Juan Hill to help the Twenty-fourth break the remaining resistance there. But by the time we reached the summit, the fighting had ended, and the Spanish flag had already been pulled down from atop the San Juan blockhouse.

Since there was no more fighting to be done, I began searching for First Sergeant Blair and the other half of our Tenth Cavalry. I held my breath every time I turned one of the dead troopers over and then felt guilty when I sensed relief that it wasn't First Sergeant Blair or one of our own from the Tenth Regiment staring up at me.

But despite my searching, it was the sergeant who found me. "Is that you, Hurricane?"

I turned, laughed, and replied, "In the flesh, Sergeant." I extended my arms. "My God, man, it's really good to see you."

The sergeant hugged me and then joked, "Where you been hiding out all this time? Never saw you again once we passed through the wire."

I pointed eastward toward Kettle Hill. "Over there, Sergeant. Got bogged down near the top; but once the Gatlings kicked in, our boys had them running like scalded dogs."

Since the energy was draining out of both us, we quickly found some shade near the blockhouse and collapsed. After catching our breath, I asked, "You seen Lieutenant Ord? I want to thank him for making all this happen. That was a helluva brave thing, first challenging the general and then leading the charge up the Heights. He's the real hero here."

The sergeant shook his head. "I'm sorry, Hurricane, but our friend didn't make it."

"Killed, Sergeant?"

"Killed, sir."

"You know what happened?"

"Saw it all. Was right there behind him. He was the first to reach the San Juan summit. Began directing fire. And just as he turned to yell a command, a bullet ripped through his throat. He stared at me. I'll never forget the look as long as I live, Hurricane. He staggered forward, dropped his pistol and sword, sat down, and clutched his throat. One of our men from D Troop swung around, shot the sniper, and turned back to help me with the lieutenant's wound. He struggled to speak. Said something about the Tenth splitting going up the hill. Said if it hadn't happened, we'd have already taken the Heights. That's all he really had time to say."

"Nothing you could do?"

"Nothing. You could see the blood gushing out the side of his neck. He just closed his eyes, gasped, and went limp."

"Sergeant, it's fitting we bury him up here. Once we know the Heights are secure, we'll get the troops together and give him the burial he deserves."

We'd made great strides on the Heights, but the war wasn't over. In fact, after the battles of San Juan and El Caney, our advance toward Santiago quickly came to a halt. The enemy had successfully defended Fort Canosa, allowing them to strengthen their defenses around the capital. In response, we lay siege to the city. While our navy was busy destroying the Spanish fleet and blockading Santiago Harbor, we were blocking overland routes and digging trenches along the city perimeter.

It then became a battle of attrition in the heat, rain, and thick mud. While we slowly went about our business starving the enemy out, we suffered daily losses from sniper fire, heat exhaustion, and debilitating tropical diseases. By the time the city fell only two weeks later, four thousand troopers had been hospitalized with typhoid, dysentery, malaria, or the yellow fever.

Finally, on the seventeenth of July, we crawled out of our trenches, paraded into the city, and saluted as the Sixth Cavalry played "The Star-Spangled Banner" and raised Old Glory above the governor's palace. And at least for a fleeting moment, our fatigue gave way to relief and a sense of pride in our achievement. We knew our mission was ending and we'd soon be heading home to a raucous hero's welcome.

But as the War Department would have it, our Negro regiments were among the last to leave. It was only in mid-August, four weeks later, we set sail for Montauk Point, New York. And when we eased into Fort Pond Bay the following week, we were quickly disabused of our earlier visions of victory parades and the warm embrace of sweethearts, families, and friends. Yes, even before reaching shore, well-meaning bureaucrats herded us onto barges to cleanse us of any threats to society including malaria and the dreaded yellow jack. And from the disinfection barges it was then on to Camp Wikoff where we endured months of detention at the windswept tip of nowhere.

So each of us had to find a way to deal with the quarantine. I chose to spend my free time painting the past and sketching the future. While out West with the Tenth Cavalry, I was convinced I'd made the right decision choosing to serve in the military. Within the chain of command our Negro regiments were highly respected and treated as equals. Even the national press wrote articles praising our success in helping tame the frontier over the past thirty years.

But during that brief stay in Florida, I got my first taste of a bitter past. Was Lakeland an anomaly or was bigotry still prevalent throughout the South? Had attitudes never really changed or had they now regressed to the mean? After helping bludgeon the Indian into submission, had our first-class soldiers now become second-class citizens again? While sailing to Cuba, I remember thinking at least we've made progress in the military. Even rebel officers who fought us during the war treat us fairly within the ranks.

But that belief quickly unraveled. When Roosevelt's Riders and the First Regulars were pinned at Las Guásimas, didn't our Tenth Cavalry drive the enemy away? Didn't our Colored Infantry overrun the Spaniards at El Caney? Didn't we lead the charge up Kettle Hill? Didn't First Lieutenant Ord and First Sergeant Blair lead the way to San Juan summit? And didn't we lose twenty-six of our own serving at the tip of the spear that day?

When thousands of our white brothers fell ill with the

fever, didn't we willingly serve as nurses and orderlies and die en masse? Didn't Pershing declare we had fought our way into America's heart? Didn't Roosevelt say we came forward with courage and offered our lives in the service of our country?

But Roosevelt, what are you saying now? How can you say my men were shirkers and would only go as far as the white officers would lead them? And what are you doing now? You know we were all there after the battle for the Heights. So what have you done to our original photograph? You know the Third Cavalry was to your left; that you were at the center surrounded by your Rough Riders; and that our Buffalo Soldiers were off to your right. But what do I see in the newspapers now? Only you and your First Volunteers. So where's the Third Cavalry now, Colonel? And what have you done with our Tenth Colored, sir?

16

THE STATION HOUSE, the shops, and the surrounding hills were much the same but just a little smaller than I'd remembered. It was as if I had left the earth for a time, toured the afterlife, and returned now to describe what I'd seen. But would anyone here believe it's a blend of good and evil? That it's just like Warfield, being shunted daily between heaven and hell? Their Bibles don't speak to this truth. So I suspect it's better to add this decade of memories to the trunk where I've already stored my uniform, my medals, and my dreams.

But one thing hadn't changed—his indomitable smile. The one I'd carried into battle. The one that encouraged me to do my best. The one that assured me that everything would be all right. Thomas had stepped out from the November shadows, flashed that resolute smile, and extended his arms. We didn't speak for the longest time; we just stood there hugging one another on the icy platform.

He finally broke the silence. "God, it's really great having you back here again, boy. Letters are good, but there's nothing like a homecoming. Everyone's looking forward to seeing you and hearing everything—and I mean everything—from the moment you left Warfield to your stepping off the train just now."

"Really not much to tell," I replied. "I went to school back East; deported folk out West; and then played a minor role in a splendid little war."

"They're expecting a lot more than that, Lil' Jim. They've all read the accounts. You're all heroes in their eyes. You've got to give them the flavoring if not the meat."

"I'll do my best, but as I explained in the letters, I'm just interested in making a clean break with the military, taking a deep breath, riding old Black Widow, visiting a fallen soldier's family, and finding my way forward. In the meantime, I thought I'd go back out to the farm, if they'll have me. Help David Lee and Theresa Anne with the winter chores and the planting next spring."

"That'll be a good thing, Lil' Jim. They'll welcome you with open arms. David Lee's no spring chicken. He's in his seventies now, and with all the sugar in his system, he's running downhill real fast. Theresa Anne's been making the trips to town, selling the butter, eggs, and milk the best she can."

"Can't someone go along to help out?" I asked.

"Hard to believe, but even after all these years, they're still having trouble finding reliable folk. So the way I see it, you'd be a godsend, doing some farming and maybe even trying your hand at selling. What do you think?"

I laughed. "That's if they'll have me. You've got to remember I was a kid in their eyes. David Lee used to take me along when he sold his wares, and before climbing down from the wagon—I mean every time—he'd say, 'Now, boy, you keep your mouth zipped. Just watch and learn.' And that's exactly what I did—just focused on David Lee. How he was acting and what he was saying. Never saw him happier than when he was driving a hard bargain. I can still hear that spiel flowing off his tongue like honey. 'I tell you, sir, that's a fair price.' And then he'd raise his voice a bit for emphasis, 'It's reasonable, reasonable.' And then after shaking on a good deal, he'd let out the biggest rebel yell you ever heard."

"A lot to be screaming about, Lil' Jim. You see, those folks doing the buying, they were wholesalers. Not buying for themselves, mind you, but buying for the stores. Buying in lots for the shops as far away as Nashville and Memphis. David Lee was making a handsome profit on every one of those sales. But it's different now. With David Lee sick and Theresa Anne selling the goods, I'm sure those buyers are taking advantage of her. Can't say I blame them. They're just driving the deal as David Lee used to do. It's just how you conduct business in this neck of the woods."

"Well, I'll try helping out. They did a lot of good by me giving me a place to stay while I was growing up and finishing school."

Thomas paused and then said, "In any event, Lil' Jim, I hope you'll stay at the house a few days before heading back out to the farm. Be good for us to get caught up and maybe even attend services together next Sunday morning. Everyone would really be happy to see you, especially the Emmetts."

"I just hope the folks there wouldn't be expecting too much. There's really not a whole lot left to say once you carve out the terror and the gore. . . ."

"Oh, there's really no need going there. They'd all be happy with you just waving the flag and speaking of heroes.

You'd be the talk of the town along with Roosevelt and his Rough Riders."

I didn't respond. I turned my head away just enough to hide a grimace.

Thomas reached down to pick up my suitcases. "Here, let me help you with your bags. Got anything stowed underneath?"

I smiled and replied ironically, "Just a trunk with some more baggage."

Thomas laughed and said, "Okay, then, we'd better find a porter to help us drag that heavy thing out to the wagon."

The few days I spent at Thomas's went quickly. I recounted some of my war stories, while he told me stories about Mama and the latest goings-on around town. There wasn't time to tell everything, and I know we both glossed over a thing or two. Yet being in his presence again helped to relieve so much of the tension I had carried ever since I first left Hurricane Creek. After all these years, he remained my best friend.

Soon enough it was Sunday and I was back to playing the role of reluctant hero. But once I had met my obligation, I climbed up onto the wagon bench next to Thomas and we drove the short distance from the church out to the farm. As we rode up the entryway past Bella's cabin and the barns, I looked over at Thomas and said, "You know, when you've been uprooted for so long, there's something really comforting about riding up to the past and finding things pretty much as you left them."

"I agree up to a point, Lil' Jim," Thomas replied. He then nodded straight ahead directing my attention toward the porch where David Lee and Theresa Anne were standing waiting. "Time's a little kinder to wood and concrete than it is to flesh and blood. You'll see."

We hitched the horse and climbed the hill toward the house. As we neared the front steps Thomas embarrassed me. "Look, y'all. The conqueror's returned home."

"Boy, you're a sight for sore eyes!" Theresa Anne exclaimed. "Come on up here and give us a big hug!" It didn't take long to see Thomas was right. Time hadn't been kind to either of them, but especially to David Lee, who was now stooped, partially blind, and missing many of his front teeth. I instinctively wrapped my arm around his waist to steady him as he turned to lead us into the house. We walked through the front bedroom and the hallway to the side entrance and took our customary winter seats near the eternal flame roaring in the potbelly stove.

Theresa Anne turned to Thomas. "I know you'll want to be getting home before dark. So why don't I whip up some ham, eggs, and biscuits right quick and then get you on your way?"

He smiled and replied, "You know as well as I if it had been anything else, I'd have respectably declined. But breakfast food for a late lunch or dinner, especially in the winter, now that's really hard to turn down. And besides, maybe Lil' Jim will tell us more about his time in Montana and Cuba."

Just then we heard the side door open. Theresa Anne turned toward the hallway entrance and joked, "Looks like my guest list and your audience just grew a bit, Lil' Jim."

"Who's that?" I asked.

"Margaret and Miss Sallie," Theresa Anne replied. "They've been at the school putting up the Thanksgiving decorations. They've both been looking forward all week to your coming home."

The two women rushed in exclaiming teasingly, "Where's our hero?"

I stood up and instinctively moved toward my old teachers.

They both gave me big hugs. "We're all so proud of you," Miss Sallie said. "I don't know if Theresa Anne or David Lee told you, but we took turns at dinner reading your letters aloud every time we got a new one. They were so exciting, hearing about the West and then the war!"

Theresa Anne jumped in. "Oh, you haven't heard anything yet, Miss Sallie! After I stir up some ham and biscuits for everybody, Lil' Jim's promised to tell us even more about his time away; only now it will be face-to-face!"

So after piling second helpings on everyone's plate, Theresa Anne sat down and signaled I should begin. But what I thought would be a straightforward narrative quickly evolved into a question-and-answer session. And I just knew that one of the first questions out of the box would be, "Did you spend any time with Roosevelt and the Rough Riders?"

Growing accustomed to the annoying but understandable question, I deflected it with aplomb. "Saw the colonel and the First Volunteers from time to time but never had occasion to speak with him personally." Why spoil the mood with the truth? After all they'd read, after all the pictures they'd seen, would they really believe the Negro Tenth Cavalry led the way up San Juan Heights and Roosevelt and his men followed on in support? Even more improbable—would they believe the Tenth Cavalry saved Roosevelt and his men from slaughter, not once, but twice? And would they think Roosevelt could be so devious as to cut everyone else out of an iconic photograph, leaving only him and his beloved Rough Riders basking in the glorious San Juan victory? No, it was better to risk boring them than cutting their adulation off at the knees. So just deflect and move on to the next off-key question about driving the Indians into submission and onto reservations.

After Thomas left and everyone else had gone to bed, Margaret and I pulled our chairs up close to the fire and reminisced about my days at Miss Sallie's one-room school where Margaret was then assisting for a second year.

She looked up into the shadows flickering on the ceiling and sighed. "You were a handful, Lil' Jim."

"I don't remember ever getting into trouble with you or Miss Sallie."

"Oh no. That's not what I meant. You were difficult to manage. Different than the other students."

"Different?"

"Yes. You had a drive about you, a drive to succeed that the others didn't have. At least, not to the same degree as was instilled in you. Yes, sir. You were driven. You wanted to learn everything you could about a subject. Always casting a wider net and digging a deeper trench. It seemed "why" was your favorite word and your favorite question. You kept Miss Sallie and me up at night, preparing, wondering what you would ask the next morning. We used to laugh in anticipation. What would be next? And we always believed you'd succeed no matter what you did in the future. And look at you now. First, West Point. Then serving on the frontier and leading men into battle. . . .”

As she relived the past, I was becoming increasingly uncomfortable—not so much with her compliments but with the anticipation of a question I knew was coming. How should I respond when there was no easy answer, in fact, no answer at all right now? It was plain to see the chronological progression from “frontier” to “battle” to “now” to “next.”

Margaret paused and gazed into my eyes. “Now that you’re back, you have any idea what you want to do next?”

I quickly wiped an incongruous smile off my face and answered her question honestly. “For right now, Margaret, I want to put some distance between me and the military. And I suspect there’s no better way to do that than helping Theresa Anne and David Lee anyway I can.”

“No doubt they can use the help. But any thoughts about what comes after that, after your stint as farmhand?”

That’s where I drew the line and dissembled—not lying, mind you, but holding back. In general, I knew where I wanted to go but just hadn’t figured out how to get there. I replied, “Oh, I’ve some ideas my Uncle Aaron put in my head years ago. I can see the Promised Land on the other side of the river there. I just haven’t found a way to get there just yet. Haven’t found the bridge.”

Margaret couldn’t resist probing. “So what big things are waiting on the other side of that bridge, Lil’ Jim?”

And unfortunately, it was now time for outright deflection. “Hard to explain. But I have one of my uncle’s old articles, which clearly lays out the goals and a path to achieve them. I'll have to dig his piece out and share it with you."

"Well, I really look forward to reading it. You know, we're all interested in what you're up to. Everyone's so proud of you, knowing you risked everything for the country. But honestly, I was more afraid than proud during the war."

"Afraid? Afraid of what?"

She reached down and spontaneously touched the scar on my hand. "That you'd be terribly maimed or, God forbid, you wouldn't come home at all." She paused and pushed back from the fire. "Don't go anywhere. I'll be right back."

Several minutes later she returned carrying a package. She pulled her chair back up to the fire and sat down beside me. "Here, this is for you. I was going to wait until Christmas, but with the cold weather already on us, I suspect you can put this to good use now."

I stuck my hand into the cloth sack and slowly pulled out a blue woolen sweater with leather buttons running down the front. I stood up, held the sweater close to my chest, and extended the arms. "It's a perfect fit! Thank you so much."

"I started knitting it when I heard you were heading off to war. It's what they call a cardigan. They're all the rage now. Decided on a cardigan for good luck because I'd read somewhere they're named after the Earl of Cardigan who'd led some famous cavalry charge with his light brigade. The earl's troops supposedly wore this style of sweater." A self-conscious smile played on Margaret's lips.

I thought, "A cardigan for good luck?" But I smiled anyway, remembering what Aunt Jane used to say—it was the thought that really counted. How was Margaret to ever know the details of a battle fought in a far-off land between the British, the Turks, and the French on the one hand and the Russians on the other? Hell, I first studied the Crimean War at West Point. So how was she to know Cardigan's Light Brigade was decimated as they charged the entrenched Russian batteries and riflemen?

I regrouped and replied, "I don't know how I'll ever repay you."

"You already have," she said. "You came home." She smiled again and added, "I'm not a religious person, Lil' Jim. But I'd knit thinking, 'Keep him safe,' and then I'd purl whispering, 'Bring him home alive.' So the cardigan was a prayer to someone somewhere who listened and stepped in."

Margaret turned and gazed into my eyes. I leaned in, cradled her head in my hands, and gently kissed her, fulfilling a dream I'd held since my schoolboy days.

17

It wasn't the first, the hundredth, or the thousandth day I realized I had begun building the bridge. I just remember how exhilarating but difficult it was helping them at the beginning. Because of the lack of reliable workers Theresa Anne didn't really have all that much to offer, and even the little she did take to market barely turned a profit. Thomas had already warned me the wholesalers were squeezing her for every dime they could.

Oh, I recall our first trip to sell the milk, eggs, and butter a few days after I arrived at the farm. Just before Theresa Anne and I left for Warfield, David Lee took me aside as he had in the past and instructed me in no uncertain terms to "keep my mouth zipped." I was to "watch Theresa Anne and learn." I was "not to interfere and lose the sale." So playing the good soldier that first day, I followed orders and gritted my teeth as the city slickers took Theresa Anne for another ride. And I remember the nightmare drive home to the farm—Theresa Anne blithely humming a favorite hymn as I seethed and promised myself they would never take advantage of her again.

Before returning to market Christmas week, I devised a plan to increase profits, which I didn't bother sharing with either David Lee or Theresa Anne. I reasoned it was far better asking for forgiveness afterward than requesting permission in advance. When Theresa Anne and I reached Warfield, I allowed things to play out as they had before. We drove up to the back of the same building, pulled off the wet canvas covering our goods, and waited for the wholesaler to arrive.

And it wasn't long before our squat, mustachioed dealer appeared wearing his customary black suit and bowler. He didn't say a word. He just tipped his hat toward Theresa Anne and then glided back to the wagon bed to inspect our latest offering. After several minutes he returned to where we were standing near the mare and immediately went on offense. "Got to be honest with you, miss, the milk's pretty thin and the eggs are small. I can't offer more than twenty dollars for the whole lot. Whaddaya say, ma'am?"

"Same little man with the same little spiel as before," I thought. "Never again, sir, never again." It was time to launch a counterattack.

Theresa Anne cleared her throat; but before she could utter a word, I stepped forward and responded, "There's been a little change in our bargaining team, Mister . . . ah . . . Mister . . ."

"Mr. Lynch, sir."

I extended my hand and responded, "Jim Taylor, Mr. Lynch. Pleased to make your acquaintance. My friends call me 'Hurricane.' From now on you'll be dealing with me, sir. But getting things off on the right foot, Mr. Lynch, I need you to repeat your offer. I'm sure I didn't hear you clearly because what I heard would be downright insulting. You mind repeating your offer for the wagonload?"

He glanced over at Theresa Anne as if pleading for help. I could tell my polite counteroffensive had set this stout little man back on his heels. He was nervously twirling the tip of his mustache. I had to give him credit, though. He took a deep breath and tried responding in kind. "With all due respect, sir, I believe twenty dollars is a fair price. When I go retailin', the margin'll be thin. You must understand I've got to make enough off the spread to feed and clothe my family."

Sensing it would now be hand-to-hand combat, I quickly struck back. "And the same goes here for Theresa Anne and her failing husband. Twenty dollars is not even a serious starting point, let alone a final offer." I paused only long enough for effect and then ratcheted up the assault employing a bit of hyperbole. "Sir, so you're aware, you're not bargaining with just anyone. With all due respect, Mr. Lynch, you're dealing with a fellow who first helped write the terms of deportation for the Cree out West and then helped negotiate the terms of surrender for Arsenio Linares y Pombo in Santiago. And again, sir, with all due respect, our bargaining here pales in comparison. So I'm prepared to step away from anything less than forty dollars for the lot. I tell you that's a fair price. Reasonable . . . reasonable."

He returned to twirling the end of his mustache for a few seconds and then stammered out, "I . . . I can only go up to thirty."

"Thirty-seven fifty."

"Thir . . . thirty-five. Honestly, that's as far as I can go."

I extended my hand. "Okay, then, Mr. Lynch. Thirty-five it is. Theresa Anne and I look forward to working with you in the future."

After offloading the milk, eggs, and butter, I helped Theresa Anne up onto the wagon bench, climbed aboard, and quickly headed out of town. When we had driven into the countryside well beyond the city limits, I stopped the mare, handed Theresa Anne the thick roll of money, lifted my arms with reins in hand, and gave out the loudest rebel yell anyone had heard since David Lee rode into town.

We made three more trips to Warfield before planting season began in earnest. Since all three of these offerings were similar to the one in December, Mr. Lynch and I quickly settled on the thirty-five-dollar amount we had negotiated the first time around. No hard bargaining, hyperbole, or brinksmanship required. In fact, the more I dealt with Mr. Lynch the more I respected him. To his credit he'd begun complimenting Theresa Anne and me on the consistent quality and quantity of our goods. And on the way home from Warfield after our March exchange, I had an epiphany: instead of considering Mr. Lynch an adversary, why not think of him as an ally, an opportunity, if you will? Besides praising our goods, hadn't he hinted he wished he had more to sell to his retailers?

The next morning, I shocked David Lee and Theresa Anne when I suggested using my military savings to attract additional workers and expand the farming operations. In his disbelief David Lee joked, "Boy, if I didn't know better, I'd say you'd contracted an exotic disease during the war, which has been slowly eating away at your brain."

I ignored the attempt at humor, looked over toward his

wife, and responded seriously, "Ask Theresa Anne. She'll tell you. More than once Mr. Lynch has expressed interest in having more of our goods to sell."

Theresa Anne nodded. "He sure did, David Lee. Mr. Lynch was pretty clear about that the last few times we've gone to market."

"You really think he's serious?" David Lee asked. "You know, Lynch could just be saying these things to butter you up. Get you to take less in the future."

"I'd say the compliments would work the opposite, would cause me to ask more for the goods, not less," I countered. "I'm pretty good at reading people. I think he's as serious as could be. Otherwise, I wouldn't be offering to put my life's savings on the line."

David Lee paused, looked down at his boots, and said, "Well, even if you think this is real, Lil' Jim, you know Theresa Anne and I haven't got anything extra to help with the added expenses."

I immediately jumped in to ease his embarrassment. "I didn't expect y'all to do anything other than give me permission to hire workers, improve the land, and then keep half the annual profits we make from the improvements."

"What you have in mind, boy?"

"I don't want to shock you into thinking this is pie in the sky and you'll turn me down. So before I say anything, I want y'all to realize we wouldn't do all this at once. . . . First, we'd have to gradually hire more help; next, improve the land an acre at a time; and then add more livestock and grow more food for market."

I reached into my pocket and pulled out a hand-drawn map of the property, on which I had penciled in my initial ideas. I spread the paper out on the table and continued. "Getting you all oriented to my hen scratching here, that rectangle over to the right there, that's Miss Sallie's School. And a little to the west of it, that's the road running back to Anderson's farm. The field lying fallow there between the school and Anderson's road, I was thinking of planting it in cotton. Then to the west of the road there, butting up to the entryway, that's the family garden.

"I've been doing some reading. There're new techniques, tools, and seed stocks we can put to good use. Increase the yield and then offer the surplus for sale. Over to the left there at the edge, that's the far field. You say it's been lying fallow now for years. We could put that in corn; and the near field there west of the entry way, we'd keep that in hay for cattle grazing. Now there's the house and behind it we've got that huge stand of timber. I suspect the oaks, pines, and walnuts haven't been touched in thirty years. Not since the war. Now whoever said money doesn't grow on trees was either lying or a damn fool. We can make good profit thinning them out.

"To the north across the highway and railroad tracks there we'd keep the open land as a forage field. And to the east of it over by the creek, we'll clear out the deadwood and expand the apple and peach orchards. So what do you think? Do I have your blessing to begin hiring and improving the land?"

"How many folk you thinking of bringing on?" David Lee asked. "You know how hard it is finding Negroes these days wanting to work for a living."

"I want to try something different—hire young tenant families. Probably three or four to start. If we do this right, we can make money from the rent and a portion of the goods."

"How you gonna convince Negroes to sign on to bringing their families here?" Theresa Anne inquired.

"Sell them honestly on a win-win. Admit we're in it to make money and expand the business, but point out what's in it for them. It's a stepping-stone for young families. Get experience here, eventually buy some land of their own, and then keep all the profits from their labor."

David Lee stroked his gray, scraggily beard while digesting what he'd heard. He looked across the table at Theresa Anne and asked, "You okay with all this? Seems like a lot we'd be biting off."

She looked toward me and then turned back to her husband. "I've watched this boy here for months, David Lee, and I'm convinced he's got the gumption to make all this happen."

David Lee slowly extended his hand and said, "Well, it looks like we're in for the long haul. So do us proud."

Since I couldn't yell after closing my biggest sale yet, I just smiled broadly and replied, "I promise you, partner. Y'all won't be sorry."

Right off the bat we put some of the timber to good use, planing it into boards to be used for building. Once we found a tenant family, we'd put them to work designing and constructing a cabin to their liking. It wasn't too long then before word got around, and we were swamped with young applicants wanting to sign on for the opportunity.

During that first planting season, we got a little of the corn and cotton in the ground. And between the planting and the harvest we made headway clearing the deadwood from the peach and apple orchards. All the while we continued making the monthly trips to Warfield selling the butter, the eggs, and milk to Mr. Lynch, who had no idea what Theresa Anne and I were cooking up on the side. Like clockwork we'd offer him our goods, and he would happily accept the standard thirty-five-dollar asking price.

When I wasn't farming, I was spending every waking hour planning. With providence shining down on us, what should we do next? The obvious answer was acquiring more land, hiring more families, and then producing more goods for market. And we followed this straightforward path the next two years. After convincing the aging Mr. Anderson to sell us his property outright, we hired five additional Negro families to work the farm. And you should have seen Mr. Lynch that third year when we revealed we had more than butter, eggs, and milk to offer him. He beamed from ear to ear and immediately began discussing potential customers for our first substantial crop of cotton and corn.

The following spring David Lee, Theresa Anne, and I began making increasingly significant moves to grow the business into something so much bigger than wholesale farming. While we continued purchasing and leasing as much land as we could get our hands on, we bought out Mr. Lynch and established ongoing brokerage contracts with most of the major farms in western Tennessee. Buying Mr. Lynch's business turned out to be a great move. During a visit to acquaint himself with our operations, he floated several outstanding ideas, which we immediately put into motion: build a shipping station; petition the railroad for a trace connecting the station to the mainline across the highway; and establish grist and saw mills producing finished goods with higher margins than we were getting for our raw materials.

Toward the end of that fourth year I realized we were growing so rapidly I would need additional supervisors to help manage the operations. As counterintuitive as it seems, I placed more value in trust than expertise. I reasoned I could always teach folks I trusted but not necessarily develop a trust for strangers who already had a good grasp of the brokerage business.

So I made two trips between Thanksgiving and Christmas that year. The first was to Saint Louis, where I spent a weekend with my old army pal, First Sergeant Blair. He had recently retired from the Tenth Cavalry and was visiting relatives in Missouri before heading out West to look for work. Since we'd kept in touch after I left the army, I believed I could persuade him to scuttle his current plans and begin a new life in the heartland mentoring young black men and making a good living to boot. And when he accepted my generous offer in Saint Louis, I shocked him and his cousins with one of David Lee's triumphant yells.

I planned the second trip for Christmas week. I didn't contact relatives or make hotel reservations in Memphis. But there was method to my madness. I knew exactly where I'd be spending that holy night. When I got to the Poplar Station, I spent a few minutes soaking up the history of the place before heading off for my destination. You see, this was the very depot where John Luther "Casey" Jones climbed aboard Engine 382 for his heroic ride to glory.

When I reached the street, I turned to the north into a brisk winter wind. I was now traveling the same route I'd followed the Christmas Eve I fled my family. Not much had changed in all those years. The rising moon still cast long shadows across the empty streets as the sweep of stars flashed assurances I wasn't alone. A left, a right, and then another left brought me again to that no-man's-land between McCreary's woods and the steep ridge overlooking the roundhouse and switching yard. Pretty much the same here too, but different in one significant way: only two shadows now huddled near the fire just beyond the evergreens.

I moved over to where the men were sitting and eased myself down next to the fire. The ghosts didn't acknowledge my arrival. They pulled their threadbare blankets up close around their necks and continued staring silently into the flames. Every so often I'd steal a glance. Even here, nothing much had changed. I was again sitting alongside scarecrows with pale, drawn faces; remarkably thin frames; long, disheveled beards; and oily hair flowing out from beneath their navy watch caps.

When a shooting star arced the sky from west to east, the fellow to my left spoke to his companion. "Looks like Jerusalem Slim's sending a message now that there are three of us and the light's blinkin'."

The other tramp replied, "Well, I suppose that calls for a change in text. So we won't use Luke this year. Let's try Matthew instead." He reached in under his blanket and retrieved a well-worn Bible. He pulled off his thin mittens and began fumbling through the pages. "Damn wind and cold's given my fingers lockjaw. . . . There now. Matthew, chapter two."

He looked toward me and then over at his partner to ensure he had our attention. He cleared his throat and began reading, "Now when Jesus was born in Bethlehem of Judaea in the days of Herod the king, behold, there came wise men from the East to Jerusalem, saying, 'Where is he that is born king of the Jews? For we have seen his star in the East and are come to worship him.'

"When Herod the king had heard these things, he was troubled and demanded of them where Christ should be born. And they said unto him, 'In Bethlehem of Judea.' . . . And he said, 'Go and search diligently for the young child; and when ye have found him, bring me word again, that I may come and worship him also.'

"When they had heard the king, they departed; and, lo, the star, which they saw in the East, went before them, till it came and stood over where the young child was. When they saw the star, they rejoiced with exceeding great joy. And when they were come into the house, they saw the young child with Mary, his mother, and fell down, and worshipped him. And when they had opened their treasures, they presented unto him gifts of gold, frankincense, and myrrh."

The hobo preacher closed the scriptures and slipped them back under his blanket. "After all these years remembering Slim here at the annual convention, I think that's enough reading for the night. Believe it's time to start planning Christmas stew for tomorrow. I've done my part, Spider, now it's your time to dole out the assignments."

"Fine by me, Sky Pilot," he responded. "Just need to know if the young man here will be joining our pot gang tomorrow for a late breakfast and dinner. With so few of us left in the jungle, we're having to do a double duty now." He looked toward me and asked, "You gonna stick with us here and help taking the whiskers off and shackling up?" Before I could answer, he added, "By the way, sir, your moniker?"

I laughed and took pride in letting my friends know I'd learned some of their lingo along the way. "Spider. Sky Pilot. I know it's been more than fifteen years now, but could I have changed all that much? My road name's Lil' Jim. 'Bos, it's Lil' Jim."

They stared across the flames at each other and shrugged. "Forgive us, Lil' Jim," Spider replied. "We've seen a lot of tourists through the years."

"I was here the Christmas that Brutus showed up. You've got to remember Brutus, the Negro, who lied about being from Corinth in the undertaking business."

They stared at each other and shrugged again. This time Sky Pilot responded, "No offense, boy, but many a son of Ham has stopped by the jungle here to nail a rattler."

Spider jumped in. "You say you've been here before around Christmas, and now you've come back again. Don't look much like you're missing a blip or two. Why you coming back here to the weeds?"

"Being really honest with you boys, to see you Wandering Willies—especially the two of you. You might not remember this young runaway, but I've carried you boys with me all these years. Out East, out West, and even to Cuba."

"But why now?" Sky Pilot asked. "Why tonight?"

I smiled. "Because it's Slim's birthday."

"You giving us some lumps or light pieces?" Spider probed.

"More than that, boys. Jobs. Real jobs for the long haul."

"Why us?" Sky Pilot asked. "We're sons of Adam— spike pitchers—and you're willing to make the two of us honest-to-God barnacles. Why?"

"What did Slim say, boys? 'Blessed are the merciful.' You see, you helped me when I was a lamb. I never forgot it. And now that I've got the means, I want to return the favor."

Spider's ears perked up. He leaned in and asked, "So, Lil' Jim, say we're interested. So whaddaya have in mind, boy?"

"Got a farming operation of sorts east of Warfield. Getting into more and more things. Got close to twenty tenant families working there now. Going to need more. I can't handle it all myself. Need folks to help manage the tenants, fellows I can count on."

"Back to my question, why us?" Sky Pilot asked.

"I recall you saying you worked a farm in between summer sermons. Believe you drove a jolt wagon."

"Happy to say more sermons than corn rows these days."

"Okay by me. You'd be supervising anyhow. And once you've farmed I hear you carry those memories in your muscles and bones."

"Leaving these parts means I'd be givin' up my preachin' . . . ."

"Being a mission stiff you know Slim will provide. Our Reverend Emmett's getting really up in age. He's hinted there's a real need for an assistant pastor—visiting the shut-ins, teaching classes, even doing some of the preaching."

"What about me?" Spider asked. "I haven't kicked the clover the way Sky Pilot's done."

"You've got something other than the farming, something easy to spot if you spend time here with you in the jungle."

"What's that, boy?"

"Putting Christmas breakfast and dinner together. Remembering precisely who did what, who fetched what the year before, everything from the gump to the pig's vest, from the cackleberries to the Irish turkey. You can learn the farming, but you were born with that organizing knack."

Spider and Sky Pilot stared through the flames at each other.

"So, boys, what do you think? We can do a lot of good together, and I'll do right by you."

A classic pantomime ensued. Spider shrugged his silent message, "Whaddaya think, Jack?"

Sky Pilot volleyed. "I dunno. Whaddaya think?"

Spider paused and then lowered his head, gesturing, "I'll leave it up to you. Whatever you wanna do is fine by me."

Sky Pilot continued staring into the fiery oracle for answers. He finally turned, removed his mitten, and extended his hand.

After shaking on the deal, I said, "Now there's one stipulation, boys."

"Oh, oh, what's that?" Sky Pilot asked.

"We're not pulling up stakes here until we've celebrated Christmas breakfast and dinner together in the jungle."

Spider smiled. "Fine by us. Let's see, now, Lil' Jim. You'll be in charge of getting the black strap and the flour for the saddle blankets."

I laughed and broke into hobo dialect, "That's okay by me too. And the morning after Christmas we'll head to the Y to scrape and polish your mugs. Next we'll pling to the main stem for new rags and then get over to the Poplar Depot and ride the cushions to Warfield."

"Oh, Lord willin'," Sky Pilot fervently prayed.

"Yes, Lord willing," I echoed.

18

I WAS LIVING the dream. There was no question now a thumb was on the scale in my favor. How could life become any sweeter? After escaping the early years of loneliness, I savored every moment interacting with friends and strangers. But loneliness always lurked in the interactions; I knew circumstances would eventually separate me from a gentle touch or smiling face. And every time it happened I relived the depths of my childhood pain. I had learned the lesson well that nothing's permanent about relationships or happiness. But now I had discovered the inverse was also true; I had managed to reconnect with old friends and reward them well for having once been there for me.

When First Sergeant Blair arrived near the end of January, he immediately took command of organizing day-to-day operations. He divided the twenty tenant families into three teams. While Spider and he would command two teams of eight families each, Sky Pilot would be responsible for only four because he also had his church duties to perform. The new managers meshed so well; they understood they could rely on each other for help. If there were a question about farming, they knew Sky Pilot would have the answers. If there were doubts about planning, they realized they could turn to Spider. And if there were concerns about tenant relations, they knew First Sergeant Blair would be their man.

It didn't take long to see the positive impact of the improvements they'd made. As productivity and margins grew, profits soared. But honestly, for me it was never about the money. In fact, before hiring my old acquaintances, I was earning enough even with the fifty-fifty split with David Lee to live comfortably the rest of my life.

So if it was not about the money, then why continue striving for increasingly more of it? Because I now understood what money could do. I could leverage my wealth to improve the lot of my people. And what did I do to advance their lives? For starters I purchased David Lee's farm and his half interest in the enterprise to ensure I could implement Uncle Aaron's vision on the farm. My objective was to be supportive without constricting the tenants' liberties. Besides providing comfortable housing and a liberal wage, we expanded Miss Sallie's school and recruited Negro teachers to educate the tenants' children. We made sure there was always enough food for everyone and enlisted Thomas's help in caring for the sick and assisting the midwives with difficult births. And with Reverend Emmett's blessing, we addressed the families' spiritual needs as well. We built a log church overlooking the family cemetery on the hill. It was all Sky Pilot's idea—the church, the location, and his appointment as pastor performing weddings, funerals, christenings, and devil-hating, hair-raising sermons.

When the wind is at your back, living and loving life is so easy. In those circumstances, sometimes even a good man's sudden death can raise the level of happiness. I found that out for myself. I had gone over to Hurricane Creek to see Thomas about initiating another vaccine program for all of us working on the farm. He had already inoculated everyone against smallpox, and I was wondering if we could introduce the new typhoid and cholera vaccines there. We had just sat down to chat when one of the church elders burst into the room insisting Thomas hurry over to the rectory. The Reverend Emmett had suffered "a spell."

Thomas grabbed his satchel, and we rushed over to the Emmett house. We found the reverend sprawled on the dining-room floor. Miss Emmett was sitting beside her husband dabbing blood from a small gash he'd suffered during his fall. Clara looked up pleadingly and said, "Please save him. He says his chest hurts and he can't breathe."

Thomas kneeled beside them, felt the reverend's pulse, listened to his heart, and murmured to himself, "Ventricular fibrillation."

"What can we do?" I asked.

"Get several pillows and some blankets, prop him up, keep him warm, and hope the rhythm rights itself."

Within minutes after we wrapped him in a heavy quilt, the reverend opened his eyes and raised his head. He reached out toward Miss Emmett and Thomas, struggled to speak, and then settled back on the pillows. He continued staring up at the couple; faintly smiled; took a long, deep breath; and closed his eyes. Thomas grasped the reverend's wrist, checked the pulse, and then slowly lowered the lifeless hand onto his still chest. Thomas looked over at Miss Emmett and whispered, "I'm sorry, Clara. He's gone." Miss Emmett buried her head in her hands and began weeping.

As you would expect, I vividly remember every detail of the reverend's death, from the minute the elder rushed in until Thomas pronounced the news. But that flickering smile still haunts me. What was the reverend trying to say? We've all heard it said folks see their lives flashing before their eyes as they grasp for life. Wouldn't the dying witness their failures and missed opportunities? Wouldn't clergymen also have regrets? So why was the reverend smiling? To this day I don't believe he was reviewing the past. I'm convinced he was foreseeing the future—not the heavenly one but the future here on earth. I'm convinced the reverend sensed the dormant love his wife and Thomas shared and was giving the benediction to their impending union. "What God hath joined together let not man put asunder."

And it wasn't long before the couple confirmed my theory. They announced their engagement only months after the reverend's demise.

Thomas's proposal and Miss Emmett's acceptance got me to thinking about my own life and ongoing relationship with Margaret. When I returned home from the war, we became friends and spent many hours together on weekend walks. We quickly overcame the difference in age and her prior role as my teacher. We lowered our guard and began sharing our most intimate thoughts.

Over time I realized I had grown to love her in my own way—a quiet, calmer way. I thought she would make a good wife. But I never acted on my feelings because I hadn't experienced the emotional intensity I'd imagined I would feel. So I was confused. Was my love based mostly on the kindness Margaret had shown me from the very beginning? From the moment I saw the hand-knit cardigan and learned she had prayed for me every night of the war? But finally, in the midst of all my ambivalence I decided to act. I would play my cards close to the vest until I was ready to reveal my vision of the future. For the next few months I would manage my projects in secret; and when all the work was done, I'd invite Thomas, Miss Emmett, and Margaret to join me for a walk in our extensive woods.

The Saturday I had long anticipated finally arrived. According to plan, Thomas and Miss Emmett got to the farm shortly after noon just as Margaret was returning from decorating her classroom to welcome in the autumn. The four of us donned our "nature clothes," grabbed our favorite walking sticks, and rushed off to ostensibly enjoy the fall foliage. I took the lead, and we followed a familiar path running southeastward toward the old Anderson farm. After a leisurely half-mile walk, we approached the clearing where Thomas and Margaret would expect to see the abandoned homestead.

"As a boy, Clara, my older brother, Robert, and I used to hike these woods," Thomas reminisced. "We imagined we were frontiersmen blazing a new trail over to Fort Anderson. When we reached the clearing up there, we'd make a run for it, sneak into the Anderson barn, climb up into the loft, and watch for hostile Chickasaws roaming these parts."

"You'll have to show me everything. The barn. The loft," Clara replied.

Thomas picked up the pace; and when he reached the tree line, he glanced out toward the farm, turned quickly back to Miss Emmett, and shouted excitedly, "The barn's right over—" He stopped midsentence as his brain registered what he'd actually seen a second earlier. "My God, Lil' Jim, where's the old barn? What's this? A new farmhouse? A new stable, shed, and barn on the other side? What have you been up to?"

Margaret rushed up to the clearing, surveyed the changes, and then whipped around in astonishment. "My God, Lil' Jim, you did all this? How? When? . . . Why?"

I sauntered up to the tree line where Thomas and Clara were standing and casually announced, "It's for y'all, a wedding gift for the two of you. I've deeded over the homestead here along with ten acres. Welcome home, Thomas. Use it on the weekends for now, if you like, and then consider moving out here permanently once you're ready to retire. But do with it as you like; it's yours."

Thomas and Miss Emmett didn't immediately respond. They just stood there facing the six-room, two-story, white clapboard farmhouse and shaking their heads in disbelief. I stepped between them, and took each by the arm. "Come on. Let's go in and have a look around."

We climbed the front steps onto the wrap-around porch and entered the house. As we moved through the first room, I suggested, "You'd probably want to use this as a front parlor for entertaining folks who drop by to visit. . . . Follow me through the doorway there into the hallway. Now if you take a left past the steps there, you'll find the first of the bedrooms." I turned to see that they were peering around wide-eyed. "Let's go upstairs and look around. Watch out now, the steps are narrow when you have an elliptical staircase. So up here we have two more bedrooms and a smaller space, which I suspect you could use as a study." Thomas just nodded. "Now let's head on back downstairs," I continued. "We'll turn left here at the bottom of the steps. . . . Now, through the doorway there." The couple followed my directions while taking everything in. "Here's the dining room. You've got a woodstove to keep everyone warm. Good for chewing the fat after dinner. And through here's the kitchen." We stopped to take everything in. "You'll see you've got a brand-new stove there, Miss Emmett. Plenty of eyes and a large oven for baking those apple pies Thomas loves. And out there you have a screened porch for feasting in the summer." Thomas and Clara were glowing while I beamed with pride. And after the shock had worn off a bit, I heard Thomas whisper, "My God, Clara, we're living a dream. . . Past is indeed prologue."

After finishing the house tour, Margaret and I escorted the amazed couple out to the corral to inspect the tool shed, the stables, and Thomas's favorite barn, which we had painstakingly dismantled and restored on the other side of the property.

"The shed and stables are new, Thomas, but everything's the same on the barn except for some cracked or rotting side boards, mostly on the north side where the moss collected. So let's go in and have a look around."

Within seconds Thomas strode over to the ladder leading up to the loft, grabbed the rails, and began climbing. He stopped midway, looked down, and said excitedly, "Come on, Clara, I'll show you where my brother and I use to stand guard watching out for the Indians."

Miss Emmett laughed and began moving toward the steps. As she passed by, she whispered, "This means all the world to him. You couldn't have given him a better gift."

As Miss Emmett started up the ladder, Margaret teased, "That's gotta be all new hay up there. Y'all have five minutes alone. Any more than that and I'm sending Lil' Jim up there after you, you hear?"

After thoroughly inspecting the outbuildings, we headed west on a trail I had blazed over the summer. "This is new," Thomas said. "Where we going now?"

I looked back and replied, "Over past the pond straddling your father's old farm and the Anderson property. I remember you saying how much you liked fishing as a boy. Imagined you might like closing the loop. Maybe weekends for now, or almost every day after you retire."

"Isn't this something, Thomas?" Miss Emmett said. "I think Lil' Jim's thought of everything!"

Since I was in the lead, my companions had no way of knowing I was grinning from ear to ear. I had pitched the fishing story, and they had bought it hook, line, and sinker. But once we reached the clearing overlooking the pond, Thomas and Margaret soon realized they had been walking the proverbial primrose path. "What's this?" Margaret exclaimed. "A second house? The spitting image of the first? So what's this all about, Lil' Jim?"

I smiled sheepishly and replied, "Well, I suspect this

hasn't happened very often, if ever at all but . . . but this is for us, Margaret. that's if you'll have me."

For an eternal second, my stunned audience stood silently gazing as if a horn had miraculously appeared between my eyes. But thankfully I didn't have to wait long for Margaret's response to my very public, unconventional proposal. She rushed over, embraced me, and repeatedly whispered, "Yes, Lil' Jim. Yes."

Miss Emmett turned to Margaret and said eagerly, "Thomas and I have planned our wedding for next spring. Wouldn't it be something to hold a double wedding right here in Magnolia County?"

Margaret looked over for my reaction. I smiled and winked. She then replied, "That'd be so kind, Miss Emmett."

"What a story for the newspapers!" Thomas interjected. "I can see the headlines now. 'Next-door Neighbors Celebrate Their Joint Wedding!'"

Miss Emmett's suggestion began snowballing with one idea quickly following on the heels of another. "We could have the ceremony right here on the property," Margaret suggested excitedly.

Miss Emmett blessed the idea. "Yes, an outdoor wedding in the spring. The magnolias and lilacs blooming. Can't imagine a prettier setting. It'll be the talk of the town."

"Your catering business can handle the meals, Lil' Jim?" Thomas asked.

I couldn't resist making the sale. "Absolutely! And that's not all. We've expanded our catering to full service. Everything you need for the nuptials—flowers, food, drinks, tents, decorations, photography, a musician or two, and even an ordained minister if you like. Not much left to do but enjoy the day. Wait a minute. Why y'all looking at me like that? You're smiling. What's the matter?"

They all three laughed aloud. "It was just funny watching you go into your sales mode," Thomas replied. "You were talking about your own wedding, selling yourself on yourself." He paused and then continued, "But you do bring up a good point. Who should officiate the weddings? The church in town hasn't filled the vacancy. The elders have been holding tryouts and haven't made up their minds. But it's got to be hard replacing someone like Reverend Emmett. So what are we going to do about a preacher?"

"You say your caterers have started doing weddings with all the trimmings, Lil' Jim. Who's the minister?" Margaret asked.

And without hesitation I calmly replied, "Sky Pilot."

My companions glanced at one another and didn't respond immediately. Their unease was palpable. So I knew I'd have to revert to selling, only this time I'd have to be subtler with my pitch.

Miss Emmett cleared her throat and responded, "You sure about that, Lil' Jim?"

"As sure as I'm standing here. I wouldn't say it if I didn't believe it. After all, it's my best friend's wedding and my own to boot. I wouldn't embarrass y'all for the world."

Thomas's concerns persisted. "No offense, Lil' Jim, but what makes you so sure Sky Pilot could handle this? I know you've been around him a lot . . . a lot more than I have; but every time I've been near him I've only heard that hobo lingo, and I can't make heads or tails out of half he's saying."

"I know this sounds strange, but let's see if I can explain it this way. We've all read about folks in Europe speaking two, three, or maybe even four languages. I saw it out West with our scouts. They'd talk to the Apaches and then turn and speak fluently in English. Saw it during the war too with some of the Cuban rebels, talking rapid-fire Spanish with the locals one minute and then translating into perfect English the next. So as I say, this may sound strange but it's the same with Sky Pilot. You'll hear him speaking hobo in his church and in the fields—it's part of his act, if you will—but I've been around him when he's been comforting folk. He knows the scriptures like the back of his hand, and his English is as precise as yours or mine. I know, I know. It shocked me the first time I heard him, but I got to thinking about it. He wasn't born speaking hobo. English is his mother tongue. And I can look y'all in the eye and tell you I have no doubt he'd conduct the dignified wedding these fine ladies here deserve."

Thomas glanced over toward the ladies and said, "Well, that settles it for me. How about for the two of you? Is Sky Pilot your man?"

Margaret and Miss Emmett looked at each other and then replied in unison, "Yes, he's our man."

We turned and began walking back arm-in-arm toward the fishing hole. Thomas stopped midstride, pointed toward the grassy knoll overlooking the pond, and suggested, "You know, we could have the wedding right here, right here in this special place holding so many memories."

"But what about the older folks?" Miss Emmett asked.

"Theresa Anne and David Lee are getting up in years. My folks aren't spring chickens either, and half the congregation are fifty years or older."

"Won't be a problem," Thomas replied. "We can ferry the folks up here in wagons. Use the back road, the one my brother and I always used to get up here to the pond and the barn."

Miss Emmett looked back toward Margaret and me. "Y'all okay with the venue?"

"It's ideal," Margaret said.

"And it'll look even better once our men give the field a good mowing a day or two before the ceremony," I said.

"Well, then, I'm glad everyone agrees," Thomas said. "It's always been a special place, and now it'll be even more so. And who knows, it may become even more special in the future. Perhaps it won't be long before the two of you bless us with some little ones who'll dip their toes in the water here, hook a big bluegill, and make their godpapa proud."

Miss Emmett laughed and added, "And godmama, too!"

Margaret replied coyly, "Don't y'all think you're getting way ahead of yourselves. We haven't even had the wedding yet, and you're already got little ones frolicking by the pond there."

I quickly changed the subject. "Let's get back to the house and let the cat out of the bag. I can see Theresa Anne now. After getting over the shock, she'll get all worked up and start talking a mile a minute about her hairdo and which dress to wear."

Thomas smiled. "Yes, and knowing David Lee, the first thing out of his mouth will be something about a 'shivaree.' You just wait and see."

By all accounts the double ceremony and wedding night were great successes. In her glowing review the society reporter included the phrases "the weather and the setting were ideal," "the catering impeccable," "the brides beautiful," and "the grooms handsome." But how did she describe Sky Pilot's performance? The one about which my companions had had so much concern?

In fits of nostalgia I will often pull out the yellowed clipping to read her praise. She called the experience "unique," "remarkable," "bold and moving." She was so struck by Sky Pilot's homily she devoted almost half her column to his words, approach, and biblical texts. "Unique" because he focused solely on Old Testament passages—verses from Genesis, Ecclesiastes, Joshua, and the Song of Solomon. "Remarkable" because he employed imagery throughout his sermon of a three-stranded cord representing the bond between a couple bound up in love:

> Two are better than one, because they have a good return for their work. If one falls down, his friend can help him up. But pity the man who falls and has no one to help him! If two lie down together, they will keep warm. But how can one keep warm alone? And though one may be overpowered, two can defend themselves. A cord of three strands is not quickly broken.

And "bold and moving" because our hobo preacher was courageous and sensitive enough to speak openly about the fierce undercurrent flowing through lovers' veins:

> Place me like a seal over your heart,
> like a seal on your arm;
> for love is as strong as death,
> its passion unyielding as the grave.
> It burns like blazing fire,
> like a mighty flame.

Of course, it wasn't the social columnist who passed judgment on our wedding night. She left that to the editor writing the birth announcements and our friends and relatives who dropped by nine months later to celebrate the birth of our healthy son, Todd. The "grandparents," David Lee and Theresa Anne, and the godparents, Clara and Thomas, were all thrilled with the prospects of caring for the little one while Margaret and I "got away" for a few days in Nashville or Memphis. But after several glasses of hard cider all around, the polite conversation embarrassingly became earthier, with many commenting on the bedroom prowess of our wedding night.

19

I DIDN'T GO to them; they came to me. It had crossed my mind a time or two, but I'd always concluded I still wasn't prepared to take the next step in fulfilling Uncle Aaron's dream. When the two strangers showed up on a blustery December day, the only thing I had on my mind was ensuring Todd enjoyed his second Christmas with a big tree, plenty of sweets, and lots of exciting gifts. I took the fellows' coats and escorted them into the front parlor where I expected to hear the usual business pitch.

"Take a seat there, gentlemen. Now you say you've come with a proposition. Well, let's hear what you have to say."

"Mr. Taylor, this here's Phillip Wrenn and I'm Meriwether Jones. We're on the council representing districts on the north side of the county."

"Pleased to meet you. So what can I do for you?"

Jones nervously pulled at his tie and responded, "I'm sure you've been reading the newspapers and would agree Winters has made a mess of things. Ya know with the embezzling, bribes, and such. Well, we've got two problems: one's economic and the other's political. First, the money problem. The county's going broke, and at some point we'll have to start laying people off. And there's no easy way to raise funds or increase revenues. With investor perception the way it is we can't float a bond, and raising taxes again is out of the question. Hell, Winters raised taxes twice in the last four years to line his pockets and pay off his friends."

"Y'all looking to me for a loan or something to help bridge the gap?"

"No, no. Ya see, it's more complicated than that. Which brings me to the second issue—the political problem. Despite the indictments, Winters says he's hell-bent on running for a second term. That'd be okay if everything was all right. No one would challenge him in the primary next spring and with him being a Democrat, he'd be a shoo-in for the fall election. But that's the rub. Everything's not all right. It's all falling apart. The county's almost bankrupt; Winters is awaiting trial; and he swears he'll hold on until they cart him off to jail. So, Mr. Taylor, if we don't do something now, our Democratic Party could lose control for the first time since Reconstruction. You smile, but it's more than possible; it's likely. I'm telling ya, people are fed up with his shenanigans."

"You working on a plan to get y'all out of this mess?" I asked.

"Sure are, and—"

"Well, I'm all ears. What's your plan?"

Jones glanced over at Wrenn, nervously adjusted his tie again, and replied, "With all due respect, sir, you . . . you're our best hope for saving the county and the party. God knows you've got the business smarts to dig us out of the financial hole. And you've also led men into battle, which speaks volumes for your leadership skills. The way we're counting, we'd say you help us kill two birds with one stone. So how does 'County Mayor Taylor' sound to you, sir?"

I didn't respond immediately. I stroked my beard, weighed the variables—mostly the economic ones—and finally fell prey to my passion for taking on thorny financial issues and turning them around. Frankly, the politics was an afterthought, a sidebar or simply a means to help get the town back on sound footing. I walked over and extended my hand. "So when do we start, Mr. Jones?"

The politician leapt from his chair. "By all means, sir, tomorrow morning! If you don't mind, we'd like you to come by the county offices for a private meeting. We have a number of financial statements we'd like to share so you can begin thinking about possible solutions."

"No worries, gentlemen," I responded. "I'll be there bright and early to get the lay of the land."

After escorting the men to the door, I raced upstairs to sell Margaret on the idea of throwing my hat in the ring. But before I could say a word, she beat me to the punch. "Who were those fellows I saw riding up the entryway a while ago?"

"Messrs. Wrenn and Jones. They're on the council representing districts on the north side of the county."

"What did they want with you?" Her angst had caused her brow to furrow. She could sense change was on the horizon.

I attempted a smile to reassure her and replied, "Do them a favor."

"Must be a big one if they came all the way out here in this December chill."

"I'm not going to lie to you, Margaret. It is a big deal."

"So what did they want?"

"They want me to save the county."

Margaret looked at me quizzically and only repeated my response, "So they want you to save the county . . ."

I jumped in. "Yes! You've read the newspapers—how the county's going broke and at some point will have to start laying people off."

"So how do they propose you right the ship?"

"Run for county mayor! Well, first challenge the current mayor, Winters, in a Democratic primary and then afterward, defeat the Republican candidate in the general election."

After pausing to process the implications for the family, the farm, and the business, Margaret responded, "You sure you can handle the politics and the responsibilities of the office without cutting into family time and harming the business?"

"I'm sure of it, Margaret. I don't really have to spend as much time running the business as before. I've got plenty of good people handling things now, including Sergeant Blair, Spider, and Sky Pilot. And I promise you that the time I'd spend as county mayor will come out of the business time not out of our family time. You and Todd mean too much to me."

Margaret gazed into my eyes and asked, "You promise?"

I smiled and replied, "I promise. . . . I promise on Sky Pilot's Bible."

"Well, okay then. You've promised, and to be honest, 'County Mayor Taylor' does have a nice ring to it."

We laughed and embraced. She then held me back at arm's length and became serious again. "You better get downstairs and tell David Lee and Theresa Anne what you're up to, reassure them that nothing around here is going to change or be harmed in any way."

I pulled Margaret back in close to me again and said, "Believe me, that was going to be my next stop."

When I arrived for the meeting the next morning, the councilmen showed me to a private office lined with ledgers. Wrenn pointed to the walls and said, "There's probably more than enough here to give you the lay of the land. I believe the records go back to the founding. The books run chronologically; so the latest entries will be in the files over there."

"I don't want to rain on your parade, gentlemen. I'm sure there's more than enough here. But I was thinking after y'all left yesterday we've first got to get the horse before the cart. Unfortunately, there's this messy thing of winning a primary and then the general election before I can legally tackle the financial issues. I could review the books and offer constructive advice in the interim; but I don't think Mayor Winters would be inclined to listen to recommendations drafted by his primary opponent. So first things first. The election's paramount, and you're the experts on that score. When it comes to elections, I don't know what I don't know. I don't even know the right questions to ask. I'm gonna need your help there before I'll be in a position to help the county. So as far as the primary's concerned, how do we get started?"

"We're willing to stick our necks out to help you," Jones answered. "But we're not really the experts at advising your campaign. That calls for a professional, and we have the right fella for you. Henry McKellar. He's been at these local wars for at least twenty years now. We'll arrange a meeting with him for tomorrow. If he's willing to manage your campaign, he'll ensure we get off on the right foot, avoiding the pitfalls of an insurgency."

It felt like a long wait, but the following afternoon, Jones, Wrenn, and I met Hank McKellar at the Tilden Hotel. After hearing our plans and learning I was a political neophyte, the veteran presented the challenges facing the campaign. He leaned back in his chair, blew several rings of cigar smoke, and said, "This is a risky proposition, ya know. Winters is going to do everything he can to hold on to his job. You have a stellar reputation in these parts, and I'll tell ya now he's going to try dirtying you up—try to make you the issue of the campaign rather than his record. Everyone around here thinks you're clean; but first of all, tell me, ya got any skeletons dancing in the closet? Steamy hot dishes on the side? A little bastard or two running around? Bribes in your business dealings?"

I shook my head and replied confidently, "No, nothing like that in the background." I knew there was no way for anyone to know anything about the years I spent at West Point and in Fishkill Landing on the Hudson.

"Well, let me tell ya, if there's nothing now, there will be after Winters and the newspapers get through with you. Hell, after this primary, you won't recognize the fella staring back at ya in the mirror. So how ya feel about that, Mr. Taylor?"

I responded resolutely, trying to sway McKellar to come on board. "Having endured the war, sir, I believe the risk from these slings and arrows is manageable."

He took a long drag on his cigar and replied, "So far

so good. Now on to the next question. How you gentlemen plan on funding the campaign?" He smiled and added half-jokingly, "I hate to be crass about this, but I expect to be rewarded handsomely for pulling ya through. All told for the advertising, the travel, the walk-around money, I put the damage at somewhere between fifteen and twenty thousand dollars."

I could read my cohorts' minds. Jones and Wrenn didn't want to handle that hot potato. They gazed over at me embarrassedly. So returning to my selling mode, I answered McKellar's question decisively: "If you'll commit to keeping the total under twenty grand, I'll foot the bill."

"Self-funding?"

"Yes, self-funding." Sensing it was time to seal the deal, I leaned forward and asked, "You ready to sign on the bottom line?"

McKellar didn't reply immediately. He took another long drag on his cigar, blew several smoke rings, and then said, "Can't deny I like what I'm hearing. So, Mr. Taylor, come hell or high water, ya willing to take my advice?"

"Being straight up front, sir, I'll tell you now I won't give you a blank check on that one. It's not like me to accept a proposal without asking questions, especially if something's not making sense. But I'll give you my word, we'll hash it out together. Now are you ready to sign?"

The adviser smiled and extended his hand. "Okay, Mr. Taylor. It's on to victory!"

"What's first?" I asked.

"Developing a strategy," McKellar replied. "We've got to

draft a game plan and then stick to it no matter how much the rough and tumble."

Jones jumped in, excitedly offering, "We're going to need a platform to run on, won't we, Hank?"

"Hold on there, Meriwether. The answer's 'yes' and 'no.' We'll need one all right, but it'll be Democrat boilerplate plain and simple. Nothing new. Nothing controversial."

"I know you're the expert here, but how do I convince people to vote for me if I'm pitching bullshit?"

McKellar leaned back in his chair, rolled the cigar between his thick fingers, and explained, "No offense, Mr. Taylor, but you could be that spittoon over there. This election shouldn't be about you. Ya see, it's gotta be about Winters, unless we do something stupid and make it about you. It's gotta be a referendum on him. A thumbs up or down on whether folks think he deserves a second term. Your job'll be to stay out of the way until the election's over. We'll let his mischief hang him."

I looked over at the councilmen and smiled. We were all three bobbing our heads like jays at a watering hole. Since we hadn't thought of something so obvious, we were privately acknowledging McKellar's superiority in drafting a winning political strategy. And over the next five months, I did a lot of dancing. When the reporters probed, I danced. When the voters inquired, I danced. When Winters attacked, I danced. McKellar had coached me well; I became very good at "fogging" or "straddling" as he called it, using worn words and phrases as "perhaps," "maybe," and "while on the one hand" and "on the other hand."

As the months passed, I saw the genius in McKellar's approach. Everyone became bored with this rambling spittoon and focused solely on savaging the incumbent mayor. So by the time the primary election rolled around, everyone in the campaign was confident we were on track to celebrate a landslide victory.

Anticipating a decisive win, I filled four wagons with family, workers, and friends and drove over to the county offices to watch the vote come in. McKellar arrived just as the polls were closing. After greeting several party bosses, he took Jones, Wrenn, and me aside and laid down the law. "I know this'll be hard for y'all, but ya see that room over there? You're to stay out. That's where the election officials will be counting the votes and I'll be analyzing precinct returns. When I've got news, I'll let ya know. I don't care if the building's on fire, ya stay out of there. Ya hear?"

We nodded and replied, "Of course."

About an hour after the polls closed, riders began arriving from the various districts in the county. One after another they strode into the office, marched directly into the backroom, and emptied their saddlebags on a long table. As the tabulation proceeded, Jones, Wrenn, and I were relegated to distractedly moving among supporters, who oddly enough, congratulated us more on the quality of the canapés and sherry than the effectiveness of our campaign and likely victory.

Being good soldiers in McKellar's army, we all accepted our fates gracefully, resigning ourselves to endless hours of anxious boredom. Margaret, Thomas, Miss Emmett, and I held our collective breath while waiting for the results. But the gods were kind that election night. Not long after the fourth rider appeared, McKellar exited the forbidden room, extended his hand, and calmly announced as if dictating a telegram, "Congratulations, Taylor. Historic margins. Winters whupped." Despite the brevity of his message, I clearly sensed the sadness lurking beneath layers of professional pride. Sadness in victory? For McKellar, yes. After primary night, there'd be little for him to do. The curtain was closing, the set struck, and the stage going dark for at least the next four years.

Since success in November was a foregone conclusion, I didn't spend much time campaigning between the primary and general elections. I immediately began developing plans to dig the county out of its financial hole. And when I took the oath thc following January, I already had drafted a proposal for the council's advice and consent. They reviewed it, honed it into legislation, and approved the bill and my budget within thirty days of my taking office. While council members then moved on to other matters, I became salesman-in-chief, traveling from town to town pitching our strategy to businessmen and other potential bond investors.

Our plan for restoring the county's prospects was very simple. The approach would be understandable to anyone keeping a household budget. We had four goals: first, the government would live within its means; second, citizens would pay less in taxes; third, we would improve investor perception of the county's financial health; and fourth, we would raise adequate capital to stimulate employment and the local economy. The actions we took to achieve these goals included approving a lean budget, cutting bloat without resorting to layoffs; passing legislation to lower property taxes; and floating a bond issue funding road and bridge projects to put the unemployed back to work.

In essence we were sending a clear message to the community: we would run the county the way local proprietors run their successful businesses. So my job selling the bond issue was easy. Once potential investors learned we were making serious cuts to the budget and lowering taxes, their perception of the county's prospects improved dramatically. And when they understood I was personally putting skin in the game purchasing a third of the bond float, they eagerly signed on; and the issue was fully subscribed within a matter of days. Behind closed doors, the council members and I congratulated one another; we strongly believed we had set the conditions for a quick and sustainable turnaround.

Success bred success, and by the close of my four-year term in office, the county was back on sound footing and I had just been elected to the Tennessee General Assembly.

Quoting Dickens, I would describe my tenure in the state Senate as the best of times and the worst of times. The main positive was we met in session a total of only ninety days over a two-year period. This meant I could spend much more time at home now overseeing my diverse businesses. I no longer had to turn over the reins to trusted managers as I had to when I was working sixteen-hour days ensuring we reversed the county's fortunes.

The primary negative was the ongoing frustration I experienced trying to move legislation through the bureaucratic

Assembly. I was no longer a leader who could cut to the chase. I was now just one of many, who spent hours kissing leaders' asses and compromising every position but my most deeply held beliefs. What veteran legislators would call "real progress" was intentionally calibrated in inches while I envisioned risking bold strokes measured in miles. So after witnessing my ongoing outbursts at home, not one of my friends and relatives was the least surprised when I privately confided that two legislative terms would be enough and my political career would be on hold after the last session in Nashville.

20

THE REVEREND'S HILLEL sermon echoes even still in my mind: "If not us, who? If not now, when?"

It's my sixteenth birthday again, Uncle Aaron. I can still hear your whispers. "It's like I've wasted ten years of my life encouraging folk to work in a rigged system. If elites can't meet their goals legally, they just step outside—trump up charges, drag us out of the jails, and beat us. No one's ever prosecuted. White folk are signaling, get back in your place and stay there."

I laid the newspaper down face up with the headline screaming SIX NEGROES DEAD AFTER BATTLE WITH CITIZEN'S POSSE and considered what this meant. *An entire family—Sarah, her daughter, and all the sons—wiped out. Over what? The eldest resisting arrest? You white folk surrounded the house; torched it; and began firing? You watched the mother drag her dying children out one by one? And when her work was done, you killed her too? Why? For what?*

You had it right, Uncle Aaron. You said white folk would use elections and violence to reset the boundaries. And they've done just that for decades. But despite your doubts, you drew the map when I was seven; and I've read it every year now on my birthday. You were writing to me then, weren't you, Uncle Aaron? "Progress depends on the Negro getting an effective education, starting his own business, becoming wealthy, and then exercising political clout." How did you boil it down, Uncle? I believe you said, "Educate, incorporate, accumulate, and legislate." Well, I've climbed the first three steps now, Uncle, and this latest lynching's telling me nothing's changed and it's now time to scale the fourth. If not me, Uncle, who? If not now, Uncle, when?

After several lengthy and sometimes painful conversations with Margaret, I finally gained her reluctant approval. I then rang up my old campaign manager and invited him out to the farm. Despite the early snow, McKellar agreed to meet on short notice since he'd been assured a free meal was in the offing. When he arrived the following afternoon, I escorted him into the study where we fired up cigars and settled into overstuffed chairs near the woodstove.

"How long has it been now since you left office, Senator?" he asked breaking the ice.

"Going on three years now, Hank."

"You don't look a day older."

I smiled and returned the compliment. "Same goes here for you too."

He nodded approvingly, took a long drag on his cigar, and blew several smoke rings into the air. "I suspect you didn't invite me out here to exchange pleasantries and reminisce about the past. What's on your mind?"

"Don't be so sure about that," I responded teasingly. "What did Shakespeare say? 'Past is prologue.' But seriously, Hank, I'm thinking about running for governor in the primary next spring. Thinking about you and me capturing lightning in the bottle one more time."

"Glad I'm sitting down, Jim. Last time we talked you said you were done with politics. But you're learning what I've known a long time. Once you've lived it, you eventually forget the pain and come back around again. Three years go by and here you are, talking about jumping back in. And not jumping into something minor either. No, sir. Something big. Real big. The governor's race."

"So you ready to roll in the hay again, Hank?"

"I'd be lying if I said I wasn't chomping at the bit." He took another long drag and blew more smoke rings. "But I'd be lying if I said I was up for it."

"It's not like you, Hank. You sick or something?"

"No, nothing like that. Ya see, my job's always been shooting straight and keeping ya out of trouble. Plain and simple, I'm not your man this time."

"What do you mean not my man? Hell, Hank, you're the best in the business."

He nodded again appreciatively. "I'd like to think so, but we all have our limits, and my job's to know mine."

"Keep talking. I'm not sure where you're headed."

"I'm your man, Jim, if you're talking about running for mayor or the legislature where the campaign's focused, local. But when you're talking statewide elections, that's where I draw the line. Doesn't mean I'm not willing to help. But I'd play second fiddle, advising on local matters, ya see. Helping a state manager to get the lay of the land. It would be his job to develop a budget, hire folk across the state, draft your message, choose the right strategy, react to the ups and downs of the campaign . . . and if he wants my help, I'll be there to speak my piece. But I'm not up for leading the charge across the state."

"If you're not the man, you got any ideas?"

"I have a couple fellas in mind. Don't know either of 'em personally. Just by word of mouth I've heard they're good. You should go to Nashville and interview 'em. Decide for yourself if you're comfortable with one or the other. But I'll tell you, running a statewide campaign is far different from what you're used to, and your manager's gonna have to be calm under pressure. Thick-skinned. Know how to inspire campaign workers to go the extra mile. And most importantly, he's got to be loyal, someone you'd trust with your life—your political life. It's like when ya went to war, Jim. Someone ya knew would be there beside ya in battle no matter what."

Within the week I traveled to Nashville and met both prospects. They appeared well qualified technically, but I remembered the emphasis McKellar had placed on trust and his comparison of the campaign to war. Perhaps I was being a bit unfair or biased because between the meeting with McKellar and my interviews with the candidates, I had pretty much made up my mind whom I wanted for the political battle of my life. Someone I'd known for years, someone who had run statewide campaigns for his father back East, someone who had also gone to war with the Buffalo Soldiers. Someone whom I loved as much as I loved myself. My only doubts—Would he accept? Would he be willing to come out to the "frontier" as he called it? Be willing to reengage mixing politics with pleasure?

My letter stimulated an immediate and positive response. Troy, all these years after West Point, was ready to "try something new and challenging." And only two weeks after our correspondence I was standing on the Warfield station platform waiting for his four o'clock. "I wonder what twenty-plus years and the war have done to my friend, the handsome Achilles to my Patroclus," I thought, "the Alexander to my Hephaestion. And what will he think of me now? I know he reminisces. His holiday greetings always mention our Christmases at Fishkill Landing. His letters allude to strolls on village streets, hikes on wooded trails, and hours alone together in the turret overlooking the Hudson. So how should I greet him? A respectful handshake or meaningful embrace? But does it really matter? After all, he could be my cousin or brother, and I want him to know clearly my love has survived our marriages and the span of separation from his Fort Totten to my Assiniboine, his Philippines to my Cuba and now his Albany to my Warfield and Hurricane Creek."

I didn't have to wait long for answers. The locomotive eased to a stop five minutes early, and Troy was the first person off the train. As he glided up the platform toward me, I thought, "My God, he's even more handsome now than during our West Point days—tall; lean; black, curly locks flowing out from beneath his cap; dark, well-trimmed beard; and that incredibly infectious smile."

Troy waved and shouted, "Hello, Governor!"

I acknowledged his optimism with an exaggerated bow and tip of my hat.

He laughed, dropped his bags, and extended his arms. We embraced. I was now home again after so many years of longing for the tender strength of his muscularity. I held him out at arm's length and gazed into his dark brown eyes asking; and he responded silently, "Yes, yes, our love endures."

I grasped his arms more tightly and whispered, "Knowing means everything."

"For me too, Jim. It's been a long time."

Bowing to social mores, I released Troy's arms and asked, "You ready to get to work?"

"Right here! Right now!" he replied enthusiastically.

"Not that fast. But how about after dinner tonight?"

"The sooner the better."

"I've asked my old campaign manager, Hank McKellar, to join us for supper and our first strategy session. I think he can help us with the local politics and the lay of the land."

"Fine by me on both counts."

"Both counts?"

He laughed and said, "Mr. McKellar's help and a fine dinner. I'm starving, Jim."

We drove out to the house where I introduced Troy to Margaret, Todd, and both sets of "grandparents." McKellar showed up fashionably late as usual just as we were about to sit down to supper. I remember observing during the meal how struck everyone appeared with Troy's good looks and charisma and thinking how my life had just reverted from openness to subtext, code, and signaling.

After Margaret's delicious meal, McKellar, Troy, and I excused ourselves and huddled near the fireplace in the study to begin work on the campaign. I opened the conversation. "Hank, for starters, why don't you give Troy here the lay of the land."

"Just in general for now, Hank," Troy interjected. "We'll get into the weeds a little later on."

"Okay. So as far as politics go, you can divide Tennessee in half. You can draw a line running north-south through Nashville from the Kentucky border to Alabama. The eastern half of the state's pretty much controlled by party bosses, and they've already announced support for Franklin Corey, our opponent in the primary. Even though Corey's not the incumbent or a member of the current administration, he starts with a sizeable advantage, which will be hard to overtake. And that's not to mention he's from Knoxville, the largest city in east Tennessee, and he's loaded with dough he inherited from his father. I've already told Jim what I think. Winning the nomination will be hard but not impossible. I believe the key to victory is exciting folk out here in western Tennessee and making damn sure we get 'em out to vote. It's pretty much gravy from then on out. Win the primary and you're sure to win the general. Republicans are just too damn weak to mount a serious challenge."

"So you see any upsides, Hank?" Troy asked lightheartedly.

"Absolutely," McKellar replied; and looking over at me, he said, "Jim's life story."

"Go on, Hank. Tell me more about our friend here. How would you frame the narrative?"

He began speaking rhetorically as if trying to persuade Troy to mark his ballot for me. "As a candidate it doesn't get much better than this. Here's a fella who's orphaned at five or six, runs away from home at sixteen, rides the rails for a spell, goes to work on a farm near Hurricane Creek, attends West Point, becomes an officer in the Indian Wars, charges up San Juan Hill with a future president of the United States, returns home to farm and build an empire, rescues his county from sure ruin, and sacrifices personally and financially by leaving his family and businesses behind to serve his district in the state legislature." And in closing the sale McKellar raised his voice and added, "So my bottom line, sir, with all things considered, how could you vote for anyone else?"

Troy and I began laughing simultaneously, rose to our feet, and cheered McKellar's persuasive performance.

"But seriously, Jim, Hank's right," Troy said. "There's a gold mine here. Hank says we've got to get folk out this way excited about voting for you; and I've found no better approach than stressing a personal narrative. Getting people to know who you are, showing them you're a man of the people, that you started with nothing and pulled yourself up by your bootstraps. Convincing voters you're more suited to helping them get out of the current economic mess than this Corey fellow who inherited his wealth. And you have the calluses to prove it!" He looked over and asked, "Where'd Hank say you landed after hoboing? Hurricane . . ."

"Hurricane Creek. It's not too far from here."

"Perfect . . . perfect," Troy mumbled as he processed my response. He then continued, "You know, we can use that."

"What do you mean?" I asked.

"Use it for your name while campaigning."

McKellar and I gazed at him quizzically.

"My name?"

Troy turned to McKellar and excitedly illustrated his point. "Sir, let me introduce you to Hurricane Jim here, who's stormed San Juan Hill and will now be storming Nashville for you!"

"Hurricane Jim. Hurricane Jim," McKellar repeated. "Has a real nice ring to it. I like it, Troy. I really like it."

21

DURING THE CAMPAIGN, Troy and I shared everything with McKellar except the real reason we always insisted on adjoining rooms at the hotels. The three of us became an effective team. The two political pros established the infrastructure, strategy, messaging, and scheduling; and I followed their direction religiously—adopting every piece of advice from what to wear, what to say during debates, and whom to flatter along the way. With three weeks remaining in the campaign, we had closed the gap and almost pulled even with Corey. But despite our momentum, Troy and McKellar felt we might need something more to put us over the top.

"Jim, we've reviewed the wires from our staff around the state," Troy said. "Hank and I have analyzed the numbers and agree we're very close to pulling ahead. So we've got to make a decision. We see two choices: we can let this thing play out and assume our momentum will carry us through the election, or we can come up with something else to ensure we put the nail in this coffin."

"What do you think we should do?" I asked.

They responded emphatically, "Nail the coffin shut!"

"If that's what we need to do, then let's do it. What do y'all have in mind?"

"Give us a little time, and we'll get back to you on that when we get into Huntingdon," Troy replied.

After a campaign stop that afternoon in Hollow Rock, we rode over to Huntingdon and registered at the hotel. Before heading off to our rooms, I pulled McKellar and Troy aside and said, "After you get settled, come on over to my suite. I want to discuss the matter you brought to my attention earlier today."

When they arrived, I showed them into the living room. "Y'all take a seat. First off, tell me where we're headed over the next few days."

McKellar pulled a folded paper from his pocket and read the schedule. "We've got stops tomorrow in Milan and Dyersburg. Then the following day we're in Blytheville and Memphis, where we'll spend Friday night. Saturday morning we'll be headed back east to—"

"That's far enough ahead," I interjected. "After the speech in Memphis day after tomorrow, I want to make a stop over at my Uncle Aaron's office. Haven't seen him in years. Since it'll be a reunion of sorts, I'll risk leaving you boys alone on the town. And by the way, y'all can move on to other issues. I have an idea how to nail the coffin shut. Leave that one to me for now." Ignoring their raised eyebrows, I quickly added, "Anything else we need to discuss? Okay, then, I'll take a catnap and see y'all for dinner."

When we finished the Memphis rally that Friday afternoon, McKellar dropped me off at Uncle Aaron's newspaper office and instructed the guard detail to secure the building. I knocked on the door, and a familiar voice rang out. "It's open; come on in." I eased the door open and entered. Uncle Aaron was sitting behind his desk with his head down, poring over some papers. He looked much the same as I had remembered except his hair was graying and beginning to recede. I cleared my throat. At first he didn't respond. But finally he looked up and gasped, "My God, my God! Is that you, Lil' Jim?"

"Sure is, Uncle Aaron."

He jumped up from his chair, rushed toward me, and gave me a big hug. "Welcome home, Lil' Jim! Welcome home!"

"It's good to see ya, Uncle."

"I heard you'd be in town today campaigning and had every intention of being there. But as you can see, I got behind on my editing, and the deadline's Sunday night."

"I'm sorry to barge in like this. Can you spare a few minutes?"

"For you, Jim? Of course I can. Here, give me your coat, and take a seat over there by the desk."

He hung my coat up and sat down. He didn't say anything for the longest time. He just sat there gazing into my eyes and shaking his head. His voice cracked as he whispered, "Why, Lil' Jim? Why did you run off to Warfield?"

"Warfield? How did you know? I didn't say anything about it in the note I left for you and Aunt Jane."

"Thomas wrote not long after you left to let us know you were safe." He paused and then repeated his cutting question: "So why, Lil' Jim, why?"

I knew exactly what he was asking. Despite my earlier letter of apology, he wanted to hear my explanation face-to-face.

He needed to hear it for himself, my justification for running away on that breathtakingly beautiful Christmas Eve over two decades ago. I hadn't anticipated his question so there was no rehearsing, no rounding the edges. It would be a spontaneous recitation of the raw, prickly truth. I swallowed hard and replied, "I never really felt I belonged, Uncle Aaron. God knows you and Aunt Jane were saints for taking me in after the fire. But despite all the kindness y'all showed me, the unbearable loneliness never stopped."

"Why, Lil' Jim?"

"To be honest, Uncle Aaron, our color."

"Our color? I don't understand. Your mother was mixed like me. We're Negroes in everyone's eyes."

"Not really, Uncle Aaron. You're dark. I'm light. And even though we were a family, we traveled in separate worlds. I could go places you, Aunt Jane, and the boys couldn't without your risking ridicule or physical harm. And it was the same for me in South Memphis. I always sensed the disdain when y'all would take me into a shop. The owner's scornful gaze asking, 'Why'd ya bring him in here? There's just too much cream in that java to my liking.' I apologize for running away. Forgive me. I didn't mean to hurt you or show you disrespect. It was just the continuous pain of feeling isolated, even in a crowded room of family and friends."

Uncle Aaron moved around the corner of his desk, embraced me again, and whispered, "Welcome home." It was his way of saying that as far as he was concerned, we had finally closed out the chapter and could now move on.

He patted me on the back several times, turned, and

walked over to the stove. "Would you like some fresh coffee?" he asked.

"By all means. It's been a long day."

"How do you take it?"

I paused and replied ironically, "With extra cream, of course."

We both laughed aloud, and then I got down to business. "On a serious note, Uncle Aaron, I need your help. My campaign manager's telling me we've just about caught Corey. We have the momentum now, but they want to be sure we bury him on election day. They say we need something extra to get our folk excited and get them out to the polls."

"What can I do?" He asked.

"Tell the truth," I replied.

"Tell the truth about what? I don't understand."

"Tell the truth about me, Uncle. Write an editorial for your Negro readers here in and around Memphis. Explain there's hope for them in the upcoming elections, that if I win the primary and the general, they'll have a governor with Negro blood coursing through his veins. You just state it as fact, without details, without sources. Nothing about a connection between you and me. No one knows that."

"It's crazy. Negroes vote Republican. You know that. They can't help you in the Democratic primary. This doesn't make sense. How's my editorial about your color going to help?"

"Been reading excerpts from an ancient treatise on war and I got to thinking, you could apply some of these strategies to politics. In a way politics is like war. One of the ideas goes something like this: 'I'll force the enemy to see our strength as weakness and then use this misperception to turn their own strength into weakness.'"

"I'm still confused. How does that logic apply here?"

"Corey's boys will get wind of your allegation and begin spreading the word that voting for this Hurricane Jim is flat-out voting for a Negro. They'll see their revelation as a strength for them and a weakness for me when, as the treatise promises, the opposite will be true."

"I'm still trying to catch up to you. So how does my assertion become a strength for you and a weakness for them? Seems impossible."

"Our side will chalk their preposterous claim up to the filthiest politics imaginable. They'll get real angry, turn out at the polls in large numbers, and turn Corey's presumed victory into an unexpected stinging defeat."

Uncle Aaron leaned back in his chair and stared up at the ceiling. I knew exactly what he was doing. He was playing out all the possibilities in his head before passing judgment on the idea. I held my breath as the seconds ticked by without a verdict. But finally I exhaled when I detected a slight conspiratorial smile forming at the corner of his mouth.

He looked squarely at me and said, "Okay, Lil' Jim. I'll do it. I still think it's crazy; but I see the method in your madness."

"You'll never regret this, Uncle Aaron. Just think of it as living out your vision, doing your part to help our people."

"I'm proud of you, Lil' Jim."

"Same goes here, Uncle. We'll make history together. You just wait and see."

When I got back to the hotel, I found McKellar and Troy doing their best to stay out of trouble. I could tell they had had a few drinks, but neither had gotten out of control. They were just more willing to say what was really on their minds. After sharing a round with them, I suggested we had better get to bed, since we had a campaign breakfast scheduled at the hotel for eight o'clock in the morning. We finished our drinks, and as we climbed the stairs, Troy signaled he wanted to see me before retiring for the night.

I had barely made it into my suite before Troy knocked on the door separating our rooms. I slid the deadbolt back and showed him into the living room. "Would you like the usual before we sit down?" I asked.

"Absolutely."

As I poured the whiskies and branch water, I probed. "Business or pleasure?"

"A little bit of both, I suppose."

I handed him his drink and led the way over to the ornate wicker settee.

"What's on your mind, Troy?"

"Thought we'd better start planning my departure without Hank around."

"I don't understand. Why tonight? November's a long way off."

"After the primary win next week, you really won't need me for the general. Hank's learned the ropes traveling the state with me. He's capable of handling anything that would come up. And besides, in the unlikely event it did, you know exactly how to reach me."

"I don't get it. My understanding was you were on board through the general in November. What's really changed your mind about staying?"

"I told you, Jim. There's no use my sticking around when Hank can handle this. Frankly, it's a waste of money you could be stashing away for your reelection campaign. And I guess if I were being totally upfront, I'd mention the obligation I'm feeling to the wife and especially my little girls. And believe me, the wife knows how to apply the pressure—having the children write letters saying how much they miss their dear father and all. I'm telling you, if you're ever away for a long time, you'll be feeling the pressure as I am right now."

"For God's sake, Troy, what about us? Go another decade without seeing each other? How do you keep love alive?"

He deflected my question with one of his own. "Don't you ever think about our luck running out?"

"Luck? About what?"

"Our not making a mistake and having someone figure this all out. Don't you have any idea what that would mean to your campaign? It would be over. No ifs, ands, or buts. Over! And even if it were two weeks before the election, the party would find a way to dump you or, even worse, find a way to make you disappear for good. They'd figure they'd win the general no matter what. Jim, there's no sense risking everything right now. And besides, what would happen after the election? You'd go to Nashville with your wife and son, and I'd go back East to my wife and little girls. So think of it this way—we're sacrificing a few months together to ensure you succeed. And believe me I want that more than anything else."

He slipped his hand onto my thigh, moved in, and kissed me softly. "You understand what I'm saying, Jim?" he whispered.

I leaned back and didn't respond.

"You gonna be okay? You know you have a primary to win."

I nodded, stood up, and showed Troy to the door between the rooms. I knew now the last real embrace and kiss we'd shared occurred years ago in the turret overlooking the Hudson. All the excuses now—McKellar's statewide capabilities, the wasted campaign funds, his obligation to wife and girls, the risk of discovery—they were all a ruse. The multiple excuses were his way of explaining our relationship had ended years ago and he really wanted more than anything to return to his current lover, the latest in a long line over the last twenty years. Oh, I knew for sure we'd make love a time or two before he departed; but it would only be a raw physical encounter for old time's sake. Nothing more. Nothing less.

22

WE HAD BOOKED the top floor of the Maxwell House in Nashville to await the primary returns. It was McKellar's job to analyze the fragmentary results, divine trends by county, and announce his findings to the entourage and me. His unspoken tasks, however, were first to report the returns publicly in a favorable light to keep supporters' spirits up and then brief Troy and me out of earshot on the actual state of affairs.

Because of an unprecedented turnout, the tabulation dragged on into the wee hours of Wednesday morning. While my supporters were hearing I had taken the lead early and had maintained it, I was hearing something quite different. In early returns from the eastern counties Corey had taken a commanding lead. But as the evening wore on and the results moved westward, I expectedly began whittling away at my rival's margin. And by the time the returns reached Memphis, McKellar described the race as "tighter than a tick on a butcher's balls."

As dawn broke, McKellar returned with the latest results, only this time he wasn't carrying his usual stack of papers. He walked over to where Troy and I were sitting, extended his hand, and said, "I don't know what you did to increase the turnout around Memphis, but your advantage just keeps growing. You're up over a thousand now; and my take on the unreported counties is your lead's insurmountable. Congratulations, Hurricane Jim! Let's join the party down the hall, and I'll introduce ya as the next governor of Tennessee!"

When McKellar made the announcement to the crowd, Margaret rushed up, wrapped her arms excitedly around my neck, and said, "I'm so proud of you." She kissed me repeatedly and whispered, "I hope you'll hurry back up to the room so we can celebrate."

I held her out at arm's length and smiled knowingly. "I'll have to chat with the party bosses downstairs for a few minutes and then I'll be all yours."

But one drink led to another, and the celebration continued in the bar until well past breakfast. We would have stayed longer, but the day manager objected to the rowdiness, cut us off, and shepherded all of us out into the lobby. Troy held up his half bottle of purloined whiskey and slurred, "Come on, Jim. Let's go upstairs for a little more fun."

We weaved our way up the staircase to the fifth floor and made it about halfway down the empty corridor before Troy pinned me against the wall and began kissing me. I still had enough wits about me to know this was dangerous. I tried pushing him away. "No, Troy. Not now. Not here." As I turned my head to the side to gain more leverage, I discovered a lone figure standing in the hallway five yards away witnessing everything. Margaret didn't say anything. She just turned, walked slowly up the hall to our room, and slammed the door.

I panicked and managed to push Troy away. "Jesus Christ, man! Get the hell to your room! Look what you've done! Now I've got a real problem on my hands."

I rushed up the hallway, stopped at the door, and took several deep breaths. I turned the knob slowly and stepped into the unknown. "Margaret? Margaret? Where are you?" She didn't respond. I moved back through the suite toward the bedroom repeating, "Margaret? Margaret?" There was still no answer. The bedroom door was shut. I tried pushing down on the handle, but it was locked. I began coaxing, "Margaret . . . Margaret, please open the door. We need to talk. I can explain everything. It isn't what it seems. Now please, Margaret, for Todd's sake, please open the door."

After hearing the lock click, I waited a few seconds, pushed down on the lever, and stepped in. Margaret was sitting on her side of the bed with her back to me. She was sobbing and rocking back and forth. Her face was buried in her hands. I moved around the end of the bed and knelt in front of her. "Margaret, it's not what it seems."

"Why, Jim? Why?"

"I'm telling you. It's not what it seems."

"Don't believe my lying eyes?"

"Margaret, for God's sake! You know I've told you this a thousand times. Troy's like a brother to me. . . ."

"Brothers don't act that way. Pushing up against each other. Kissing that way."

"We were drunk, Margaret."

"Not drunk enough to keep on rubbing up against each other and ignoring me. No! You knew what you were doing."

"My God, Margaret, we've got a fall campaign to run beginning today. How can I make this right?"

She didn't hesitate. "Admit the truth, to start."

I paused, calculating how to negotiate the mine field. I decided to step tentatively with a question rather than an outright admission. "What would you say if I were to tell you there's always been a certain flexibility in my nature?"

She parried my question with one of her own. "What do you mean, Jim?"

"I'm just saying I grew up in a world of men without a mother's love. I've always felt comfortable being around them, whether it was when I was hoboing, serving in the military, or conducting business. Nothing improper. Just my nature."

She pushed harder. "But that's not what I saw in the hallway just now, was it, Jim? You might as well be honest because I'm not believing your 'nothing improper' story with Troy."

Inching closer to a declaration, I asked, "What would you think then, Margaret?"

Increasingly regaining her composure she turned to the scriptures. "I'd say you needed to confess to the reverend. Do a lot of talking and praying with him to rid your soul of this evil. You know the Bible condemns you for committing unseemly acts with other men. You're risking hell, Jim. You have to repent for your lusting."

"If I confessed and repented, what then? Would you be willing to forgive and stay?"

"Too early to say. But one thing has to happen for sure. Troy's got to leave Memphis, go back home now."

"Have my manager leave in the middle of the campaign?"

"There's no other way I'd consider staying. And you need to be thinking about protecting Todd from this mess. Maybe not so much now, but in the future. What would he think if he found out?"

I seized the opening. "It'd be a big risk having Troy leave now. You know that." I smiled guiltily and continued, "But if the choice is Troy or Todd and you, there's no question I'd come down on the side of the angels. So you'd stay?"

"We'll see. Only after he's on the train headed home."

"Then I'll make it happen."

It took several days to wrap things up with Troy—get his opinions about messaging and financing the fall campaign. But the day that in the past I'd hoped would never come had now arrived, and we were standing on the platform waiting for his one o'clock. He looked directly into my eyes and apologized. "I'm sorry for causing you trouble, Jim. Nothing more or less than the whiskey. So I guess it's a good thing I'd already decided on going home rather than seeing this through to November. But I know you'll do just fine. Hank's learned a lot from the primary. I have no doubts he'll come through for you in the general. He's a good man, loyal and smart."

I smiled and replied, "If I hadn't believed your assessment, I never would have agreed to let you leave. . . . That is, until all this blew up."

"Believe me, Jim. I'm really sorry."

So his departure was nothing as I had imagined. Our conversation was all business. There was no talk about separation, loneliness, or our prospects for the future. There were no tears or regrets. Honestly, I don't think his train could have come any sooner for him or me. Just before boarding, he extended his arms and we quietly hugged as brothers, soldiers, and close friends. He climbed the coach steps, turned, and saluted. I didn't respond. But moments later as his train disappeared into the curve, I slowly raised my hand and returned the salute, not signaling farewell to a lover but to the fading memory of a distant past.

23

WHEN I RETURNED home from the depot, I found McKellar pacing in my office. I'd never seen him so anxious. I joked, "Troy's been gone less than an hour, and you're already showing the strain. What's up?"

He held out a folded newspaper and replied, "I think you better see this. It could mean trouble. Something I'm sure the reporters will be asking you about this afternoon."

"I'll read it later. What's this about?"

"The local paper here's picked up a wire report about a bunch of murders in Memphis the night before the election. Lynched three fellows in a publishing office and then proceeded to the poor fellows' homes, torched the houses one by one, and fired a lot of rounds into the flames. Apparently most of the family members died too."

"So what does this have to do with me or the campaign? Why would the reporters be asking questions?"

"Well, this wire service story says that several days after the murders, the police rounded up several men who've now admitted to being a part of the plot. They've told police they were 'whipped into a fury' by an editorial in a local journal, which falsely claimed you had Negro blood in you. They said the piece angered them so much they followed the journalists around for a day or two to find out where they lived. They wanted to exact the most painful revenge possible—kill their families and burn down their houses."

"My God! Our supporters?"

"No question, Hurricane. They've confessed to the police."

"You know we had nothing to do with this. How you think we should handle it?"

"Get out in front of the story. When you meet with the reporters, make a statement mourning the loss of life, offer condolences to any surviving family members, and condemn the attacks outright. Emphasize there's never any justification for violence in politics. Then I suggest you let the reporters ask all the questions they want. Stay as long as it takes to sap their enthusiasm and curiosity. I'm sure it'll all die down in a day or two. . . . You know, this kind of thing wouldn't have boiled up outside of Memphis if the wire service hadn't been interested in making us southerners look real bad up North. This'll just add fuel to the fire, just strengthen the impression we're all savages down here. That was the bastard's intention from the start putting this bullshit out on the wire."

"Okay. I hear you. Sounds like a good way to handle the press. We'll just play the cards the way they've been dealt." I paused and smiled as confidently as I could. "You see, Hank, Troy was right. You'll do a great job with the campaign."

He smiled appreciatively. "Thanks for the trust, Hurricane." He then paused and said, "I better get back to work on your acceptance speech. Just a few more edits to the first draft. We've got an election to win. I'll see you at two o'clock on the front lawn when you have to feed the beast." Then he was gone.

After McKellar left, I collapsed into the chair behind my desk. I could now let my guard down and react to the personal side of his reporting. "My God, what have I done? Uncle Aaron lynched; Aunt Jane possibly murdered; and it sounds like Marcus, Daniel, and Lil' John might have died in the fire too. They could've come home for their mother's birthday. Gone. The Memphis family all gone! And now I've got to go out there in front of those snakes and act like nothing's happened? . . . But it's got to be done. Got to put my feelings in the box and move on."

As expected, the reporters weren't interested in my five-point plan to strengthen the state economy. No, they only wanted to cross-examine me about any potential role I might have played in the murders and how any involvement would impact my campaign. Following McKellar's advice I began the news conference with a brief statement mourning the loss of life, condemning the violence, extending condolences, and praising the police for their quick resolution of these heinous crimes. And then the barrage began. One incriminating question after another spun to lure me into a mistake.

One reporter asked, "Mr. Taylor, you ever met the publisher or journalists who were dragged out into the street and lynched?"

I responded reflexively, "No, I—" And then I caught myself midsentence. Someone might have seen my security detail or me when Uncle Aaron and I hatched the plot. I self-corrected and continued, "As a matter of fact, I may have sat for an interview before the primary. I remember holding campaign rallies in Memphis, and I may have entertained a few questions at their offices."

Another probed, "Mr. Taylor, you and the publisher of the Negro journal share the same surname. Are you related to him some way?"

Understanding any hesitancy could be fatal, I looked the fellow in the eye and answered crisply, "No, sir. You and I both know life is filled with coincidences every day."

And then a wire reporter asked the final and most cutting question, "Mr. Taylor, with all the rumors circulating about you around the state, do you want to once and for all clearly state you're not of a mixed race?"

Knowing sarcastic humor strengthens counterattacks, I scowled at him defiantly; slowly transformed my frown into a sardonic smile; extended my arms out to the side; and replied through gritted teeth, "With all due respect, sir, do you see an ounce of Negro in this handsome frame? In the nose, sir? In the hair, sir? In the skin, sir? Anywhere, sir? Anywhere?" Following this definitive denial and bitter exchange, the reporters raised the white flag and slithered away—at least for the time being.

When I'd finished with the newsmen, I returned to my study and closed the door. I wanted to be alone with my thoughts. As I sparred with the reporters, I'd heard Saint Peter cursing repeatedly, "I don't know the man!" I now stared into the mirror on the far wall. "And how many times did I deny my uncle and my lineage today to save my political hide? But perhaps a means to an end, collateral damage or the trailhead to redemption? And if denials suggest deliverance, then the path? The prescription? The text says Peter 'went outside and wept bitterly' after his denials. Wasn't that his pivot from self to Christ? And then once converted, his divine mission? Clearly 'to strengthen his brethren.' Haven't I now reached the end of self and stand primed for my own conversion? If so, then what? Follow Peter's lead? Weave my uncle's dream? Strengthen my people?"

There was a soft knock at the door. "Hurricane. Hurricane, you in there?"

Transitioning quickly from penitent to confident politician, I shouted, "Is that you, Hank? Come in! Come in!"

He extended his hand. "I've finished the second draft of your convention speech. I've made all the changes you suggested. I hope I'm beginning to capture the spirit of what you're driving at."

"What do you think so far?"

He replied lightheartedly, "We're getting there. I'd say close to mesmerizing, but not yet Jennings Bryan. But seriously, while I don't agree with everything you have to say, I like the way you sandwiched the bitter pill between acknowledged goals—erasing poverty and transforming our political past. Artfully done. The crowd will hear the first and last and miss that one in the middle. Overall, your words pack a punch. The power's there in the vision, in the dreams, and frankly, inspirational speeches work in our trade."

"I'll review the draft this evening after dinner and get it back to you tomorrow morning, hopefully with final changes. There's precious little time until the convention."

McKellar moved toward the door.

"Hank, one more thing before you go. How do ya think we did this afternoon? I tell ya that was a grilling. Sharks were circling. They thought they were smelling blood."

"We did fine. You followed the plan. . . ."

"So you think I handled their questions well? Well enough to put this Memphis mess to bed?"

"Yes, but let me offer one piece of advice for the future."

"What's that, Hank?"

He smiled knowingly and said, "Something I've learned over the years. There are no coincidences in politics." He slowly turned away and exited the room.

24

THE PARTY CHAIRMAN poked his head through the doorway and announced, "It's time to go downstairs. They've finished the formal vote, and Senator Chase is about to start the introduction. By the way, Mrs. Taylor, when your husband finishes his speech, that's the cue for you and Todd to join him on stage for the family portrait. And don't forget to smile and wave. Your picture will be front-page in every newspaper across the state tomorrow morning."

We arrived just as the senator was taking the stage. I moved away from my entourage to a spot near the curtain so I could hear his remarks. He began: "Fellow delegates, I'm truly optimistic about the fall campaign and our state's future. The voters have spoken, and they've chosen wisely. We have a strong candidate who's been tested both in politics and in life. He's a man who was orphaned at an early age . . ."

As the senator spoke, I thought, *"Yes, abandoned by a mixed mother and a missing father."*

"He's a man who left home to ride the rails and see America . . ."

"No, to flee the pain of race."

"He's a man who attended West Point to become a leader . . ."

"No, to be with my kind and to find a lover."

"He's a man who fought the savages and won the West . . ."

"No, never fired a shot but dragged women and children out into the cold."

"He's a man who supported our president's charge up San Juan Hill . . ."

"No, you got that wrong; it was the other way around."

"He's a man who built a small farm into an enterprise . . ."

"No, the workers did that."

"He's a devout man who attends every Sunday . . ."

"No, a doubter who sees evil and asks, 'Why?'"

"And most importantly, he's a family man who loves his wife and son . . ."

"Yes, and took a male lover."

"So, fellow delegates, we have the right man for our time. The man who'll sweep away the past and build a brighter future. And that man is Hurricane . . . Jim . . . Taylor!"

As the cheering reached its crescendo, I stepped out onto the stage, smiled broadly, and thrust my arms into the air. I grasped the podium tightly with both hands, waved occasionally, and waited until the shouting quieted down. After signaling the delegates take their seats, I launched into my acceptance speech: "Mr. Chairman, Senator Chase, and fellow delegates, it's with great pride and humility I accept your nomination to become the Democratic candidate for governor of the great state of Tennessee."

I responded to their loud applause. "Thank you. Thank you. Please be seated. . . . Thank you. Thank you." I then continued, "Fellow delegates, my uncle used to say that bridges are dreams we've turned to steel. I envision building a lot of bridges, bridges spanning poverty, prejudice, and our political past. And with your help and God's blessings we'll cast off the yokes and begin to build. Will you join us now in our crusade?"

The hall erupted in a sustained chant of "Yes! Yes! Yes!"

www.ingramcontent.com/pod-product-compliance
Lightning Source LLC
LaVergne TN
LVHW091031080826
845145LV00002B/440

* 9 7 8 0 9 9 0 9 4 9 9 6 1 *